BETWEEN

FRIENDS

Champion Books Publishing Company

NATALIEBANKSNOVELS.COM

Printed in the United States of America

The Library of Congress has catalogued this edition as follows:

Between Friends/Natalie Banks

ISBN- 979-8-9927098-4-1

Other titles by Natalie Banks:

The Water is Wide

The Dark Room

The Canary's Song

The Moments Between

House of Lights

Connect with Natalie:

WWW.NATALIEBANKSNOVELS.COM

INSTAGRAM: OFFICIALNATALIEBANKS

FACEBOOK: NATALIE BANKS TOMANY

TIKTOK: AUTHORNATALIEBANKS

NATALIEBANKSNOVELS@GMAIL.COM

Sign up for her newsletter for free short stories.

Early Praise for Between Friends*:*

Between Friends keeps you on the edge of your seat with every twist and turn. Natalie Banks' writing is lyrical, haunting, and beautifully immersive. A must-read for thriller lovers, it has the nostalgic suspense of a '90s classic, like I Know What You Did Last Summer, but with a voice all her own.

-International Bestselling Author Jessica Dodge

Jessica is an international bestselling author whose stories blend the wonder of magical realism with the heart of human connection. With a background in film and art and a gift for storytelling, she creates immersive worlds that readers return to again and again.
www.theforgottenwitch.com

Darkly thoughtful and absorbing. Banks pulls no punches in this haunting tale of family dysfunction, buried secrets, and friendships gone wrong. I couldn't read it fast enough.

-Lanie Mores
Lanie is a retired psychotherapist and the award-winning author of the science fiction and fantasy series, Father of Contention.
www.laniemores.com

Riveting and lyrical storytelling, with intriguing characters, Banks' prose is sharp and smooth all at once.

-Canadian Author Michelle Young

Michelle is a Canadian author of multiple books. She has been featured in The Globe and Mail, appeared on television and podcasts, and is passionately seeking new ways to bring invisible battles into the light through her stories.

Follow her on Instagram or Facebook

BETWEEN

FRIENDS

Natalie Banks

A CHAMPION BOOKS PUBLICATION

For the little girl inside of me,

The one who stayed up late with a notebook in her lap.
Who breathed in stories like air and spilled her heart onto paper
in ink before she even knew what it meant to be brave.

I saw you then and I see you now.

You dreamed of this.
And you never let go.

Look what you are doing.

I am so proud.

PROLOGUE

Madison

They never found the body.
Twelve years, four months, two weeks, and three days had passed since the night she disappeared. And according to Google, Olivia Mariner was still a missing person.

Most days I didn't think about her. Not anymore.
But for many years, her face was all I could see, haunting me in the dark hours.
Waiting for the quiet to slip in.

Blonde waves frayed with humidity.
Her expression frozen in confusion.
Her perfect skull split open, gaping like a cut watermelon.
Bright red blood trickled down her face, as her lifeless eyes locked with mine.
Accusing.

She'd fallen to the ground in perfect poise.
Just like everything else Olivia had done.
It was flawless.
She landed as if she'd been placed delicately there.
Lips slightly parted, eyes wide open.
Completely beautiful, even in death.

CHAPTER 1

Madison

Present day

The plane's wheels thudded against the runway, stirring me from a hazy sleep. A sharp groan echoed through the cabin, as the brakes seized against the tarmac. My head swam, thick with the lingering haze of Valium and cheap whiskey.

For a moment, I didn't know where I was.

The air felt too cold. The light too bright. And a low mechanical hum pressed against my ears, steady and unnatural.

Then everything came back into focus.

LA to Raleigh, North Carolina.
American Airlines. Economy class.
Row 11, seat B.

I blinked, swallowing against tightness in my throat, gaining my bearings. To my left, a chubby-cheeked Asian man wearing wire-rimmed glasses texted furiously on his phone. And on my right, a middle-aged blonde woman with a pixie cut and a Botox frozen face clutched an e-reader between manicured fingers.

Neither of my travel mates acknowledged my existence when I slid into the seat between them a few hours ago, and I hadn't bothered to break the illusion that there was no more than two inches of space separating us. We all agreed in silence, to pretend we were alone.

I exhaled, feeling the drugged weight of my limbs. The last thing I remembered was tossing back my second shot of whiskey, letting the burn carry me under right after take-off. It felt like only minutes had passed, yet here we were.

Landed.

As the plane taxied, I reached into my pocket, fingers fumbling for my phone. I pulled it out and the screen blinked to life, the harsh light burning my eyes in the dimly lit cabin.

7:00 PM flashed across the screen, bannered over a blurry selfie of me and Adrienne, a girl from work. New Year's Eve. Two single women drinking away our loneliness. When we snapped the photo, I was three sheets to the wind, wearing a crooked crown that said *2025*, and Adrienne was about thirty seconds away from throwing up. Which she did, right on the shoes of the guy that was standing right behind us.

Afterward, I got her into a cab and walked the six blocks home alone, my heels clicking against the damp sidewalk, each step more irritating than the last.

I was mad at myself. Again.

I hated girls' nights. All the high-pitched laughter and oversharing, the clink of martini glasses and false intimacy. I only ever went for the drinks. And I always regretted going.
This night ended the way so many did.
Pointless.

I put my phone back in my pocket, as the pilot's voice echoed over the loudspeaker.

"Welcome to the East Coast."

4

His words sent a slow, creeping chill down my spine. They were meant to be warm, inviting. Instead, they felt like a prison sentence.

I was only here out of necessity.

My mother was gone. And now, her house, the place I swore I'd never return to, was mine.

A sharp breath rattled through my chest as I leaned back in my seat, staring at the terminal building in the distance. The RDU airport loomed beyond the rain-streaked window, squat and gray beneath the encroaching dusk. Shadows pooled over the pavement, spilling toward the plane. Toward me.

I swallowed a rush of claustrophobia, bracing myself for what lay ahead.

The house had been re-mortgaged two to three times. Selling it wouldn't leave me rich, just barely breaking even. But it had to be done.

My childhood home.

The phrase felt foreign, like it belonged to someone else. I had no nostalgia for that place. My mother made sure of that. She'd left me just as alone as the father who abandoned us right after my birth.

Men had been more important to my mother, than raising a daughter. The cycle repeated over and over. Different names, different faces, the same stench of aftershave clinging to the walls. And in the end, after all the husbands and boyfriends, she died alone in a hotel in Florida. At some singles' retreat, no less.

I let out a sharp, humorless breath. That was so her. Always searching for something, or someone, who would never be enough. Her heart just gave out, they said. Went to sleep and never woke up. Quite ironic, given her circumstances.

I thought I would feel something. Some flicker of sadness. Some loss. The only parent I'd ever known was gone.

Yet I felt nothing.

Maybe I was just jaded now. After what happened to Olivia back in high school, I was never the same.

Or maybe it was because there was nothing to grieve.

All I could feel was the unbearable weight of obligation pressing against my chest. Thirty years of dust and ghosts waited for me in that house. And I would have to face them alone. I had no siblings. No grandparents. No partner. It was just me.

I curled my fingers around my phone, forcing the tension from my hands. Four weeks. That was all I had. Four weeks to box up the past, sign the papers, and return to my real life.

Back to Muse Magazine.

Back to LA.

I never intended to work for a magazine. Photography was supposed to be an escape, not a career. But the universe had other plans.

I'd been in the park that day, my camera fixed on the toothless bag lady feeding pigeons, when Sally Hertz spotted me. Sally Hertz, the editor-in-chief of Muse, the woman with razor-sharp cheekbones and a reputation for making grown men cry.

She'd been there for a cover shoot, screaming at her photographer, berating him in front of the entire crew. I remembered the way his face twisted with rage before he spat at her feet and stormed off, cursing her in French.

And she turned her sights toward me.

She plucked the camera straight from my hands, her scarlet-painted nails scrolling through the images with an unreadable expression.

"You're hired. Start now," she said. A statement. Not a question.

I followed behind her and snapped pictures of a gaunt, wide-eyed model from Eastern Europe. When I was finished, Sally was noticeably pleased.

The next day, she called me to Muse Headquarters. My first paycheck was $1,500 for two hours' worth of work. More money than I'd made in a month of waiting tables.

And just like that, my future had been rewritten.

I'd traveled the world since then. Paris. Tokyo. Santorini. I stood in the shadows of marble palaces and photographed faces that graced the covers of Muse's glossy magazines. My world had been loud, bright, and full of movement.

And yet, not once in the past decade had I stepped foot in North Carolina. Not even to visit.

Now, here I was.

The airport loomed closer, and the plane slowed to a crawl and the clicks of unbuckling seatbelts, and the soft rush of conversation echoed through the cabin. As the people around me stirred, stretching, yawning, unbuckling their seatbelts, my fingers curled into the armrest, eyes fixed on the headrest in front of me.

Outside, the sky was bleeding into night. Heavy, thick clouds churned in the distance, swallowing what little light remained. It was an omen. I was sure of it.

The house was waiting.

The past was waiting.

And I had no choice but to face it. Whether I liked it or not.

As the airplane rolled to a final stop, a wave of commotion surged through the cabin. Passengers stood too quickly, elbows jutting, bags unzipped in frantic hands. Overhead compartments creaked open one by one, as the line formed to exit. I sat still, as if movement might rush me more quickly into the inevitable. A little delay was fine with me.

When we finally began to shuffle off the plane, the first thing that hit me was the air-conditioned chill of the jet bridge. Overhead, the fluorescent lights buzzed faintly, flickering once before settling into a steady hum. Beneath my feet, the suitcase wheels clattered rhythmically against the tile, echoing like a heartbeat. The sound synced with a new thud in my temples, creating a slow, gnawing unease in my stomach.

Once we hit the terminal, the high-pitched squeal of a child echoed off the polished floor, and I winced. A door slammed somewhere down the concourse. The scent of over-roasted coffee and greasy pretzels twisted my stomach, churning with whatever mix of pills and whiskey still lingered in my bloodstream.

I stopped walking, blinking against the brightness of it all. Too many lights, too much noise, too many people moving in all directions at once. My body swayed slightly. I gripped the handle of my rolling suitcase just to stay upright. For a split second, I thought I might vomit right there on the tile.

"Madison!" a female voice called out, echoing off the walls.

I froze. The sound of my name sliced clean through the chaos. My pulse skipped, as I turned my head, dread pooling low in my belly. A woman I didn't recognize, a wide smile plastered across her face, weaved through the crowd toward me. My chest tightened. There was no way to avoid her.

But at the last second, she veered. Right past me. To another Madison. Her arms flung around the girl who had been walking just behind me. A high schooler in a hoodie and flip flops. The two of them squealed with joy, laughter trailing off behind them as they disappeared into the current of people.

I exhaled, breath sharp and unsteady. My hands, shaking from relief.

I didn't want to see anyone. Not yet. Maybe not ever.

The Raleigh-Durham airport wasn't big, but it felt endless. I wandered past signs and slow-moving travelers, each step echoed louder than it should've.

And right before veering off toward the baggage claim, I saw it.

Through the tall windows at the far end of the terminal, a baggage cart curved around the belly of a parked plane. On the last trailer, a long, narrow box rested alone. Matte gray. No markings. Two ground crew workers stood at either end, heads bowed against the wind and misting rain.

It took me a second to register what it was.

A casket. Being wheeled off the back of a plane.

The sight of it jarred me. A harsh reminder of why I was here.

I squared my shoulders, muttering under my breath, as I walked toward the escalator.

Welcome home, Maddie.

CHAPTER 2

Madison

The girl behind the rental car counter couldn't have been more than twenty, small-framed with permed brown curls and an eager smile. She slid the keys to a blue Ford Focus across the counter, her heavily enunciated Southern drawl thick and sweet.

"Have a great day," she said, as I walked away.

Instead of stepping out of the building, I turned toward the hallway beside the customer service counter and ducked into the women's restroom, needing a moment.

The light inside the bathroom was cruel, fluorescent, sharp, unflattering. It bounced off the mirrors like an interrogation lamp, spotlighting every flaw I'd tried to ignore the last few years. I dropped my bag by the sink and leaned in.

My dark brown hair hung in loose, waves around my shoulders, still faintly disheveled from the airplane headrest. Freckles that were remnants of a sun-drenched childhood, dotted the bridge of my nose, faded but stubborn. I'd always hated them. The kind of thing people called cute when you were six and tried to airbrush out when you were thirty. My teeth were straight, thanks to three years of braces and a mother who thought appearances were everything...until she stopped caring about anything but herself.

But it was my eyes that gave me away. They couldn't decide if they were green or hazel, and right now, they looked both, and neither. Dull. Exhausted.

There were shadows beneath them I hadn't noticed before. I didn't look sad. I didn't look angry. I just looked... tired. The kind of tired that couldn't be slept off.

I splashed cold water on my face, patted it dry with a thin paper towel, and took a long breath that didn't help me feel better.

This was who I was now.

Thirty, frayed at the edges, coming home to bury the ghost of a mother that never was.

The door squeaked, as I stepped back out. The rental keys jingled, feeling heavier in my hand than they should have. I moved past the row of cracked plastic chairs, past the faded posters of tropical beaches no one working there had ever seen, or probably ever would.

The woman behind the counter looked up just as I reached the door.

"Have a nice day," she called again, as if she hadn't said it to me once already.

Her voice was friendly enough, but the words felt off.

Hollow.

I stepped out into smothering Carolina humidity and the doors hissed closed behind me. The rain had stopped, leaving mugginess in its wake and the thick evening air pressed in from all sides.

BETWEEN FRIENDS

I navigated the parking lot, struggling to catch my breath, switching my bag from one shoulder to the other. The wheels of my carry-on suitcase snapped and clattered across the uneven asphalt, rattling my teeth. Sweat prickled at the back of my neck, but I kept moving.

After several grueling minutes, I finally found my rental car space, B-3341. The car was parked in the farthest row, against the chain-link fence separating it from the short-term lot. A flimsy barrier between movement and permanence. I heaved my suitcase and bag into the trunk, slamming the lid harder than necessary.

Before climbing into the driver's seat, my gaze drifted beyond the fence. Reunions played out in soft-focus just yards away, people collapsing into each other's arms, holding hands, pressing foreheads together. Laughter. Relief.

Smiling faces illuminated by the glow of happiness. Separation over.

I watched for longer than I should have. A boy sobbed into his father's shirt. A woman threw her arms around a soldier. Even the tired-looking couple who barely touched still shared something.
I gritted my teeth, pushing against the rush of loneliness curling in my gut. A feeling I hadn't allowed myself to acknowledge in years, pressing hard against the walls I'd carefully built.

In LA, I was too busy to be lonely. I was a strong, independent woman. I didn't need a man.
Or a mother.
Or a best friend.
Half an hour in North Carolina and my entire personality was dismantling.

———••◆◆••———

The drive to Fairfield only took an hour and a half. Yet, the road seemed to stretch endlessly beneath me, headlights cutting through the emerging night.

Deep woods lined either side of the two-lane highway, dense and closing in.
Branches tangled and thick, blocked out most of the evening light. It felt darker than it should have been. Still. Too still. The forest stretched on for miles.

My headlights caught the eyes of a creature on the edge of the woods. I startled, passing a lone opossum, yellow glowing orbs peering, tail switching.

Every once in a while, a mailbox appeared, leaning from the weight of time, most of them marked with names that sounded vaguely familiar.
Holloway. Barnes. L. Stewart.
Names whispered in school hallways, scribbled in yearbooks.

People that never left. I sucked in a shallow breath, as the trees seemed to press closer. Like they remembered something I was trying to forget.

I almost didn't recognize the place when I crossed the county line.
Fairfield always looked a little tired, the kind of town that didn't move with the natural course of time, and porches that leaned with age. But now, wedged between the sagging rooftops and rain-streaked siding, there were coffee shops with glass walls and a yoga studio where the old hardware store used to be. It looked strange, like someone had patched a torn sweater with the wrong color, mismatched and obvious.

The gas station was still there, only the pumps had been replaced.
The old Methodist church stood tall, but its doors were locked and looked they had been for a while. Even the trees lining Main Street looked confused, their roots tangled between past and present.

BETWEEN FRIENDS

It was the same town.
And it wasn't.

There was a brand-new shopping center where the arcade and bowling alley used to be. A Publix supermarket, a frozen yogurt shop, a UPS store, among other shops now stood in the place where I spent many of my middle school Friday nights.
New neighborhoods had popped up where cows used to graze.

And the Piggly Wiggly was gone too. In its place, a sprawling mega-church with massive glass windows and an illuminated cross that loomed high against the night sky.

It didn't feel real. Not until I passed the old wooden sign, leaning slightly to one side, weathered and splintering at the edges.
Welcome to Fairfield.
Jesus Loves You.

The sign had been there since I was a kid, put up by the First Baptist Church decades ago. I'd never liked it. But tonight, it was the only thing that anchored me into recognition.

Not much of what I remembered was left now.

The old pharmacy sat gutted, windows papered over with curling eviction notices. A once-thriving diner we used to go to was now boarded up, the words **CLOSED FOR GOOD** spray-painted across the side like a eulogy.

My shoulders sagged as a sudden rush of nostalgia curled around me and I pushed it away. I had no reason to care if this place burned to the ground. I wasn't staying.
I didn't belong here.

As I neared the opening to my old neighborhood, I passed the sheriff's office, the windows illuminated almost as brightly as the mega church's cross next door. My pulse quickened in an uneasy rhythm against my ribs, and I pressed the gas, rushing the tour down memory lane.

My blinker clicked too loudly as I waited to turn. Cars whipped past, their headlights cutting long, sharp streaks through the dark. It was after nine now and irritation buzzed through my mind. My body ached from exhaustion. The Valium had worn off hours ago, as had the whiskey. I debated finding a bar, drowning out the night with something strong and warm or go straight to bed. Either way, I needed an escape.

When the traffic finally broke, I opted for sleep and turned down Magnolia Lane.

This used to be *our* street when we were kids. Three of us in total. Me, Imogen, and Andy. Our summers had been endless, the woods behind our houses a world all our own. We played for hours, losing time in the thick brush and towering trees, only remembering to go home when the fireflies came out and the crickets sang their evening song. And usually well after the sun had set. I wondered now why none of our parents ever worried about us.

I eased my foot off the gas as I passed Imogen's old house.

For a moment, I could see her, seventeen again, stepping out onto the porch. Hair tied in two tight braids, a mini skirt riding high on her thighs, gum snapping between her teeth. She'd spot me, her eyes narrowing in that familiar, scrutinizing way, a silent declaration that I was, yet again, a disappointment to her.
But then she'd smile. Because we were best friends.

At least, we used to be.

Now, I could barely remember the sound of her voice. She was an echo of the past. All that was left of her was a few images carved into my consciousness. Permanent markings of Imogen.
The way she used to cut her sandwich diagonally. How she wrote her name on the bottom of Oliva's sneakers in purple Sharpie. The way she moved through the halls of our high school like she owned them. Doors just opened for her. People stepped aside. Even silence bent a little when she passed. And I just trailed behind.

Two houses down, hidden in the dark, was home.
Or what was left of it.

I pulled into the driveway and sat unmoving, the car's headlights illuminating the weathered garage door. Shutters were barely clinging on, some missing entirely. Siding had darkened with time, streaked with water stains and neglect.
My mother let it rot.
I wanted to yell at her for it. For giving up on this place. For giving up on everything.
But she was dead.
And you can't yell at the dead.

I shut off the car, and for a brief second, the house disappeared into the dark. A quiet moment of relief.

Luggage in hand, I walked up the porch steps. The wood groaned beneath my weight, brittle and weak. The key slid into the lock with an eerie familiarity, and when the door swung open, the air inside wrapped around me…thick, stale, suffocating along with the scent of must and something rotting.

Like old apples left to sour. Or forgotten lunch meat in the back of a fridge. It clawed into my nose and settled in the back of my throat. I had to breathe through my mouth to survive it.

I turned on the lights and saw something that looked like a scene from a hoarder's television show. Boxes and bags were stacked everywhere. Junk toppled over, spilling onto the floor.

I turned the lights back off. I wasn't ready to see more of my mother's handiwork. Not yet. Instead, I moved through the house by memory, guided by years of practiced childhood routine. I carefully made my way up the stairs and turned left. My bedroom door loomed at the end of the hall. The handle was cold as I turned it. The overhead light flickered to life, bathing the room in a washed-out glow.
I stopped.

The room was exactly as I left it. The same posters on the wall. The same worn-out cheer trophy on the bookshelf, the metal glinting in the dim light. My bookshelf, lined with Harry Potter books, scattered movie theater tickets, and framed pictures I didn't dare look at, were all still there. Neatly lined up and freshly wiped down. Not a speck of dust appeared to have touched this room.

Even my bed was neatly made, sheets crisp and fresh. The comforter, freshly laundered.
It was as if it had been prepared for my arrival.

A slow, unnatural chill traced down my spine. Something was off.

I froze. Listening.
And the house held its breath.

Maybe I should have questioned it.
Maybe checked the rest of the house.

But exhaustion pulled me under instead.
I popped another Valium, crawled into bed fully clothed, and let sleep take me.

And just as I slipped from awake to dreaming, I saw Olivia's face again.
Still very dead.
But instead of her usual accusatory expression, this time, she was smiling.

CHAPTER 3

Madison

Sunlight slanted through the blinds, cutting across my face in thin, illuminated strips. The warmth stirred me, dragging me from the depths of sleep.

For the first time in a long time, I slept through the night.
A miracle.

I rolled over, blinking up at the ceiling. My gaze settled on the old water stain above my bed, soft edged and brown. It had been there since I was five. A relic from a storm that tore shingles from the roof and let the rain seep through. The damage had been repaired, but no one ever bothered to paint over the mark.

I'd always seen a face in it. Even now, in the soft morning light, the warped discoloration still resembled something humanoid. A slanted, jagged mouth, two hollow eyes, and a stretched forehead where the water bled outward in uneven tendrils. As a child, I found comfort in it, believing it watched over me like some kind of silent guardian angel. Now, I wasn't sure why I ever thought that twisted thing looked kind.

A mockingbird shrieked outside the window, shattering the moment.
I stretched under the blanket, yawning, my body heavy with the remnants of sleep. I felt hungover, though I knew two ounces of whiskey on the plane wasn't nearly enough to cause one.

The house around me creaked with a soft groan. Not in a charming, old-home sort of way...but like it was adjusting to my presence. Wood popping, air shifting.

I reached for my phone.
4:00 AM in LA. 7:00 AM here.
Time to get up. Four weeks wasn't a lot of time to do everything necessary.

Dragging myself out of bed, I stumbled downstairs, stepping around the piles of junk my mother accumulated. Bags. Boxes. Stacks of things whose purpose I couldn't guess. I barely paid them attention as I made my way through the house.

It was like walking through someone else's mind...disjointed, nonsensical, the logic long gone. Pill bottles. A broken clock. A framed quote that read "Live. Laugh. Love," with a dead fly stuck between the glass and the backing.

I stopped short of the kitchen, realizing that I didn't have my two-thousand-dollar espresso maker for my morning ritual. The machine was a gift from Sally. Well, a regift. People were always giving her gifts she didn't want. I inherited many of those said gifts. Most recently, a Tiffany's bracelet, a Prada clutch, and a five-hundred-dollar bottle of Merlot. It was the only bottle of alcohol in my house I never opened. I kept asking myself what could possibly be worth a $125 glass of wine. So, it sat there on the kitchen counter, taunting me day after day, while I drank cheap wine and even cheaper vodka and whiskey.

My apartment in LA was small. Just 650 square feet, all my own. I loved my tiny place. It overlooked Benton Park and was in walking distance of a couple of bars and restaurants. There was even a little bookshop down the block that I stopped in occasionally.

Though I'd only lived there a few years, it was comfortable.

Unlike the house I grew up in. I felt more like a stranger standing in this kitchen than anything else. It was like stepping into a pocket of time that had stopped, just after midnight. Nothing had moved forward, but everything had grown older. Crooked. Dimmer.

And yet... it still somehow seemed to *remember* me.
The floorboards creaked in all the same places. The wall by the fridge still had the faint outline of the growth chart I used to pencil in myself, when my mother forgot to. My old soccer cleats were still hanging on the mudroom peg, hardened by age, like they'd been left there yesterday instead of two decades ago.

Some rooms felt like they were stuck in 1999. Others felt like no one had breathed inside them in a hundred years. I wasn't sure which unsettled me more.

I drifted through the house, unsure if I was moving forward or slipping back.

I stopped in the doorway of the kitchen.

It couldn't have been me, could it? The little girl that stood on tippy toes making her own dinners while her mom was out on the town.

I looked around the dingy space, my gaze landing on every surface. I stopped when I saw the sink. It was full of dishes haphazardly stacked and submerged in murky, gelatinous water that had been left to fester. The smell was thick, almost tangible, an acidic mix of rot and mildew. I clapped a hand over my mouth and turned away. My mom had never been much of a housekeeper, but this was really bad, even for her.

I swallowed, I couldn't imagine my mother cooking, much less eating in here. There was mold curling along the baseboards. A broken lightbulb in the ceiling fan. A rogue sock on the counter. The wallpaper was stained around the edges. Floor tiles' grout stained and discolored. And the appliances, still the same ones from my childhood, were worn down, yellowing with age. The refrigerator hummed in the corner with a weak and uneven sound, like it was struggling to stay alive.

Who was ever going to want to buy this dump? I thought, grimly. I scanned the countertop, the desperation for coffee, getting worse after the tour de horror.

And then I saw it. A Mr. Coffee machine. My heart leapt with something close to hope.

It was beige, and the decanter pot was cracked near the handle. But somehow it was standing, like a relic from some ancient world that still knew how to function.

I shuffled toward the pantry to search for coffee grounds but found nothing. No coffee. No filters. Just an expired box of saltine crackers, six cans of tuna, and a Ziploc bag filled with takeout napkins and plastic cutlery.

My throat tightened. I hadn't cried when I heard my mother died. But this, this was certainly something to grieve.

I closed the pantry door with a slam, feeling the weight of everything press down on me. The house. The mess. The obligation. For half a second, I considered setting the whole place on fire, booking a flight back to LA, and pretending none of this ever existed. But that was just the coffee withdrawal talking.

I exhaled sharply, turning away from the disaster of a kitchen. The only solution was to leave to get supplies, get coffee, and get through this day without completely unraveling.

24

After a quick shower and a change of clothes, I felt slightly more capable of facing the hell that awaited me. I grabbed my purse and stepped onto the porch, shivering as a brisk morning breeze wrapped around me.

It was then that I noticed them.
The newspapers.
Stacked neatly to the right of the door, worn, yellowed, and breaking down at the edges. There were so many. At least a hundred, maybe more. All local papers.
I bent down, running my fingers along the brittle edges. Some were so old the ink bled into the fibers, creating dark, blurry smudges.

They smelled like attic and mildew, like stories that had been hidden too long.
A few had pages torn out. Folded and refolded. I saw one with a headline about a local missing dog. Years ago. But something about it made my stomach knot. Why did my mother keep all this junk?

Suddenly, a whisper of movement caught my attention. I froze, listening.
The wind? No…

I heard it again. Softer this time. A small, plaintive sound.
A mew.
I turned toward the sound, stepping off the porch, scanning the yard.
Then I saw it…
A small orange tabby, its fur scruffy, ears slightly too big for its head. He blinked at me from the edge of the overgrown flower bed, tail twitching, ready to bolt.

"Here, kitty, kitty," I said, crouching, extending a hand.
The cat hesitated and darted away.

I sighed, shaking my head, giving up immediately.

I made my way toward the driveway, the blue hue of the rental car blinding me in the harsh sunlight. Something about it felt too bright, too clean. Out of place against the peeling paint and decay of the house.

Just before I reached the car, I heard the mew again.
The cat had followed me.

He came all the way in and pressed against my leg, tail curling around my ankle, purring, a deep, rhythmic vibration that sent warmth through my fingers as I scratched under its chin.

"Hi, there," I murmured. "So, now you want to be friends?"

Something about the way it looked at me, head slightly tilted, gaze unwavering, made me wonder if he somehow understood.

I straightened, dusting off my hands. "I gotta go."

I stopped, just as I opened the car door, his eyes ever present on me.

"Hey, listen, if my mom was feeding you, don't count on me to follow in her footsteps," I muttered.

He sat there, still watching me with inquisitive eyes. I waved my hands, shooing him away, but he didn't budge. Not until I got into the car and turned on the ignition. Even then, he only slinked back toward the porch, settling onto the stack of newspapers like he belonged there.
I shook my head and pulled out of the driveway.

By the time I hit the main road, my focus shifted to the essentials. Food, cleaning supplies, and, most importantly, alcohol. If I was going to get through today, I was going to need all three.

BETWEEN FRIENDS

The Publix parking lot was half full when I pulled in, claiming a spot near the buggy coral. I sat there for a second, gripping the steering wheel, staring out at the clean, bright storefront...the new that paved over the old. And for a moment, I felt a world away from the cluttered house waiting for me down Magnolia Lane filled with unwanted junk and unwanted memories.

I exhaled sharply and stepped out of the car just as my phone rang.

The vibration rattled in my pocket, sharp and jarring against my leg. I pulled it out, frowning at the screen. A local number. Not one I recognized.

I hesitated.

For a moment, I considered letting it go to voicemail. But something made me press accept instead.

"Hello?" I said tentatively.

All I heard was a crackle of static.

And breathing. Slow. Measured.

The kind of silence that wasn't really silent at all.

I pulled the phone away, checking the screen. The call was still connected.

"Hello?" I tried again, sharper now.

Nothing.

Just that steady, rhythmic breathing.

A shiver ran down my spine, my fingers tightening around the phone.

I exhaled sharply and ended the call, shoving my phone back into my pocket.

I'd barely taken a step toward the store when it rang again.

My stomach twisted.

Without checking the incoming number, I answered with, "Listen, if this is some kind of..."

"Ms. Andrews?"

I froze, stopping behind a white Jetta with a license plate that read, MOMOF2. The voice on the line was male, professional, carefully polite.

"This is Richard from Harper Funeral Home. I apologize for the intrusion, but I wanted to inform you that your mother's remains are ready for pickup at your earliest convenience."

The breath I'd been holding left me all at once. For a second, I couldn't speak. I turned my back to the Jetta, the store looming in the distance, pressing my fingers against my temple.

Of course, it was the funeral home. Of course, it was something I hadn't prepared myself for.

"Right," I said finally, my voice flatter than I intended. "I'll come by soon."

"Take your time," the man said gently, as if I needed comfort. "We're open until five today and from nine to noon on Saturday. If you'd prefer, we can also arrange for delivery."

A dry, bitter laugh almost escaped my lips. Delivery. Like she was a flipping Amazon package.
"I'll pick it up," I muttered.

"Of course. Whenever you're ready."

I ended the call before he could say anything else.

For a long moment, I stood there, gripping my phone, staring at nothing. *She was really gone.*
Not that there had ever been any doubt. But this made it real. A box of ashes waiting for me to come claim it. A gust of wind cut through the parking lot, carrying the faint scent of something burning.

BETWEEN FRIENDS

I turned, scanning the sky, but there was no smoke.

I swallowed hard and turned back toward the store, the world feeling just a little less solid beneath my feet.

Behind me, down Magnolia Lane, the house waited.
Not patiently. Not silently.
It waited the way something breathes just under the surface. Steady, deliberate, and watching.

I could already picture it, sitting heavy in the morning light, shutters sagging, roofline sinking.
But it wasn't the decay that unnerved me.
It was the feeling that inside those walls, time still refused to move.
Like the house hadn't accepted she was gone.

Peeling at the edges. Rotting from the inside. But still pretending to be whole.

Even when I wasn't inside, I could hear it.
Floorboards settling when no one was walking.
The faint rattle of a window I knew was nailed shut. The same sounds that used to scare me when I was a child, home alone.

I shuddered against a sudden cold gust that whipped through the parking lot.
The gust caught a shopping cart and launched it across the asphalt.
It slammed into the side of the MOMOF2's Volvo causing the car alarm to explode into sound…blaring, shrill, deafening.

The wind intensified, thrashing the limbs of the surrounding trees. Leaves and bark pelted the pavement like shrapnel. I bolted for the sliding doors of Publix, slipping inside just as a massive branch cracked and came crashing down, landing on the exact spot where I had been standing seconds before.

Onlookers turned. Stared. A few pointed, whispering behind cupped hands. I was the miracle survivor.

But I didn't look back.

I grabbed a cart and pushed toward the beer and wine section, ignoring the pounding behind my eyes. A dull, pulsing warning that the branch was only the beginning.

CHAPTER 4

Imogen

I stared at my reflection in the mirror and sighed. The face staring back looked like me but there was a shift.
I could see it, just beneath the surface.
Maybe the lighting was bad.
Or maybe time was finally daring to touch me.

I wasn't sure how thirty got here so fast, but it did, and it did so without mercy.
I leaned closer to the mirror, tilting my head, inspecting the small line between my brows.
Frowning at myself only made it worse.
I stepped back, smoothing my expression.

Botox had been on my mind for months now, lingering at the edge of my vanity like a whisper.
It was time to stop considering and start doing.

Especially now that Madison, *my Maddie,* was back in town.
Because the last thing I needed was for her to see me looking less than perfect.

Twelve years had passed since I last saw her, and truth be told, there was a lot more to worry about than fine lines and aging skin.
I wondered, sometimes, if it was the guilt that was aging me.
Carrying someone else's sins was heavy.
But the weight of my own? That was unbearable.

Because I had a hand in it.
More than I wanted to admit.

I leaned into the mirror again, patting my cheeks as if that would bring something youthful back to the surface.
Once upon a time, I'd been Miss Pender County. Twice.
I'd even been prom queen our senior year.

I'd been envied.
Talked about. Admired. Feared.
Back when those things still mattered.

Now? I was just another rich soccer mom in the carpool line trying desperately to hold onto her youth.

Brassy blonde hair, breast implants that didn't quite sit right, a house in a gated neighborhood, two boys, seven and nine, and a husband who only married me because he had to.

A good life, for some.
For me?

A beautifully decorated cage.

Maybe that's what I deserved. One life for another?

Truth be told, if it weren't for the boys, I would've left Chris years ago.
I would've kicked the dirt off my heels and forgotten this washed-out town.
Like Olivia wanted to.

Too bad she didn't.
She just had to stay one more night.
And it was her last.

BETWEEN FRIENDS

A cold shiver slid down my spine.
Twelve years, and I still couldn't get her face out of my head.
Her cold, lifeless expression…frozen in time in my mind.

Her mouth slightly open. Her eyes closed.
She'd looked undeniably beautiful. How I hated her for that. How could
she be that beautiful when she was dead? Covered in dirt and blood and
still prettier than any of us could hope to be.

Olivia had been naturally stunning.
The most attractive of the three of us, by far.

But we never let her know that.

Madison and I always acted like we were the best. The smartest. The prettiest.
Of course, none of that was true.
She was all those things, times ten.

She walked into a room and people noticed.
And that kind of attention didn't come with money or designer clothes
or a last name that meant something.
It just came with her.
And I hated that.
We both did.

The only thing we had on her was money.
She didn't live on Magnolia Lane like the rest of us.
She lived in Hillshire Mobile Home Park, in a musty old trailer with tin
walls and broken steps.

How she ever ended up being our friend in the first place, I'll never know.

We were petty, stuck-up girls.
Cruel in ways we barely understood back then.

But not cruel without reason.
Not without provocation.
At least… that's what I told myself.

Being poor wasn't a crime.
And it sure didn't sentence her to death.

But here we were.

All of us still breathing, with Olivia's bones mixed in the dirt somewhere in the forest where we used to play.
A place only we knew about.
That's where we left her.
And that's where she's stayed.

We got to grow up.
She got to rot.

I can't say she didn't have something coming for what she did. She thought no one knew. But I did.

But still…
She shouldn't have died.

I've wondered what my life might have turned out like if she hadn't.
If things had been different for all of us. If she'd gone on to New York and I hadn't lived my life riddled with guilt. I pushed out the questions that couldn't be answered and stepped out into the hallway, forcing Olivia's name back into the dark corner of my mind where I liked to keep the memories buried.
Straightening my back, I made my way out to the patio.

Chris was sitting there, hunched over his phone, not noticing me.

BETWEEN FRIENDS

Our boys ran across the yard, their laughter cutting through the warm evening air.
Sharp and bright, like the church bells I no longer believed in.

The boys were the only thing in my life I loved without regret.

Even if I sometimes felt like I was watching from behind glass.
Even if some days I wasn't sure whether I was raising them or performing motherhood for the neighbors.

I took a seat at the patio table across from Chris, waiting for him to notice.
He didn't look up.

I tapped my acrylic nails against the glass tabletop.

Once.
Twice.
Over and over.

Finally, he sighed and looked at me.

"What?" he asked, not bothering to mask the contempt in his voice.

"Nothing," I replied, not masking mine either.

It wasn't a lie.
I didn't want his attention.
I wanted to interrupt him because I knew it would irritate him.

And it did. His brow twitched. His thumb stilled mid-scroll.
Small victories. That's what marriage was now.

That's what we'd been reduced to.
Two people locked in a silent battle, seeing who could make the other more miserable.

I married Chris after college because I was pregnant.
Our parents insisted it was the right thing to do.
Because what would people think if we didn't do what was right in the Lord's eyes?

Never mind what was right for us.

I was six months along when I stood in the First Baptist Church sanctuary, repeating worn-out wedding vows in front of sixty-five guests.

My eyes had drifted to the wooden sanctuary double doors multiple times. I wanted to run like Julia Roberts in *Runaway Bride*. I wanted to be that brazen. That bold. Take a stand for what I wanted. To be the girl I pretended I was in high school.

But I swallowed it all down and said *I do*.

Across from me, I watched my groom, his eyes far away, counting down the minutes until he could drink away reality with his college buddies.

And he did. Our reception had an after party. Long after all the church loving guests had gone home. The rest of the night resembled a frat party far more than a celebration of love.
That night, my new husband passed out in his tux, reeking of bourbon.

I sat on the edge of the bed, eating the cheap chocolates the hotel left on the pillows.
A *Congratulations!* card sat untouched beside me.

Six weeks later, I lost the baby.
A little girl. Barely three pounds.

But I still didn't run.

BETWEEN FRIENDS

I cried in the shower until the water ran cold.
And I dried off, put on makeup, and went grocery shopping like nothing had happened.

I should have left.
Instead, I spent years trying to fill the empty space inside of me.
Trying to get pregnant again.

It took two fertility treatments before I had Chris Jr.
Then, by some miracle, Layden came next.

I had my boys.

But my womb still felt empty.

Like something had set up camp in the hollow space where she should have been.
A daughter-shaped absence that clung to me more tightly than memory.

Chris refused to try for a girl.
"Two is plenty," he said. And I silently accepted, nursing resentment and disillusionment.

I looked across the table at him now…his tawny hair receding at the temples, his face illuminated by the glow of his phone. The only thing that seemed to matter to him. That phone and his job as a corporate realtor.

I looked across the yard. The sun was setting, sending a thread of golden light rippling through the trees.
It was nearing that time to bring the boys in and get them ready for bed.
But just before I stood to call their names, Chris spoke.

"Did you hear your old friend Madison is back in town?" he said, not looking up.

His voice was casual, but the words ripped something open inside me…just like he knew they would.

He liked to drop bombs like that.
Small, deliberate detonations.
Just to watch the twitch in my jaw.

He was well aware how much I'd missed Madison all these years, and how she'd erased me.

He just didn't know why she erased me. He didn't know our secret.

I shifted in my seat. "Yeah, I heard."

Chris fell silent. No more daggers to throw. And I was grateful.

I never talked about Madison to him anymore.
Because talking about her always led my mind back to the past. To the burden of truth.

To Olivia.

No one really looked for her after she went missing on graduation night. Not the police. Not her grandparents. No one.

That still stunned me. Made my stomach flip.

Where we'd hidden the body would have been easily found if anyone had actually searched for her.

Everyone knew she was planning on skipping out of town right after graduation.
She'd made that clear to the whole town.

BETWEEN FRIENDS

She wasn't even supposed to be at the party that night in the woods.
She was supposed to be getting ready to board a Greyhound bus headed
to New York City.
She had the ticket.
She'd sent me a selfie, ticket in hand, with the words:
See you *never,* typed under it.

I told myself it was a joke. A final jab.
But it didn't feel like a joke.
Not then.
Not now.

But she never made it out of the woods that night.
Her grandparents told the cops she was wild as a mustang, probably
already long gone.

And that was the end of it.

No search parties.
No missing posters.
Just silence.

But we knew the truth.

Madison couldn't live with it.
That's why she left.

My best friend since elementary school left me here, holding all the guilt.

Or at least… half of it. The part she didn't take with her.

She had escaped.
Built a whole new life in L.A.
Left this town and everything in it behind her.

But now she was back.

My heart thudded, anticipation curling hot and tight in my stomach.

I really wanted to see her.
But the question was… did she want to see me?

Five friend requests denied on Facebook in the last twelve years didn't bode well. And I didn't dare text her, though I still had her number saved in my phone.

What would we even say to each other?

It had been twelve years since we last saw each other.
Twelve years since we stood over Olivia's lifeless body.
Since we pressed our palms together in a silent oath of secrecy and prayed no one would come looking.
Since then everything changed, and none of us could still say out loud what we did.

Madison was only back because her mother died.

Poor thing.
I heard it happened in some run-down singles' resort in Florida.
Alone, of course.
Chasing love, like always.

That woman never had a shred of class, not even when she tried. Her parents died and left her a huge inheritance. That's how she got into our circle, but money couldn't hide her true nature.
She wore leather boots to church and flirted with gas station attendants like they were rock stars.
Always chasing some man or some dream, and in the end, neither one chased her back.

BETWEEN FRIENDS

No wonder Maddie turned out the way she did.

But still I had to admit, in some small way, I did miss her.
Missed the way we were back then.
When we still believed we were untouchable.

But things are different now.
We're grown.
We have lives.
We have secrets that have been kept so long they've hardened into truth.
Maddie could play dumb in California, like nothing ever happened. But she was home now. She was in my territory. And if she thinks she can come back here just to sell the house, shake a few hands, and run off again like none of it matters, she's got another thing coming.

Secrets bind and it's time she faced that. She couldn't run from what she did.

The woods remember it well.
And so do I.

CHAPTER 5

Madison

I pulled back into the driveway with three crinkled Publix bags rolling around in the trunk. I turned off the engine but didn't move.

The sun had shifted since this morning, casting long, angular shadows across the siding. The house looked different now. Not just empty. Not just neglected. But…something else I couldn't name.

My eyes locked on the crooked garage door. I stared at the small gap underneath the bottom, just as a lizard darted across the yellowing grass and slipped in through the opening.

The movement startled me, not because it was unexpected, but because I'd seen it a hundred times as a child. Lizards slipping beneath doors, under porches, into the cracks of the world that adults never seemed to notice.

But now, it felt wrong. Like even the lizard knew this place was trying to pull me back in time and it was part of the scam. To bring me back to the girl I no longer was.

I shivered.

The air was thicker now. The kind of heavy that pressed on your chest like a warning. The house loomed quiet, but not still. And I felt it. Something in the darkened windows felt watchful. Alive.

And…I started to cry. Real tears. Heavy ones. The kind that burned your cheeks as they slid down. It began with a tremble in my bottom lip, the echo of the funeral home director's voice looping in my head.
"Your mother's remains are ready to be picked up."
The tremble cracked wide into full-blown sobs.

"Why did you leave me alone to clean up this awful mess?" I cried out, slamming my fist against the steering wheel.

This house. This town. This godforsaken place was full of ghosts. The last place on earth I wanted to be, and yet, without my consent, here I was.

The trees whispered it. The cracked pavement beneath my tires echoed it.

Welcome home, Maddie. Welcome home, Maddie. Welcome home, Maddie.

I didn't want to be here. I didn't want to face anything from the past. I wanted it all to go away.

I wanted to be like Sally. She never let anything shake her. I'd been on a shoot in New York with her the day she got the call about her brother. He had been hit by a car as he was bicycling in San Francisco and killed instantly.

I could still hear her voice in the back of my mind. Cool, collected. She stood in the middle of Times Square, shed a single tear, brushed it away, and turned to the group like nothing had happened.
"No sense in crying like a child. There's work to be done, and it won't do itself."

That was Sally. Unbothered. Unshakable.
I reached for a crumpled tissue in my purse and wiped my face.

BETWEEN FRIENDS

Straightened my spine, pushed open the car door, and stepped into the blinding Carolina sunlight.

Despite it being springtime, the heat wrapped around me, thick and relentless. The air shimmered above the driveway, warping the edges of the house like a mirage I couldn't wake from.

I looked at the worn garage door again. And nodded to myself.
Yes. There was work to be done. And I was the only one here to do it.
It was time to stop feeling sorry for myself.

As I popped open the trunk, something brushed against my legs.
I flinched. My heart skipped, and I almost shrieked, thinking of the lizard and its long tail and clawed toes. My breath caught sharp in my throat. That same tight, childlike panic. Quick and irrational. Like I was ten again, barefoot on this driveway, terrified of cicada shells and shadows and the fact that no one was home.

But when I looked down, I saw it was the orange tabby cat.
He weaved between my ankles, purring like he knew me.

The sound was rough, vibrating through his ribs and onto my legs.
There was something oddly comforting about it. It was surprising that something in this place could still move my heart toward warmth.

I reached for the grocery bags and pulled one out with the bright Meow Mix cat food label showing.
"Are you happy? You won," I muttered.

His tail flicked as if he were answering me.

I slammed the trunk shut and headed toward the house. He trotted after me as if he'd done it a hundred times before.

His paws were nearly silent on the cracked pavement, but I could feel him anyway. That soft thump-thump of something following me.

I shook my head.
Of course. My mother had to have been feeding him.
Of course she would care for some stray cat, then disappear and leave it to starve.

She did it to me.
Why not to him?

Only difference was, he waited.
And I left.

------------◆◆◆------------

An hour later, I stood in the wreck of her kitchen, wearing yellow plastic gloves that were now stained brown at the fingertips. They squeaked when I moved, slick with a film I couldn't identify, and didn't want to.

I'd unclogged the sink and washed all the rancid dishes, aside from two storage containers that smelled like death that went straight into the trash. I didn't open them. Just felt their weight and knew. Whatever was inside had passed the point of being identified. Beyond food, beyond trash, just… wrong.

In hindsight, I should've thrown everything out, dishes included.

It would've been faster. Cleaner. Less personal.
But part of me needed to suffer through the mess. To rub my fingers raw under my gloves like penance.
She made the mess.
Yet I still had to clean it.

Leech, the name I'd given the orange tabby, in honor of his succubus nature, had eaten two bowls of fishy-smelling kibble and downed a full bowl of water.

He was now sprawled out on the kitchen mat, licking his paws, perfectly content, while I choked on bleach fumes and regret.

My mother's energy was all around me, pulsing.

I almost turned once, remembering the sound of her laugh.
The memory, vivid and alive.
Laughter echoing from the living room...sharp, breathless, curled around the voice of a man I couldn't place now.

I'd been banished to my room that night, like many other nights, but in desperation, I crept down the hall barefoot, stomach growling, slipping into the kitchen like a thief.

She hadn't heard me. Or maybe she had. And didn't care. As long as I didn't interfere with her date.

I crouched by the fridge, small and alone, eating cold cuts with my hands. The tile freezing beneath me in the dark. The yellowed light over the stove cast long shadows across the floor. I sat in those shadows, the only sound, my own chewing...slow and ashamed.

Suddenly, a bluebird slammed into the windowpane over the sink, the sharp crack snapping me out of the memory. Jarred, I sucked in a sharp breath.

I stood on tippy toes and leaned against the sink, peering through the window where it had hit. I pressed my face against the pane, straining to see. The coolness of the glass startled my skin, grounding me for a second. The pane warped with a faint fog from my breath. Outside the window, the yard blurred at the edges, warped by grime and sunlight.

I went outside to get a better look.

The air was still.
The sky soft, in the wash of daylight.
And there was no bird in sight. No feathers. Not even a mark on the glass.
As if it had never been there at all.
Just a flash of color and sound. A ghost with wings.

After I went back inside, I made my way through the house, removing the first layer of trash. Leech followed me like a shadow. Room to room, never more than a few steps behind, as I threw out half-drunk Diet Cokes, dozens of empty Amazon envelopes, and fast-food wrappers with grease stains bleeding through the paper. When I was done, three garbage bags had been filled to the brim.

I dragged the heavy bags out the side door, Leech trotting faithfully behind.

I opened the outdoor trash can parked next the garage and instantly recoiled. The stench hit me like a tidal wave. With one arm over my nose, I jammed my elbow into the lid and shoved it open, flinging the bags inside. They each slumped in with a wet, hollow thud, sinking into layers of old garbage that had turned soft at the edges.

When I tried to wheel the can to the curb, it wouldn't budge.
The plastic thudded against the driveway with a stubborn grind, refusing to move. With a quick investigation I saw the issue. A missing wheel.

Just like everything else around here…crooked, cracked, and impossible to fix without a fight.

I gritted my teeth. "Figures she'd leave me with a homeless cat and a one-wheeled trash can to clean up her mess," I said out loud.

I grabbed the handle with both hands and tipped it sideways, the lid clapping open and shut. The vile odor escaped in bursts. I gagged, as I ripped it from its comfortable spot exposing brittle yellow grass flattened beneath it. There was a sudden scattering of silverfish and beetles, as they darted out in every direction. I'd disturbed an entire kingdom of rot.

I dragged the can to the street, the lopsided frame scraping against the cracked pavement. The friction vibrated up my arm, jarring, stubborn, like the house itself didn't want to let anything go. I passed over cracks in the driveway with brown weeds popping through. Everything about this place was in a state of decay. *Even the weeds were dying.*

When I finally made it to the street, I dragged the can up, leaving it beside the red mailbox. The mailbox itself leaned at a crooked angle, the flag rusted in place like it hadn't moved in years. The house numbers were missing, and the black spray-painted lettering someone had scrawled on the back long ago had bled into a smudged, unreadable stain.

It looked like it was trying to forget who it belonged to. Just like I was.

I shook my head and turned to head back toward the house.

A few steps from the porch, Leech suddenly darted ahead, disappearing into the bushes with a rustle. And I heard a voice sliding across the grass.

"Excuse me, ma'am..."

It trickled in from the neighboring yard, soft at first. Sweetly poisonous.

I picked up my pace toward the house but froze mid-step. It was too late to get inside.
A cold flush moved through my chest, tightening around my ribs.

She was already coming across the lawn, each step deliberate.

I couldn't move. My feet stayed planted, heart thudding hard against the sound of her voice.

Colleen.

Just as nosy as ever, only now older.
Her hair was nearly white, her face heavy with age and time. But her walk hadn't changed. Still stiff with importance. Still convinced the neighborhood was hers to govern.

"Excuse me, ma'am. This is private property," she called out.

The hair on the back of my neck prickled, as I looked up at her with a forced smile.

"Miss Colleen, it's me, Madison." The words came out thick and foreign. I almost didn't recognize the sound of my own voice.

She blinked, thrown. The authoritative edge dropped from her expression.

"Madison?" she breathed. "My goodness, child. I'd have never recognized you."

I took a small step toward the porch, hoping she'd get the hint.
I was not in the mood for reunions. The house loomed ahead, quiet and waiting for me, but somehow still safer than the conversation coming my way.

"You've grown up so much, Maddie Bear," she said, stepping closer.

I flinched. No one had called me that in years. A name that belonged to another girl. A girl who used to press her palms against the porch screen door on summer nights, watching the fireflies and waiting for her mother's headlights long after bedtime. A girl who believed promises, even after they were broken. A girl I didn't know anymore.

"It's been twelve years," I said, looking at the house instead of her, wishing it would reach out and swallow me whole.

"Twelve years. My goodness, child. Where does the time go?"

"Straight to hell, I suppose," I said, forgetting my Cali wit might not be appreciated here.
She blinked at me but didn't miss a beat.

"Where's your momma? I've got eight Amazon packages at my place. She asked me to pick them up while she was gone on vacation. And Lord, two of them are heavy. It hurt my old back to carry them over to my house."

The breath left my chest in a tight coil.

In my absence, apparently, they had gotten closer. And she didn't know about my mother. Which meant I had to tell her.

"Would you be a dear and come grab them? They're just too..."

"Miss Colleen," I said, cutting her off. "My mother," I said, hesitating. "My mother is gone."

She frowned. "Yes, dear, I know. But I expected her back by now," Colleen said, looking toward the porch, as if she expected my mother to come sashaying out the door to greet her.

I looked over at the porch too. The porch light flickered once. A single bulb coated in a thin veil of spiderwebs. It cast a weak golden haze down the wall, just enough to make the wood grain siding ripple like water in late afternoon shadows.

And for a split second, I could see my mother standing there in black jeans and scuffed leather boots, her hair pulled high into a loose ponytail. Her latest getup to fit the image of a dream girl for some man. This time, a rodeo cowboy from Selma.

She'd smeared on blush and bright red lipstick, and there was a smudge on her front tooth. A tiny blot of red, right in the center. I remember staring at it, fixated, while she rattled off my instructions for the night: *Don't answer the door. Do your homework. Go to bed by nine.*

Instead of listening to her words, all I could think about was that smudge…like maybe if I stared hard enough, it might tell me everything I needed to know about who she really was.

Back then, I never knew if she was coming home that night. Though she always promised she would. Only the morning and her empty bed would tell.

That was how it always was. Her voice echoing down the hallway before she disappeared, chasing something wilder than motherhood.

Some nights, I used to whisper into the silence, just to hear something answer back. Even if it was only the fridge humming, or the sound of a hoot owl calling from the trees.
It was better than nothing.

"Madison, dear. When will she be home then?" Colleen asked interrupting my thoughts.

"She won't be," I said gently, the words tasting like oil. "She's dead."

Silence fell between us, cold and heavy. Colleen blinked and shook her head.

"That can't be right. No. No, I just saw her…"

"I'm sorry," I said, retreating onto the porch steps.

My hand found the doorframe before my body did. I steadied myself, fingers trembling slightly. Not from grief. From the weight of saying it out loud. Again. It didn't get easier.

I shut the door behind me and stood there, breathing hard, watching Colleen through the side window. She stood still for a long time. Then her shoulders sagged, and she disappeared into her yard, swallowed by her own grief.

I stayed by the door even after she was gone, Leech weaving between my legs. The house felt quieter now. Heavier, as if it just found out too.

Outside, the wind picked up, rustling the dried azaleas against the porch rail. Something sharp pressed behind my eyes. Not tears. Just pressure. Like a headache waiting to bloom.
I turned the lock on the door and whispered to the room behind me.

"I'm not here to stay."

But the air didn't shift.
The house didn't believe me.

———————•◆✦◆•———————

Hours later, I sat on the floor of the living room surrounded by opened Amazon boxes and a cup of Folgers. At least forty of them were toppled on the floor. From the looks of things, my mother had become some sort of shopaholic. She'd ordered everything from a DIY suncatcher kit to a crevice-sized mini vacuum. Socks with sarcastic sayings. A boxed facial steamer. A wall decal that read "Let it Be" in glitter script.

All of it junk. Meaningless, plastic, consumer trash.
And I packed it all up for donation.

The floor around me looked like the aftermath of a lonely birthday party. Torn cardboard, bits of packing tape, things that will never be touched or loved. I wondered what she was trying to fill. What she thought might finally show up at her door and save her. I almost felt sorry for her in that moment.

———————•◆◆•———————

Later, I stood in the hallway, steadily darkening as the sun set outside. I looked up at the photos lining the dimly lit wall of the hallway.
Me in diapers, my mom's eighties prom picture, and a photo of a fuzzy mixed-breed dog from her childhood.
My eyes glazed over all of them and landed on the infamous picture of my grandmother. My mom's mom in the early seventies.
Bell-bottom jeans and oversized sunglasses. She was smiling, leaning on the hood of a '65 Mustang. She looked like someone out of a movie. Carefree. Untouchable. An undeniable doppelganger twin of Farrah Fawcett.

I never met my grandmother. She passed when my mother was only ten. This image on the wall is how I always saw her in my mind. Radiant and young. Full of life.
Something otherworldly.
A better version of my own mother.

Maybe that's who my mother was trying to become. Carefree. Unreachable.

BETWEEN FRIENDS

I moved past the photos and stood at the edge of the hallway, my heart pounding just slightly faster than before. With one more room left to inspect, I paused. It was the only door I hadn't opened. Not because I forgot it but because I didn't want to see what might be behind it.
But it was there. Not going away. Closed tight, waiting for me.

So, I pushed open the door to my mother's office.

The air inside was still. Like it had paused, waiting for her return.
The desk was buried under magazines and receipts, takeout menus, and unopened bills. Everything stuck in mid-motion.

I walked over to the desk, pushed aside an unopened electric bill, and picked up a magazine from the top of the stack.
The title glistened in the low lighting. *Muse Magazine.*
Last month's issue sitting on top of several back issues.
Judging by the stack, she seemed to have collected every single one they'd released that year.

There were dog-ears on some of the pages, smudges of fast-food grease on the covers.

A neon pink sticky note peeked from the side of the one in my hand. I opened it to the page she'd marked.

And there it was.
One of my shoots. A red-haired, omnisexual model in a highlighter-yellow suit, chunky earrings hanging like chandeliers.
I'd hated that shoot. It wasn't my best work. The colors were all wrong, the lighting was off, and the model had refused to follow direction.

Still. She'd marked my work.

I sucked in a sharp breath.

55

The tears came without resistance this time.
They were quiet.
No heaving sobs, no drama.
Just the kind of tears that slipped out when there was no more pretending
that everything was okay.
Because it wasn't.

Because this house still felt like her.
Because she tried in her own strange, broken way.
Because she was gone, and she still left a mess. And a part of me missed
her. At least missed what I thought she should've been. A mother.

When the tears dried, I made my way to the kitchen and reached for the
bottle of wine.
I set it right back down.

My head hung low with a knowing. This was not going to cut it.
I needed something stronger than wine tonight.

I changed clothes, grabbed my keys, and stepped out into the thick
evening air.
I was just looking for a bar and a strong cocktail.

Somewhere dark. Somewhere with neon lighting and bad music and the
dull comfort of strangers.

But what I didn't know…
I was about to walk straight into the arms of fate.

CHAPTER 6

Madison

The sign for The Drunken Parrot flickered. Neon letters blinked, green, then red, then green again, casting a low glow across the gravel lot. The bar sat off the main road, forgotten by time, slouching into itself like an old forgotten relic.

The parking lot was fuller than I expected. Especially for a Wednesday night.

Shouldn't sinners be in church? I wondered.

When I passed by First Baptist Church, mid-week services were in full swing. Voices lifted hymns into the sky, floating into the air, hollow and strained.

Of course, if I still lived in this town, you'd find me here too.
Not clapping along in the pews. Not folding my hands under stained glass.
But here.

Among the drifters and the lifers.
The real believers.
The ones who wore their sins on the outside for the world to see.

If there was a God, I was sure He wasn't behind the church walls where the tithing plate always needed filling and the preacher's hands were a little too grabby with the young girls.

No. God was more likely to be found in places like this.

In dimly lit corners of dark bars where people lingered, drinking away their sorrows. Where the lights buzzed, the wallpaper peeled, and the truth slipped out easier than it ever did in a confessional box.

The air was thick with humidity, and the ground crunched under my flats as I stepped out the car.
Cricket songs rasped from the trees behind the building, their night songs rising and falling. The true song of the south.

The warped wooden door of the Drunken Parrot creaked as I stepped inside. The air was thick, stagnant and stale. The smell of smoke, old liquor, and must filled my nose. Everything around me was muted and ambered, like a memory pressed in wax. The light was low, but not cozy. Just dark enough to hide in.

I made my way to the bar, letting my fingers trail over the worn edge of the counter as I passed, the grain smooth in some places, splintering in others. Years of stories and time soaked into it. Cheap lacquer and secrets.

I slid onto an empty stool next to an old man, leaning against the bar, half asleep, the remnant of beer in front of him. The seat was cracked vinyl, warm beneath me, a faint stickiness clinging to the backs of my thighs. Somehow, that felt right. Familiar and comforting.

"Stand by Your Man" played on the jukebox, its slow drawl curling like a smoky ribbon through the room, reinforcing the time warped theme of this place.

I glanced around.

No one else seemed bothered by the twangy whine or the patriarchal lyrics echoing off the walls.

A few women swayed in their barstools, mouthing every word like it was an anthem.

If this were California, a protest would've broken out mid-chorus. Maybe even made the news.

Behind the bar, a short blonde bartender reached up on tiptoe for a bottle of Evan Williams 65 perched on the top shelf. She finessed the bottle with her fingers, and it seemed to float down straight into her hands.

She poured a perfect shot without even glancing at the glass, eyes fixed on the woman across from her. They were shouting over the music, something about a high school football game and crooked referees.

The woman leaned heavily on the counter, shouting at the bartender, nails chipped, sun-streaked hair swept into a messy knot. She wore a faded Panthers sweatshirt and denim shorts that had seen too many summers. Probably had three kids in Little League and a husband who still talked about his glory days like they mattered. She had that brittle kind of energy...the kind built from PTA meetings and barely sleeping.

They continued their conversation like the words they spoke held the balance of world peace and I rolled my eyes.

Small-town drama. Small-town minds.
They never changed.

The bartender slid the whiskey across the bar to a man three stools down, his NC State ball cap pulled low, shadowing his face. His head was buried in his phone, and he didn't look up, as he grabbed the glass and muttered something drowned out by Patsy Cline.

The bartender made her way over to me, green eyes sparkling in the glow of the neon lights. As she did, the song ended. And another one didn't start. The silence fell sudden and heavy, like the whole bar paused.

Within a few seconds, the soft clutter of bar sounds began to creep back in. Ice shifting in glasses, the low thud of a bottle being set down too hard. Muffled conversation swelled in the corners, like voices drifting underwater. A burst of laughter rang out, too loud, and vanished just as fast. Somewhere behind me, a barstool squeaked on the floor, and the faint clatter of a dropped spoon echoed sharp against the quiet.

I wished someone would put money in the jukebox.
Soured country music was better than this.
But no one moved. Everyone too broke or too proud to feed the machine.

"What can I get ya?" the bartender asked without a smile.

She was pretty.
Not LA pretty, but something softer. Familiar.
There was something in her face I couldn't quite place. Like I knew her. But of course, I didn't.

Still, something about her eyes pulled at something buried. Like déjà vu you couldn't trace.

"Jack neat with a lime. And anything local you've got on draft," I said, still watching her.

"We've got a brown ale, a lager, and a pretty nice IPA. The Mango Bango's decent, most people seem to like it," she offered.

"That's a bold-faced lie, Kristen," said the guy in the ballcap without looking up. "That stuff's too sweet. Especially for someone drinking straight whiskey."

The old man that had been sitting beside me, finished his beer, slammed down a crumpled ten, and left without a word, like we had offended him.
The door creaked open, letting in a rush of warm air before it shut again with a thud.

The man in the cap got up from where he was sitting and slid into the now empty seat beside me, like it belonged to him.

"Get her a Coors Light. She'll love it," he told the bartender.

I held up a hand.
"No, I do not want a Coors Light, actually. But thanks."

He chuckled, deep and unbothered.

"Aww, come on, Maddie. You don't drink Coors anymore? That California life got you all high and mighty?"

The sound of the name jarred me.
Maddie.
Second time today someone had called me that.

"How do you know my name? I mean... my old name. I don't go by that anymore."

He looked up.
Deep brown eyes. Familiar.

"You don't recognize me? I'm truly hurt," he said, grinning.

"Andy?" I asked, leaning closer. "Is that you?"

"Yes, it's me. Am I that old looking that you didn't know your own old best friend?"

"Well, I wouldn't quite call you *my* best friend. After all, you were dating Imogen last I knew."

"God! Seriously? That was a lifetime ago. She's married now. Couple kids. Get with the times, Maddie," he said with a laugh.

The way he said my name had a worn-in ease, and I couldn't help but smile.

"And anyway, did you forget I was the one that bailed you out of that mud pit when you were twelve? If it hadn't been for me, you'd be buried under all that mud."

"It was your idea for us to swim there, you know!" I said, laughing now.

"I didn't know it was only three feet deep, and you jumped in first!"

"Yeah, yeah, blame me, Andy. You know it was your fault," I said, with feigned offense.

We laughed again. And just like that, the years fell away, and we were two kids again.
For a second, I let myself float in it. The kind of memory that softened you without permission.

Kristen came back and dropped off a Coors Light and my shot of whiskey, no lime. I opened my mouth to correct her, but Andy was still smiling, caught in some nostalgic joy, and I let it go.

"Hey Kristen," Andy called. "This is Madison Andrews. Fresh in from the West Coast."

Kristen turned around and looked at me, her eyes darkened.

"Maddie, this is Kristen. You remember her, right? Olivia's kid sister."

The words sliced through me before I could brace.
The bar began to shrink around me, squeezing.
I closed my eyes for a moment, wishing everything would disappear.

Kristen stepped closer. Her voice cool, even. "Yeah. I remembered you right away."

I swallowed. *No wonder she looked so familiar.*

The resemblance was impossible to miss now. She had Olivia's jawline. The same almond-shaped eyes, but hers were harder. And her lips pressed into a tight line that Olivia never wore. Olivia had smiled wide. Kristen did not.

"Wow. I wouldn't have recognized you, Kristen. Last time I saw you, you were what, ten?" I sputtered.

She didn't answer.
Just turned and walked away like she had somewhere better to be.
Like being near me left a bad taste in her mouth.

Andy kept talking, something about the mud incident again, but I couldn't hear him.
There was a buzzing in my ears.
A pressure building in my chest.

I stood abruptly.
"Excuse me, I have to pee. Be right back."

I ducked into the tiny back bathroom, sliding the rusty lock closed behind me.

The latch stuck at first, groaning like it hadn't moved in years before finally clicking into place.

The air was thick with the sharp stink of urine, half-masked by flowery-scented air freshener.
The combination was offensive.

The mirror was permanently fogged, but I saw enough. I looked terrified. And tired. Worn through by memories I'd spent over a decade trying to bury. I splashed cold water on my face and pressed my palms against the sink. The porcelain was cracked in the corners, cold and trembling beneath my hands.

No one knows anything, I told myself.
No one except Imogen.
And me.
And I didn't plan on running into Imogen on this trip. Or ever.

As far as everyone else was concerned, Olivia had run away to New York and vanished.
That was the story. And that was the end of it.

But deep inside I knew it wasn't the end. It never was. It would always be there, hanging over me. Waiting to strike.

I dried my face with a rough brown paper towel and unlatched the door. An older woman waited outside the door, leaning against the wall, eyeliner smeared into the lines on her face, wobbling and reeking of gin.

"'Bout time," she muttered, brushing past me into the stall and dropping her pants without bothering to shut the door.

I didn't look back.

Andy was still waiting for me at the bar when I came out.
He sat, one elbow resting on the counter, his fingers tracing circles in the condensation on his beer glass.
The seat beside him still warm.
Still open.

My heart stuttered.

Andy.

The secret crush I'd nursed from second grade to senior year. The one boy who stole my heart. And truth be told, I'd never felt the same about another guy, even to this day. What I'd felt for him had been strong. Encompassing.

Imogen knew how I felt about him, and she took him anyway.
Just because she could.
She could've had her pick of any guy in the school, but she picked Andy.

My Andy.

And now here he was.
All these years later.

Older. Broader. But the same familiar softness behind the eyes.
Like time had layered him but hadn't changed the center.

For a second, I didn't move. I just watched him.
The way he leaned forward a little when someone spoke beside him, polite even when disinterested. The curve of his shoulders, broader than I remembered, filled out now by time and whatever life he'd been living.

His profile was different now...less boyish...but there was something steady about it.

Something inside of me shifted. What it meant, I didn't know.
But I found myself floating back toward my seat.

The jukebox had started again...something slower now, softer...a voice
like silk drifting beneath the murmur of conversation.

I passed by Kristen, and she glared at me. Like she knew the truth. About
what I'd done.
But maybe it was my imagination, guilt skewing my perception.

But whatever it was, I ignored it. Andy was there. Waiting. Nostalgia
called me back to him.

As I slipped back into my seat, he flashed that same charming grin that
got to me all those years ago. It was softer now, lived-in, but it still
landed like a spark against my skin.

I looked at him, searching, as his warm eyes met mine.
Steady and unblinking, like no time had passed.

My pulse quickened. Just slightly. Just enough to notice.
There was a flutter in my chest, light and uneasy.
My breath caught in my throat and suddenly I felt something I hadn't
felt in a very, very long time. Something that whispered hope. That this
could be something. We could be something.

But the truth pulsed in the background reminding me that it couldn't
happen.

Not now. Not ever.

Not after what happened that night in the woods.

Messing around with Andy was like playing with fire. Eventually I was
going to get burned.

CHAPTER 7

Madison

We were on our second round of drinks when Kristen's shift ended. She stopped on her way out, her hand resting lightly on Andy's shoulder, ignoring me completely.

"You on duty tomorrow?" she asked.

"Yup. Night shift, so I won't see you," he answered.

She nodded and smiled. The first smile I'd seen on her face all night. She turned before I could make sense of it. The sound of her heels echoed on the hardwood as she crossed the bar to the exit. She disappeared out the door without another word, leaving the air colder than before.

As soon as she disappeared, Andy turned to me.

"She sure has grown up, hasn't she?" His voice was light, as he said it, but his expression shifted ever so slightly, something flickering in his eyes that I couldn't read.

"So, you did it? You're really on the force?" I asked, changing the subject.

He nodded. "Yes, ma'am. Deputy Sheriff, as of last year. And I love every second of it."

The pride in his voice was impossible to miss. I remembered how determined he'd been to get into the police academy…how nothing was going to stop him. It had been his dream for as long as I could remember, even back when we were still swimming in creeks and climbing trees, mud streaked up our legs and tree branches tangled in our hair.

"I knew you would make it. Even back then. I knew you would be somebody."

"Well, hey, look who's talking…Miss West Coast fancy-pants photographer!"

"It's never boring. I have met some pretty unusual people," I said with a laugh. "And it pays the bills, so that helps."

He lifted his beer glass. "Cheers to us. We turned out pretty dang cool, if I do say so myself."

I clinked my glass against his. The tap of glass meeting glass echoed sharper than it should've, hollow and cold. And as the echo rang out, Olivia's face flashed in my mind.

Cold. Still. She was out there in the woods. In our woods. The very ones we played in when innocence reigned supreme.

And little did Deputy Sheriff Andy Marson know…

He was sitting across from the girl who helped put her there.

The bar grew quieter as the night wore on. Conversations dipped into murmurs, laughter thinned to occasional chuckles. Even the jukebox went silent again, leaving only the clink of glass and the low hum of the beer cooler to fill the space between us.

"You know, I never gave up," Andy said suddenly, pushing away his empty glass.

"Gave up on what?" I asked, sipping on my beer casually, still half full. I was pacing myself.

"On Olivia, of course," he continued.

The sound of her name echoed through my mind, rattling me. Condensation from my glass slid down my fingers, cold and slick. Across the room, someone laughed too loudly and fell quiet again.

I picked up the remnants of my drink and swallowed it in one go. *Had he read my mind during the toast?*

"They closed her case within days of her going missing," Andy continued. "No one really looked for her. Even from day one. Everyone assumed she really ran off to New York. But I wasn't convinced."

He leaned in slightly, voice lowering. "I tried to re-open the investigation once I joined the force. They said it wasn't worth the time. No evidence. No trail. Just another runaway kid."

"Well," I said carefully, "she always said she was leaving after graduation. Maybe she just... meant it."

The lie scraped against my throat, ragged and tough, and I coughed.

"You, okay?"

"Yeah. Just tired. Jet lag, you know? It's catching up to me."

The stool creaked beneath me as I shifted, suddenly too aware of how close we were sitting. The air felt heavier now. Thicker. Like the walls were closing in.

He put his hand on my arm. The feel of his skin on mine, sent a jolt of electricity through me.

 "Maddie, I'm really sorry about your momma."

"Thanks," I said, pulling away from his touch.

I was ready to leave.

Kristen's replacement stood behind the bar. I watched, as he worked methodically hand drying cocktail glasses with a white towel. Slow but precise, with broad shoulders and a face weathered from years of smoke and long nights. His graying beard was trimmed close, and a faded tattoo curled above his shirt collar.

I signaled to him for the check, and he nodded in silent understanding.

"No way," Andy said, waving off my attempt to pay.

"This one's on me. For old time's sake," he insisted.

I accepted because it gave me an opportunity for a quick exit.

A kindness I didn't deserve.
But I took it anyway, because it gave me a chance to leave while he was distracted.

I gave him a quick side hug and darted for the door before he could say anything else.
Before my resolve grew weaker.

The door slammed behind me, sharp and final.
And I made a run for it.

BETWEEN FRIENDS

Running from the memories.
Running from my feelings.
Running from the look in his eyes that almost made me stay.

But just as my hand touched the car door handle, I heard his voice behind me.

"Dang, you ran out of there fast."

I turned. Andy stood behind me in the parking lot, hands in his pockets, smiling. He pulled his ball cap off and ran his hands through his thick brown hair.

His stare penetrated my soul, weaking my resolve.

"I told you I'm tired," I said, forcing a laugh. It sounded brittle but it was the best I could do.

"I'd like to see you again, Maddie. How long will you be in town?"

"What? For old time's sake?" I asked, sharper than I meant to.

"Aww. Don't give me a hard time. Just say yes," he said, his eyes pleading.

Everything in me screamed to say no.

He was a cop. And if he ever found out what I did, I'd be behind bars for the rest of my life.

But the words that came out were:

"I'd like that."

We exchanged numbers and I climbed into the rental and drove off in silence.

The air in the car was suffocating me. I cracked a window to catch my breath. And the second I pulled onto the main road, Olivia's name whispered through my mind like a ghost dragging a finger across my shoulder. Like she was judging me for coming back to this town. For trying to reclaim anything I left behind. My exile had been my punishment. And now I was trying to take it back.

The drive back felt different than the night before. The town was even more hollow than it had been when I arrived with California glitter on my shoes. I passed the First Baptist Church. Now dark, the steeple looming against the cloudy ebony sky like an omen. A warning I wasn't heeding.

I turned onto Magnolia Lane, cursing myself. Of all the bars in town. Of all the nights. Of all the people to run into…Why Andy? And why did I turn into a stupid adolescent child again the moment he looked at me?

As I pulled into the driveway, the headlights swept across the darkened yard like a searchlight in a forgotten place. While I was gone, the porch light finally burned out, leaving the house in a quiet, dark silhouette.

I turned off the engine and silence fell. The kind that felt too still. Imposing and cold.

The yard looked different now too. Wrong somehow.
I looked around slowly, and every shape seemed off...like the night had warped them.
What had been trees this morning now looked like figures. Everything had morphed into eerie silhouettes. Twisted limbs. Gnarled shadows. Things that had occupied my childhood nightmares.

BETWEEN FRIENDS

The woods at the edge of the yard, the ones I used to run through barefoot, felt like they were leaning in... pressing closer with every passing breath.

I gripped the steering wheel tighter, a fearful pulse ticking in my throat.

A sudden flash of movement caught my attention. My eyes darted to the wood line.

Then flash of something moved between the branches.

I told myself it was nothing.
That I was just tired.
Jet lag. Whiskey. Old ghosts.

Then a sudden boom sounded directly in front of me, and I screamed. My body jerked back into the seat, as Leech leapt up from the shadows, landing squarely on the hood, tail puffed, eyes wild. He hissed, low and guttural, like he didn't recognize me anymore. His ears flattened as he stared through the windshield, unblinking.

I didn't move. Just stared back.
For a moment, neither of us did anything.

He slipped off the side, vanishing into the dark with no sound at all.

I exhaled, slow and shaky, and got out.

The moon peeked out from behind the clouds. It cast a sickly light over the front stoop, making the peeling paint and warped boards look even more distorted. The house stared back at me, every window dark, each one like an empty, watching eye, as I fumbled for the keys.

Leech jumped onto the porch and sat beside me like nothing had happened. I wanted to be mad at him for scaring me but was grateful for his company. I opened the door, and he brushed right past me without hesitation. Like this was his domain now.

Inside, the air hadn't moved since I left. It was stale, but something else was here now too. Like I'd dragged something in with me.
Or maybe it had been waiting here all along.

I dropped my purse on the side table and leaned against the door, exhaling through my nose.
But the guilt didn't release.
It stayed close.

Olivia.

Her name moved through my mind like a ripple across still water.
Her voice in the quiet. Her shadow on the stairs.

The lights buzzed faintly when I flipped the switch, casting a yellow wash across the hall. I didn't move for a long moment.

I didn't want to keep going.
Didn't want to be in this house.
Didn't want to be in this skin.

But I was here.
And the ghosts were too.

I went straight to the kitchen, popped the cork off the wine bottle, poured some into a plastic cup, and sank onto the cold linoleum floor.
I drank it in a haze, the wine sharp and thin on my tongue, barely tasting it.

BETWEEN FRIENDS

The unwanted cat curled up in my lap like he belonged there, his body warm against mine.
His rough purring filled the silence...deep, steady, and unbothered.

The only sound of life in the house. And somehow... soothing.

I let my eyes close, just for a moment. Just long enough to catch my breath. And without warning, the past came rushing in.
Uninvited, unrelenting.
Opening all of the wounds, I'd worked so hard to close.

With Leech in my lap and wine in my throat, the night of the senior graduation party unveiled itself across the theater of my mind. Grainy and distorted. But relentless in its pursuit of me. It clamped down on me like a vice, forcing me to watch. Frame by brutal frame, I relived the moment everything changed...

The bonfire crackled in the center of the clearing, casting long, flickering shadows that danced across the damp earth. The smell of smoke, sweat, cheap beer, and pine sap hung in the humid air, as moonlight filtered through the trees in thin, crooked blades. Music pulsed from someone's car speakers, distorted through the distance. Too loud. Too fast.

Laughter rang out from every direction, echoing like it was circling me. Everyone was drinking too much. Including me. The bottle had been passed around so many times I'd forgotten what was in it.

My thoughts swam sideways. Everything was soft around the edges, but the heat, the noise, the light...it was all too bright.

Imogen was the only one not drunk. She paced around the edge of the fire, talking too fast, her hands flying. Her jaw was locked, eyes wild, pupils sparking, catching the flames.

She was furious with Andy. Mad that he hadn't come.
Mad that he'd stayed home to study for the academy test.
She called him a coward. Said he'd rather chase a badge than be with her.

I sat on the edge of a log, watching her unravel, one thread at a time.
I should have defended him. He was doing something with his life.
He was going to Raleigh. He was going to make a difference.

But my tongue felt thick, and the fire was mesmerizing.
Everything she said started to smear at the edges like watercolor bleeding.

I took another drink. And another.

I was mad at her. Mad for being mad at him. Mad because nothing about that night felt right, but I was too slow and heavy to stop it.

The bottle tilted again.
And I couldn't find Imogen anymore.
She was gone. I could've sworn she'd just been there. Shadows moved along the edge of the fire instead, blurring in my mind. The bottle was in my hands again, and I took another swig.

One minute I was staring into the fire, the embers swimming like red stars, and the next…
I was in the woods.

Alone.

The trees were too close. The air was tighter, strangling me. Every twig snap felt like a threat.

Every whisper of wind through the branches sounded like someone saying my name.

Something was wrong. I knew it in my bones. But nothing made sense.

The trees leaned in, swaying. Closer than they should have been. The moonlight couldn't quite reach me here. A cold sweat broke across my skin, even though the air was warm.
My legs were unsteady, like the ground might tilt at any second.

Shadows moved slowly, and all at once.

There was a scream...sharp and sudden...
but it got swallowed whole by the music.
And then...
Blood.
So much blood.

But I didn't know whose.
But it was all over me.

Crimson glinted in the moonlight. It was on leaves. On bark.
On my hands.

Or maybe that part wasn't real. Maybe it was the drink.
Maybe it was the moonlight playing tricks.

I tried to breathe, but the air tasted like ash.
Something rustled just beyond the trees.
A shape. A shadow. A girl running. Or falling.

The woods stretched out silent and endless in every direction. But then...a voice. Distorted and echoing. Like it was being piped in through a broken speaker deep in the trees.

Imogen's voice stretched thin, reaching me. She said, "Olivia's not...
breathing..."

The leaves stirred violently. A branch snapped.
Somewhere, something crashed through the underbrush.

"Maddie! Don't just stand there. Help me..." her voice louder now.

The rest was swallowed by the pounding in my ears. Or maybe the
music, still faint in the distance. I staggered forward a step and the world
tilted again.
And then...nothing.

Just the trees. The hush of the now silent woods. And the thick,
thrumming terror curling hot at the base of my spine that jarred me back
into the present.

I opened my eyes, and the wine bottle sat empty in my lap.
I hadn't even realized I'd finished it.

Leech stirred, yawned, stretching against me with talon like claws
grazing my thigh. His purring was low now, nearly imperceptible.

I blinked in the dark kitchen, echoes floating around me.
The fire. The blood. Imogen's voice.
"Help me..."

Her words clung to me like a mist. I pressed my palms to my face, trying
to will it away.
But the woods were still in my throat. And Olivia's scream echoed
behind my eyes.

I got up on shaky legs, Leech trailing close behind. Each step up the
staircase felt like walking through molasses. The house creaked around

me...soft, settling groans...but tonight it sounded different. Not like settling. More like it was trying to wrap around me. Trying to grab me.

I moved with a purpose. I didn't turn on the hallway light. I didn't want to see the photographs. To catch my own reflection in the glass. I just opened the bedroom door and dropped onto the bed without changing clothes. Leech hopped up beside me and curled into the dip near my pillow, his body warm and anchoring. My head sank into the pillow.

I was just on the edge of sleep, teetering...when the phone rang.

The ringtone shattered the silence, piercing and shrill in the dark. My heart leapt to my throat as I fumbled blindly for the screen, blinking against the harsh glow.

A local number.
Again.

"Hello?" I asked, my voice small. Thin.

On the other end...nothing. Just static.

Then breathing. Raspy. Rhythmic.
Too slow. Too deliberate.

Just like earlier today at Publix.

"What do you want?!" I snapped, voice cracking from the strain.

The breathing grew louder.
Like whoever it was had leaned closer to the receiver.
I hung up.

My hands shook as I stared at the screen, the glow seeming to pulse in the darkness.

I wasn't sure what I was trying to accomplish but I couldn't stop myself. I called the number back. Ready to fight. To admonish this childish behavior.

It trilled in my ear. Ringing and ringing.
But no one answered.

The silence that followed felt heavy.
Like some unseen threat had settled over me.

Leech purred softly beside me, the sound a slow, vibrating thrum.
I stared into the dark. Waiting for... something.

Finally, I opened Google, fingers trembling, and ran a reverse search. One result.

Number not found.

That was worse somehow. Worse than a name. Worse than a blocked caller.
Like it had never existed.

I laid back down, but the room didn't feel right. I lie quietly in the dark, phone still glowing in my lap. The house around me was quiet. Too quiet. Leech's tail flicked against my arm, but I didn't move. I lay there, plagued by flickers of red splattered blood against leaves, the sound of breathing on the phone line, and the sickening weight of the woods closing in around me.

Sleep only came when the sky began to pale.

CHAPTER 8

Imogen

I couldn't sleep, so I slipped out from underneath the covers, careful not to wake Chris. I tiptoed down the stairs into the hush of the night. The house was silent, blanketed in stillness, except for the soft mechanical hum of the refrigerator and the occasional creak of settling floors.

I opened the back door and stepped out into the cool air, grateful for the rush of night against my skin. I looked up at the sky, riddled with millions of stars. They watched me, as I reached under a planter pot and grabbed a pack of Marlboro cigarettes I kept hidden from Chris and the boys. I lit the cigarette with a rusty blue Bic lighter and took a long drag, as the orange tip glowed against the darkness. I exhaled a long plume of smoke, my mood sour, bitterness biting the back of my throat.

Maddie had been back in town over twenty-four hours, and I hadn't heard from her. That really burned me. And it didn't help that she was the talk of the town. Everyone was talking about Madison Andrews the hometown girl turned West Coast goddess. I heard about her in the bank and the grocery store. The woman behind me in line at Walgreens said her cousin saw Maddie at the Publix and swore she looked like a movie star.

Everyone acted like they personally knew her.

But they didn't know Madison. They didn't know Maddie. Not like I did. And even if she had been gone from here for over a decade, the west coast wasn't going to save her from her roots.

From the truth.

Ignoring my friend requests was one thing.

But she was home now.

I thought maybe she'd stop by. Or call. But she did neither.

And she was all I could think about. I was consumed, thinking about the last night I saw her.

Of what we did.

You would think something like that would bond people, not make them turn their back on you.

We had been through so much together. All of us kids. An entire childhood of memories. And all it took was one night to destroy everything. And I was left holding the bag.

Yes, I was guilty too, but they should be the ones carrying the burden, not me. They should be the ones suffering with the daily panic attacks and the shame. Instead, they are parading around town like they're some kind of celebrity. A local hero. Pretending like what we did that night never happened.

I took another long drag on the cigarette balanced delicately between my fingers. I would have to throw the butt over the fence, so Chris wouldn't find the evidence in the morning.

He would be up early. Saturday morning. He would be out here mowing his precious lawn and then sit in the recliner the rest of the day watching sports and drinking beer. Praising himself for quality family time.

I guessed I should be grateful, at least Chris was faithful. At least as far as I knew.

That was something, right?

Becky down the street had just been left by her husband, for their twenty-two-year-old Russian nanny, no less. Now she drove through the neighborhood like an apparition in her Porsche, mascara smudged, smile brittle. The child support and alimony, not enough to maintain the life she was used to.

Chris might not be in love with me, that I couldn't deny, but he took great care of me and the boys. We at least had that. We never lacked for anything in the finances department. In every other department we were truly bankrupt, but at least I had a brand-new Range Rover parked in the driveway, a Nordstrom account, and curated life with soccer schedules and silk throw pillows.

It could be better. But it could also be a lot worse.

When I was younger, I always thought I would marry some celebrity or pro ball player. I was too big for this town. At least that's what I told myself.

In high school, I dated Andy, a member of our childhood neighborhood gang, now the town's beloved Deputy Sheriff. He should've been off limits. But I couldn't help myself. To show Maddie I could have whatever I wanted.

Even so, Andy was just a distraction. A plaything. I could never seriously consider someone whose only ambition was to become a cop.

An owl hooted from one of the trees along the fence line, sharp and sudden, slicing through my thoughts. I jumped, the cigarette trembling between my fingers. I took one last drag and extinguished it against a tree. I flicked the butt over the fence and hid the pack and lighter back under the planter pot, pleased with myself.

My secret sin. Smoking.

I sighed. I wished that was my only secret. A smoking mom in the backyard. But I had more secrets. I had done worse things. Much worse things.

I closed my eyes, trying to push it all back down but the memories broke through.
Maddie drunk. Stumbling. Her hands shaking. Me, cold and breathless with shock.

And Olivia. God, Olivia. Lying there like a broken doll.

Blood soaking into the earth.

I shivered in the night breeze. The stars were still watching me. Just like they had been watching that night. That horrible night. Bearing witness to the unthinkable.

Twelve years had passed and now Maddie and I were under the same sky again.

My mom called me earlier today, asking if I'd seen Maddie yet. I lied and told her that we had plans to meet up on Sunday. I couldn't let my mother think that Madison was just ignoring my very existence.

Even though she was.

And the thought of that suddenly flamed me. Like, how dare she? Back in high school, I would've never tolerated being ignored. I was the one everyone orbited around. Even Maddie.

Especially Maddie.

But now who was the golden girl? The west coast wonder. Jetsetter. Photographer to the stars.

Okay, maybe I was a little jealous. No, a lot jealous.

But if she would at least be cordial, I could forgive her for having such an amazing life. Leaving me stuck in nowhere-ville while she lives it up, forgetting every single thing that led her there. I mean, she wouldn't even have had a single bit of style sense if it wasn't for me. She wouldn't even have had half a personality if I hadn't given her one to wear.

I stepped through the back door back into the house, walking over cold Italian travertine tile, and stopped mid-step. I looked around the dark kitchen. Marble countertops. Crown molding. The leftover faint scent of the hibiscus candle I burned today.

On paper, I had it all. But who was I kidding trying to gas myself up?

Imogen, the prom queen had been traded in for the carpool queen and there were no returns.

But that didn't mean that Maddie didn't have to face the past and the consequences of that said past that she was so conveniently ignoring.

We all died a little that night. And she left me to hold the wreckage.

Because unlike her, I didn't run.
I stayed.

I *lived here*. With it.

Every day. Alone.

I stood in the dark kitchen, lit only by the glow of the fridge light, and something inside me clicked into place.

Carrying this alone. That was over now.

What happened between friends, needed to *stay* between friends.

So, if Maddie thought she could come back and pretend like nothing happened, she had another thing coming.

I didn't have to keep waiting for her to show up.

I, at the least, had power over that.

It was time to plan a little...reunion.

CHAPTER 9

Madison

The morning sun warmed my pillow, as I opened my eyes. I reached for my phone. Nine AM. The day was already getting away from me. I stretched as the unknown caller incident from last night quickly faded into the back of my mind. In the light of day, it no longer felt urgent or concerning.

I had my coffee on the porch with Leech, who had let the fact that I let him sleep in my bed go to his head. He was curled up next to me, his body, the perfect c shape, purring loudly. I dropped my hand to his silken fur and stroked his face. I thought I heard him sigh. I questioned it. Did cats even sigh? Still, I withdrew my hand.

"Don't get too comfortable. I am not sticking around," I told him. But he ignored me, too deep in cat dreams to listen to my warning.

The rumble of tires caught my attention, and I looked up just as the mailman stopped in front of the house, pushing some envelopes into what I could tell was a very full mailbox. He glanced my direction, looking like he might say something, and I looked away. I didn't look back until I heard the rumble of tires moving further away.

After he was well out of sight, I walked out to the mailbox and emptied it of its burden. It was loaded with a bunch of sales flyers and a couple of unpaid bills marked past due. As I turned away, the big black scrape on the side of the mailbox post caught my attention. The scrape that ten-year old Andy made when he crashed his bike into it, trying to show off his wheelie to me.

Andy.

My heart squeezed at the thought of him. He still had me hooked. Wrapped up in every glance, every breath. The way he looked at me last night. Warm and familiar, full of things I used to dream about in secret. It was the look I used to beg the stars for.

Being with him gave me that same feeling I had when I scribbled in hearts along the margins of my notebook.
Maddie loves Andy.
I had written it over and over, like writing it could make it real.

Back then, I had truly loved everything about him. His laugh. His drive. His dedication to wanting to be a police officer. He was good to the core.

And that was the exact problem today. Someone like Andy would never be with someone like me. If he knew what I'd done, if he had even the slightest clue, he wouldn't come within a mile of me. No matter how much history we had together. No amount of nostalgia was going to wash away the guilt.

So, there was no point in crying over spilled milk. I was a nightly drunk and a runaway criminal. I needed to stay focused on why I was here. To get my mother's house cleared and sold. And get myself back to California where I belonged. Like I told Leech. I wouldn't be here long. And the faster I got this house cleared, the faster I could leave.

I walked straight inside past all of the boxes and bags of crap my mom had accumulated and called 1-800-GOT-JUNK. It was time to get this ball rolling.

———— ◆◆◆ ————

Even if I could get my mother's stuff cleared out by the junk haulers, I still had to face my old bedroom. A room full of memories I didn't want to face and the belongings of a girl that I left behind.

I started in the closet.

Dust clung to the hems of old dresses...the ones I hadn't worn since high school. The kind with spaghetti straps and floral prints, ones I thought made me look older, more mysterious. Now, they just looked... outdated. Like they belonged to someone else.

I tossed them into a donation pile without really looking, letting the fabric slump into a heap on the bed. But when I reached behind a stack of shoeboxes in the closet, my fingers brushed something stiff and curled.

A Polaroid photograph.

I tugged it free, heart already tightening.

It was the three of us. Me, Imogen, Olivia. Taken in the backyard one afternoon in late spring, everything in bloom. Imogen was in the center, of course...hand on her hip, a glint in her eye that dared the world to ignore her.

I was on the left, laughing at something out of frame, hair wind-tangled, no makeup, eyes squinting against the sun. I looked... alive. Happy, maybe.

And then there was Olivia.

Tucked on the right, half in shadow, arms folded loosely across her stomach like she wasn't sure what to do with herself. Her blonde hair fell in soft waves down her back, thick, like she'd just stepped out of the ocean. Her eyes...those impossibly clear sea-green eyes...held a thousand things she'd never say out loud. Her skin was warm and sun-kissed, glowing even in the dull paper print.

Imogen always acted like Olivia was the least of us. Quiet. Mousy. But looking at this picture now, it was obvious...Olivia was radiant. Ethereal. She didn't need to demand attention. She just existed, and that was enough.

I stared at her for a long time. Then I stared at the three of us...ghosts in cheap Polaroid ink.

With trembling hands, the ache in my chest, gnawing, I dropped the picture into the trash can beside the dresser. It landed face-down, caught on the edge of the can.

I turned to take in the rest of the room. Still so clean, it didn't belong in this house. The rest of the place was breaking down...dusty baseboards, cracked wallpaper, rooms that smelled like time. But my bedroom looked untouched. Preserved. Like I might come back at any minute, throw my backpack on the bed and start complaining about algebra.

Trophies lined the dresser...cheer, track, even one for "Most Spirited," which was laughable now. Little gold-plated girls frozen mid-jump or holding plastic batons. Their shine hadn't dulled at all. Unlike me.

A framed photo of Andy sat tucked into the corner of the mirror. He was in his football uniform, helmet under one arm, grin crooked and carefree. I reached for it, thumb grazing the edge of the glass. His eyes looked different back then. Brighter. So different than the Andy from last night. His eyes now carried the weight of the world.

Next to the photo sat a bottle of perfume...Sunflowers. One of those cheap but wildly popular scents from the 90s that I wore like it was a religion. I popped the cap and inhaled, instantly slammed by memories. Pep rallies. Locker rooms. Glitter lip gloss. The smell of too many teenage girls crammed into a car with the windows down and the radio too loud. I set the bottle down fast, releasing the memories, too strong, too bright.

BETWEEN FRIENDS

In the back of the closet, the real ghosts waited.

My old cheer uniform hung limply on a padded hanger, the fabric faded but still proud in its colors. Red and gold. I traced the embroidered lettering with my fingertip, for a moment, not sure if I missed the girl who wore it or pitied her.

As I dug deeper, I found it. Wedged in the back corner of the closet, half buried beneath some old winter coats and a torn garment bag.
The dress.
Satin, soft blush pink, wrinkled now in places where it used to cling tight to skin and hope.

I hadn't laid eyes on it in over a decade.
But I could still remember the way it felt on. How I spun in front of the mirror that night, thinking this dress would surely do it.

I'd bought it thinking maybe… maybe this time he'd really see me.
Maybe if I looked beautiful enough, he'd stop choosing her.

I touched the fabric now, fingertips grazing the bodice, the loose thread near the hem.
It smelled like dust and time and a little bit of that perfume.
I'd smiled too much that night.
Laughed too loud.
Tried too hard.

And he danced with Imogen anyway.

I let the skirt fall.

I walked out of the closet and my eyes landed on the trashcan, the Polaroid sticking to the edge.

The guilt stirred again, curling low and sick in my gut.
I grabbed the trashcan by its edges and carried it downstairs, careful not to look too long at what I'd buried. At the bottom, the Polaroid waited.

I tipped the can over the kitchen bag and let it fall, silent, weightless. A single flutter of glossy paper. I closed the lid quickly, but not before my eyes caught hers.

Olivia. Still smiling in that frozen, golden light. Still haunting.

I turned away fast, breath held tight in my chest and hurried for the stairs. I passed the photo of my grandmother in the hallway. And stopped.

Without thinking twice, I reached up and pulled it from the wall. The frame gave easily, lighter than it looked. She stared out through the glass, still and strong. The kind of woman who didn't ask permission. The woman my mother never talked about, at least not without a sharp edge.

But there was something in her eyes I recognized.
Something I needed.

I tucked the frame under my arm and kept walking.

Back upstairs, I nestled it into my suitcase between folded sweaters and clothes I wasn't sure I'd wear again and closed the lid.

That's when I heard it.

A low groaning sound outside. Tires squealing. The heavy grind of machinery out back.

I stood still, my pulse ticking in my ears.

The woods. It was coming from the woods…

BETWEEN FRIENDS

My feet moved before I could think. Down the stairs. Through the back door. The air outside was heavy with heat and the tang of disturbed ground.

The earth was soft beneath my steps, still damp from a late morning rain shower. Grass brushed against my shins, wild and overgrown, twining itself around my ankles as if trying to slow me down. Here and there, bursts of color bloomed from the weeds. Small, stubborn flowers that hadn't been planted but had claimed the land anyway.

I paused at the edge of the property where the trimmed lawn gave way to a patch of open land. It had once been cleared for planting a garden. When my mom dated the horticulturist. But now tufts of grass reached skyward, swaying like whispers. Beyond it, the tree line loomed. Familiar, yet foreign. I hadn't been this way into the woods in years. Not since I was a girl chasing shadows with Imogen and Andy, pretending the forest was full of magic. Back then, we had come hunting for secrets...mushrooms shaped like moons, magical pools of water, stories buried in the bark of stumps.

But back then the woods felt different. Friendly and full of life.

I pushed through the brush, branches snapping at my arms, leaves wet with leftover rain dripped onto my skin. The trail was barely visible now, choked with growth...but I knew the way.

My body remembered.

The tractor's hum came again, low and distant, threading through the trees like a call. I drew in a breath and picking up my pace, my heart kicking up in my chest as the memory of bare feet and laughter trailed just behind me.

Every step toward the sound of the machinery felt like slipping deeper into something I couldn't name. Sharp branches snagged my arms as I pushed through, thorns catching on my shirt, but I didn't stop. I couldn't.

The trees thinned.

And suddenly there it was.

A massive tractor sat in a newly formed clearing. Its clawed arm dragged deep into the earth, piles of torn roots and splintered bark lying like bones around it. The trees we used to sit beneath were gone. Gone, like they'd never been there.

Limbs scattered, covering the ground. Massive tire tracks crisscrossed the soft earth, and in the center of it all.

They were clearing everything.

Here…

They were digging *right here*.

I stood at the edge of the clearing, heart slamming in my chest, breath tight in my throat. The smell of wet soil and split pines filled the air.

I froze at the edge of the clearing, my breath caught somewhere between my ribs and the past.

This was the place.

Where it happened.

Where we ended our childhoods. Our innocence.

The earth was being split open, layer by layer, and all I could think, all I could pray, was that the secrets would stay buried. That Olivia's body would stay where we left it.

That none of this would ever come back to light.

Because I knew, if even one thing surfaced, even one scrap of fabric or forgotten hair clip...

Everything would come undone.

And this time, there'd be no way to bury it again.

CHAPTER 10

Madison

The sun hung lower now, casting long shadows across the floor. The tractors had gone quiet, the work suspended for the day, but the echo of screeching tires still lingered in my mind, sharp and shrill, like they'd carved themselves into the lining of my thoughts.

I'd come in through the back door, brushed leaves and dirt from my jeans. Leech blinked at me from the windowsill, like he knew where I'd been.

I opened a can of tuna, meant for me, but now destined to top Leech's dinner. He meowed at my feet like he'd been personally wronged by my lateness of feeding him, his tail flicking with judgment as I scraped the tuna into his bowl.

"Bon appétit," I muttered, giving the can one last shake.

I was halfway up the stairs, thinking only of a shower and silence, when my phone buzzed on the hall table. I stopped and picked it up, looking at the screen.

A local number again.

I froze, my grip tightening.

My stomach flipped the way it had the night before when the same area code lit up my screen. That call had ended in silence...but not empty silence. I'd heard the breath. Steady. Waiting.

The phone buzzed again.

I hovered for a second longer, then answered.

"Hello?"

Another beat of silence. Half a second. Just long enough to feel it again...panic, memory, the edge of something wrong.

Then his voice broke through.

"Maddie?"

It was Andy's voice. The sound of him saying my name struck me like a boom of thunder.

"It's me, Andy," he said, softer now. "That sounds weird, introducing myself," he said with a laugh. "But I figured you might not have my number saved yet."

"I don't," I said, then immediately regretted how flat it sounded.

There was a pause. "Right. Makes sense."

I pressed my fingers to my temple and sighed. "Sorry. I just... wasn't expecting a call."

For a second, neither of us said anything. Then I asked, "Why are you calling?"

"I was hoping I could see you," he said. "Just for a little while. I remembered this place we used to go, and thought maybe…maybe we could go back, just for few hours."

My throat tightened.

"I don't know, Andy."

"You don't have to talk," he cut in gently. "We can just… sit. Look at the water. It's not a big deal."

I hesitated, heart thudding. I'd told myself I was going to just leave. That I didn't need closure. That seeing him again would only stir up everything I'd already worked so hard to put behind me.

But his voice…it was softer than I remembered. Worn at the edges. And there was something about the way he said "we" that cracked open a door I thought I'd nailed shut.

And somehow, that was exactly what made me say yes.

———————•◆◆•———————

I heard the rumble of his truck before I saw it…low and familiar, like it belonged to this place as much as the pine trees or the relentless summer heat. He pulled up to the curb in a four-wheel drive black Dodge Ram with the ease of someone who'd done it a thousand times before.

I stepped out onto the porch, just as he opened the driver's side door. And then he was there.

Even though I had just seen him last night, the sight of Andy standing in my front yard again jarred me. In my mind he was still supposed to be teenage Andy. Long. Lanky. Hair in his eyes. But a man stood on the lawn.

Though he looked different now, somehow, he also looked exactly the same. A little older, a little broader in the shoulders, like time had tried to rewrite him but couldn't quite let go of the original draft.

His hair was shorter now but those eyes, those eyes still made my knees go weak.

He gave a small nod. "Hey."

"Hey," I echoed, hoping my voice didn't betray the sudden rush of nerves hammering through my chest like I was seventeen again.

I climbed into the passenger seat, the door clicking shut behind me with weighted finality. The cab smelled like cedar and something I couldn't quite place...faint and familiar.

The truck rolled through town, tires humming over pavement, windows cracked just enough to let in the warm dusk air. He didn't say much as we drove. The local country music station played songs I didn't recognize, as I leaned against the passenger door, watching the familiar blur of storefronts. Trees slid past, leaning into dusk, orange and red streaking across the sky like splattered paint.

"They're tearing up the woods," I said after a while. "Our old stomping grounds."

Andy glanced over, one hand loose on the wheel. "Yeah. I heard."

I hesitated. The image of the churned-up clearing flashed behind my eyes. Dirt spilling from the bucket.

I swallowed hard. "I went back there. They've already destroyed so much."

He gave a low whistle. "More of the growth coming into the area," he said with a dry laugh. "I heard they're putting in a gated neighborhood back there. Whole thing is going to be luxury homes, saltwater Olympic pool, clubhouse, tennis courts. The works."

I turned back toward the window. "Of course they are."

"Well, where I'm taking you today, hasn't been touched by change. Not yet anyway."

"Where are you taking me?" I asked.

"You will just have to wait and see," he said, that same old boyish charm breaking through.

My pulse tapped at my neck as I sat just inches away from him, close enough to feel the heat of him in the small space between us. I kept my eyes forward, but I could feel his gaze flicker toward me every so often, then back to the road. I couldn't breathe right. It was stupid. It was everything.

As we drove, the sun filtered through the trees, warm and low, making everything outside look softer than it really was. It was one of those Carolina afternoons that made you fall in love with its rolling hills and miles of green forest. But I knew better.

This place had a way of pulling you under.
Of sweet-talking you into staying just a little longer.
Just one more week. One more season.
Then one day you'd look up and realize you'd never left.

I wasn't letting that happen.

I wasn't staying.

The old Madison lived here permanently.

And if I stayed too long, she'd find her way back to me and hold me captive.

We hit the dirt road that led to a little private lake on the backside of an old tobacco farm. A place we had hung out many times as teens.

The truck jolted slightly, the tires crunching against gravel and dust. I let out a small laugh, more air than sound. "I can't believe they still haven't paved this."

Andy smiled. "Just like I told you, some things haven't changed."

We rounded a bend, the trees pulling in closer, their branches tangled like whispered secrets. That's when we saw it.

A deer stood in the middle of the path, bathed in the last strands of sunlight.

It was still. Poised. Its body slender and taut like a breath held too long. Its coat glowed gold in the dying light, the softness of it almost unreal, like velvet stretched overshadow. Antlers arched from its head like a crown, delicate and defiant. But its eyes… its eyes were wide and alert, like it knew it was always being hunted. Even in the quiet. Even in the calm.

Andy eased the truck to a stop.

We sat there in silence, both of us watching it.

"It's beautiful," I whispered.

He nodded slowly. "Yeah, sure is."

The deer twitched an ear, turned and vanished into the woods with a single, elegant bound.

BETWEEN FRIENDS

We didn't speak again until the trees opened up, and the lake came into view.

The lake was quieter than I remembered. The kind of quiet that made you breathe softer, like the air itself was lighter here. I stepped onto the dock slowly, my shoes thudding against the worn wood. And there it was…the canoe. Green, chipped along the sides, waiting like it knew me. And it did, in a way. We had taken it out so many times in the past.

Andy stood beside it, one hand resting on the edge like this was just another summer night. Like time hadn't slid in and separated us.

"I thought maybe you'd like to come back to this spot," he said, voice low, almost careful. "You used to say the fireflies looked like stars on the water."

My chest tightened. That memory lived in some dusty corner of me, curled up and forgotten until now.

"I *did* say that," I whispered.

"Wanna go out?" he offered, his smile broad and impossibly handsome.

"Sure, but are you sure that thing is seaworthy still?" I asked, eyeing the canoe as he slipped it into the water.

"Don't you trust me?" he asked, holding out his hand.

"Not really," I said, laughing and put my hand into his.

I stepped into the canoe first, steadying myself with the edge before lowering onto the wooden seat. Andy climbed in behind me, the boat rocking gently beneath us, the rhythm slow and familiar. We drifted out, the paddles dipping into the water leaving a trail of ripples behind us.

Neither of us talked much. The silence wasn't uncomfortable, just full. Full of things we weren't ready to say yet. The kind of silence that understood time.

By the time we reached the middle of the lake, the sun had fully sunk into the trees, leaving behind the soft violet hush of dusk. I pulled the thin blanket he'd packed over my lap, fingers brushing the edge of the thermos he'd stashed beside me full of whiskey.

We drifted for a while until the water was still, touched by the light of the first stars. Fireflies began to rise from the tall grasses along the shore, blinking to life like sparks from something long burned out.

"It's exactly how I remembered it," I said, eyes fixed on their reflection dancing across the black surface of the water. "Maybe even better."

Andy smiled faintly. "I used to wonder if this place would feel different with time. Like maybe it was only magic because we were young."

I turned to look at him, the lines around his eyes deeper now, but his gaze steady. "It still feels like magic."

We sat there like that, the lake holding us, the stars above and below. And for a moment, I let myself believe it was okay to feel something again.

Andy shifted, setting the paddle across his lap and letting the canoe drift, slow and aimless, like it had nowhere better to be.

The moon had risen higher now, casting a soft silver over the water, turning everything quiet and sacred. The fireflies blinked like tiny stars caught between sky and earth, and I could feel the warmth of him, even though we weren't touching.

"I missed this," he said suddenly. "Not just the lake. You."

My breath caught.

I turned to look at him, and there was something in his eyes. Something open and raw, like he wasn't hiding anymore.

"I know I don't deserve to ask for anything," he continued, "but if I had the chance to go back, if I could change things, I would. I just want you to know, it was always you, Maddie."

I didn't know what to say to that. So, I didn't say anything.

He leaned in slowly, like he was giving me time to stop him.

But I didn't.

His lips touched mine, soft at first, gentle, like the brush of a memory. Then deeper, like he was searching for something in me he'd lost long ago.

And for one impossibly fragile second, I kissed him back.

The ripples shifted with the movement of the canoe, distorting the sky reflected there. But in the flicker of moonlight and memory, I glanced down toward the water and suddenly I saw her.

Olivia.

Her face, pale and blurred, rising through the murky black water. Eyes wide. Hair floating like seaweed. Lips slightly parted like she wanted to speak or scream but couldn't.

I gasped out loud.

The canoe rocked hard as I scrambled back, the world tilting under me. "Stop. Stop, Andy!"

He lunged forward, steadying the boat before we tipped. "Maddie, hey...what's wrong?"

"I want to go back," I said, breath short. "Take me back. Please."

He hesitated, eyes searching mine, but then nodded and reached for the paddle without a word.

The ride back to my house was quiet. Not the kind of quiet we'd shared on the way there. This one was hollow. It echoed. I kept my eyes on the silhouettes of the trees slipping past the window, pretending I didn't feel the phantom press of his lips still lingering on mine.

Andy didn't say a word. He just drove, knuckles tight on the steering wheel, gaze fixed ahead like the road might break apart if he looked at me.

When he pulled up to the curb in front of the house, the truck idled for a second before he finally cut the engine. The stillness settled heavy between us.

He exhaled deep and long, like he'd been holding it the whole drive.

"I'm sorry," he said, turning toward me. "I shouldn't have kissed you."

I blinked. "It's not that."

His brow furrowed. "Then what is it?"

I hesitated, fingers curled tight in my lap, unable to form words.

"Is it because I chose to date Imogen back in high school?" he asked, his voice softer now. "I'm sorry. It's just we were... too close? You and me. It always felt like we were more like..."

"Don't," I said sharply. "Don't say brother and sister."

He stopped, seemingly surprised.

I turned to face him fully. "Imogen chose *you,* Andy. Not the other way around. And just for the record, you were *never* like a brother to me."

The silence that followed was different this time. Charged.

"So…" he said, a half-smile tugging at the corner of his mouth, "what you're saying is you like me too then?"

I rolled my eyes, but it didn't land. Not really. My heart was still racing.

"You're impossible!" I said.

Before I could open the door, he leaned over and kissed me again. This time slower, surer. There was no question in it, no hesitation. And for a breath, I kissed him back like I meant it.

Because maybe I did. I let myself get lost in that kiss. But then reality called me back and I pulled away.

A shadow moved across the steps, as I stepped out of the truck. For a split second, my heart slammed in my chest, until I realized it was just Leech. He stretched out and yawned, tail flicking lazily, glowing eyes trained on me like he'd been expecting us.

Andy climbed out too, squinting toward the house. "Friend of yours?"

"Something like that," I murmured. "He was here when I came back. Now he's kind of adopted me."

Andy moved toward me, slipping his hand around my waist and pulled me in closer. His lips had just grazed mine as Leech let out a long, dramatic yowl, like he'd been deeply inconvenienced by our delay. Then he stood, shook himself off, and turned toward the door, clearly expecting me to follow.

I pulled away from Andy, thankful for the distraction.

"Thank you for tonight," I offered.

"Can I see you again tomorrow? I am off one more day and I'd really like to spend it with you."

"I'm really busy, Andy. There's a lot to do here still," I said, knowing full well that teenage me, would've killed for this opportunity, and here I was, squandering it.

"Hey, I totally understand," he said, shoving his hands into his pockets.

"I'll text you," I offered, though I knew I wouldn't.

He let out a half laugh. "No, you won't."

I raised my brows. "Wow, you have absolutely no faith in me, do you?"

"How about dinner, then? I mean, you have to eat, don't you?"

I glanced back toward the house. Leech was pacing the porch, tail twitching in disapproval. I looked back at Andy.

"Maybe," I said with a soft smile, turning to walk away.

"I'll take it!" Andy called, triumphant. "it's better than a no!"

"Get out of here," I yelled over my shoulder as he climbed into his truck.

I stood there for a long moment, watching his taillights disappear into the dark, the red glow fading like the end of a dream. I turned back to the porch, where Leech was waiting, eyes bright, tail flicking.

"Don't look at me like that," I muttered, stepping up beside him.

He didn't answer. Just blinked, like he knew more than he should. He waited until I opened the door before slipping inside.

I followed, heart still thudding in my chest, not from fear this time, but from everything I still didn't know how to feel.

Leech slipped inside ahead of me, his tail flicking once as he disappeared into the dark. I followed, the door creaking shut behind me with a soft thud that seemed to echo.

The house was quiet. Too dark.

I cursed myself for not leaving any lights on.

I reached for the light switch, fingertips skimming the wall. I stopped suddenly, fingertips hovering. The room was cloaked in darkness. And for just a moment, in that space between breath and thought, I saw her again.

Olivia's face.

Eyes empty, skin bluish, lips parted, ready to scream.

I backed into the wall, pressing my palm to my chest.

"It's not real," I whispered.

My hand rushed, fumbling against the wall, and found the switch. Light spilled across the room, warm and sudden. The image vanished, leaving just me. Just the living room. And just the shadows that curled around the stairwell, familiar but suddenly feeling full of menace.

Leech stood on the arm of the couch, watching me, like nothing had happened at all.

But my pulse was still pounding.

And Olivia disappeared somewhere, still in the dark.

CHAPTER 11

Imogen

I leaned in close to the mirror, steadying my hand, as I traced the liquid eyeliner along the curve of my lash line. The brush moved in a smooth arc, winging up just enough at the outer corner. I held still, watching it dry, then dipped the brush again and with practiced precision went over the line a second time. Just to be sure. The silence in the bathroom air stifled me, thick, heavy, and buzzing with the low hum of a world that never stopped judging.

I always started with the eyes. Same process every single morning...concealer, foundation, brows, eyeliner, mascara, then highlighter last. A soft dusting on my cheekbones, the bridge of my nose, a touch above my lip. Not too much. Just enough to catch the light when I turned my head.

Everything had its place. Everything in balance.

There was something comforting about the whole process. About making things look perfect. No matter how things really were. No matter how out of control I felt. This. This I could control.
Makeup was like an act of power over my life. While other moms were running around town looking haggard and worn, I looked put together every single day.

I applied lipstick last from a Chanel tube. Red and dewy. I pressed my lips together and tilted my head. Pleased with the reflection looking back at me.

I'd done my hair hours earlier. Before the boys left for school. Loose curls, the kind that looked like they happened naturally, even though it took two different irons and a round brush to get there. I tugged at the collar of my cream silk top and smoothed down the white fabric of my slacks. Fitted. Not tight.

I still had an enviable figure. People said so. I saw it too, in the way men looked at me in public, trying to pretend they weren't. Even the married ones. They always looked too. Maybe even more so, wondering how Chris ever got so lucky.

But I didn't mind. That's why I did Pilates five times a week. Why I skipped bread and sugar and drank that super green powder every morning. Why my jeans still hugged my hips like a glove.

I was still trophy wife material. Even if my husband didn't notice. Or care.

He saw me the way people see anything else in life they've gotten used to. Just part of the background. He didn't have a clue how other men desired me.

Honestly, I knew that I could have any man in town if I wanted them. From the mayor to every man at the Country Club. Even the good old Deputy Sheriff Andy Goody Two Shoes.

If I wanted him again.

Not that I did. But knowing that I could have him was enough for me. At least that's what I told myself.

I sprayed a mist of hair spray around my head like a halo, sealing the smoothed cuticles into place. It hovered for a moment in the air like a cloud, then vanished.

I caught my reflection again and paused.

Still no word from Madison.

She hadn't called. Hadn't texted. Not even a polite drive-by to say she was in town.

After all this time.

I turned my head slightly, watching the shimmer catch on my cheekbone. I looked good. Better than I even had in high school.

She'd see that.

Even though she worked for a magazine, hung out with models and lived a fancy glamorous life. Deep down, I knew that I still had her beat. I always would. She was Maddie and would always be so…well…Maddie. A little off-center, a little behind. Like a painting hung just a few inches too low. Pretty enough, but just not quite there.

I walked through the house slowly, letting my fingertips trail along the edge of the hallway table. The place was quiet, still, and perfectly kept. Not a throw pillow out of place. Not a smudge on the glass. I liked it that way. Order. Beauty. It kept the chaos from creeping into my mind. It kept the memories tucked in tightly to the corners where light didn't reach. Where no one could see.

As I passed the sitting room, I paused in front of a painting hanging above the fireplace. A piece I'd won at an art auction in Charleston. Luc Kaisin…not quite a Monet, but close enough that people pretended to know his name. He'd studied in Belgium, painted light like it was something he could trap on canvas and keep for himself.

This one was a soft ocean scene. Washed-out blues, golden sunrays, and flecks of white. Sea spray some said. Others said, it was the clouds dropping closer to touch the ocean waves.

I didn't care what it meant or said or could be interpreted as. It was nothing more than a show piece. It made the room look expensive. That was enough.

Meaning didn't matter. Appearance did. Always.

I kept walking, sling back kitten heels clicking softly against the hardwood.

In the foyer, I passed the large mirror that stretched nearly floor to ceiling, framed in antique gold leaf, carved with little clusters of fruit and curling vines. I caught a glimpse of myself as I passed and stopped.

I turned around admiring my shape. I pulled my shoulders back, stood straighter. Only a few more Pilates classes and I'd be perfectly bikini-ready for Aruba next month. The girls had already started shopping for resort wear.

I wasn't about to be the one in a cover-up, hiding that extra five pounds. They'd whisper about it, if I was. They always found someone in the group to judge.

I turned away from the mirror, and hesitated.

Something pulled me back.

My gaze flicked over my reflection again. Shoulders back, lips glossed, curls still holding place. I looked good. Perfect, even. But something... something in the glass felt off.

And then...*there she was.*

Just for a breath. A blink.

A figure behind me in the reflection. Slight. Still. Head tilted just enough to suggest she was watching me. *Waiting.*

BETWEEN FRIENDS

Olivia.

In a pink floral sundress.

The same one she wore that night.

I spun around, checking the space behind me. The was nothing there. The hallway stood empty. Quiet. No sound but the ticking of the antique wall clock and the hum of air conditioning. My chest rose and fell once. Twice. I touched my collarbone, grounding myself.

I shook my head, told myself it was the lighting. The mirror. My imagination.

Because the alternative was impossible.

I turned again, grabbed my Louis Vuitton bag off the hook by the door, and stepped outside into the blaring sun. The sunlight struck me like a bolt of lightning, like it was trying to burn away the shadow still clinging to the edge of my mirror vision. I shook it off…hard. Whatever that was, it wasn't real. Just a trick of the mirror. The past trying to claw its way back through the glass.

The light seared my eyes, and I resisted the urge to squint. Squinting caused lines, and I already had too many. I slipped on my sunglasses, oversized, dark, sophisticated, and made my way down the front steps, the concrete already warm beneath my heels. The inground sprinklers had just watered the lawn and misted the walkway, leaving air smelling like summer and chlorine.

My silver Range Rover waited in the driveway, spotless, shining in the light like a trophy. I climbed in, shut the door, and sat for a second in the cool silence of the car.

I sunk into the rich leather seat. Every seam tailored, every detail whispered luxury around me. The air inside was still the same, untouched. But something about it felt different now. Like the ghost of what I saw in the mirror had followed me out here, curling into the passenger seat beside me.

Olivia. A wisp of her dress. A glint of something behind the eyes. Just enough to remind me that the past doesn't stay buried. Maybe I'd imagined it. But either way, it was a reminder that the past was not gone.

And maybe it was time Maddie faced that.

As I cinched the seatbelt around my waist, I looked into the rearview mirror and nodded to myself. I pushed the start button and put it in reverse.

Before letting off the brake, I took a deep breath.

Then said, just loud enough to break the stillness,
"Maddie... ready or not, here I come."

————————◆◆◆————————

It was as if the car knew the way back to the old neighborhood. I hadn't been back here since my parents died eight years ago. They were killed in a helicopter tour accident in San Francisco. They had been on a trip to celebrate their 24th wedding anniversary. My mom hadn't wanted to go but went against her will. My father had insisted on taking her. Touting it being the next thing to liven up their marriage. He had been trying to save their marriage since high school, but nothing ever quite worked. That was his last effort.

One minute they were here. The next they were gone.

I turned off my street and headed across town, the wheel cool beneath my hands, the road rising in soft memory beneath the tires. The Range Rover glided across the road as if on air and in a blink, I found myself on Magnolia Lane.

It had been years since I'd driven through the old neighborhood. Magnolia Crest. Once the epitome of wealth and status, back when brick homes and two-car garages meant something.

As I turned in, I felt it...that disorienting sting of memory meeting reality. The houses looked so much smaller now. Worn. The shutters were faded. The lawns patchy with crabgrass. It was jarring...the way the past shrinks when you finally face it.

This used to be *the* place all the girls in town wanted to grow up in. We had made it seem like royalty. But looking at it now, with the life I lived and the home I had, it all felt… sad.
Beneath me.

I slowed as I passed my old house.

Someone else lived there now. The blinds were crooked in the front window, and a plastic flamingo stood in the yard.

It stunned me, the sight of it. I used to think we were the rich kids living on this street. And maybe we were for this town. But now, the sight of it, was just embarrassing.

I kept driving.

Madison had lived in the neighborhood with me. Six houses down, in a smaller house than ours, but she still lived on *this* street.

But Olivia?

She didn't grow up here. She didn't belong here.

She lived in the trailer park down the road, past the last turnoff. A rusted swing set in her yard and a porch held up by cinderblocks.

She didn't grow up with us.

Olivia wasn't clueless...she was calculated. She knew what she was doing. She wanted our world, and she knew exactly how to get it. She played pathetic. Played poor. That sniveling little act Maddie always fell for. I never did.

And still...Maddie, of all people had the nerve to do what she did that night without blinking.

Well, I guess, what *we* did.

And then had the audacity to leave me with the guilt.

Me.

Like I was supposed to shoulder the blame all by myself.

Like I was the villain in this story.

No. I had no choice but to do what I did. Anyone in my shoes would've done the same for the person they were closest to in the whole wide world.

I was definitely not the villain. No matter who said otherwise.

Some crimes were in fact self-defense.

I spotted Maddie's rental car before I even reached the driveway, some piece-of-crap American thing, dusty blue with plastic fenders and hubcaps. I parked behind it, frowning. Of all the cars in the world, *this* is what she picked? Certainly, she could've afforded the upgrade.

I looked up at the house and stilled.

The porch sagged on one side. Shutters hung at awkward angles like they were one breath from falling off. The flowerbeds had long been swallowed by weeds, and one of the window screens flapped in the breeze like a ragged flag.

This was the house I used to love. The house where my best friend lived.

And now...

It looked like something out of a foreclosure brochure.

I closed my eyes for a second, and in the quiet behind my lids I saw it: Maddie and me barefoot in the grass, tumbling in synchronized cartwheels, shrieking and laughing and cheering each other on. Cheerleading tryouts were the next day, and we were determined to be perfect.

We were perfect back then.

A pang of something twisted in my chest. Nostalgia, maybe. Or the desperate hope that she'd be excited to see me. That I didn't look older. That she'd remember who we used to be.

And just as quickly, the anger snapped back into place.

She *hadn't* called.
She *hadn't* texted.
She hadn't done anything but pretend I didn't exist.

Fine.

I got out of the car, smoothing the wrinkles from my pants with slow, practiced hands. I adjusted my blouse, lifted my chin, and walked up the front steps, careful not to scuff my heels on the cracked concrete.

I didn't remove my sunglasses. They gave me a step up. A power move.

I rang the doorbell. And heard nothing.

Impatient, I rang it again.

Somewhere inside, I heard the dull thudding of footsteps, and the door swung open with a jolt.

A blur of orange fur shot past me with a hiss, brushing against me and scratching my exposed ankle.

I screamed, my voice rising, echoing.

"Oh my *God,* get that disease-ridden thing away from me!"

I stumbled back, heels catching on the edge of the top step, clutching the porch rail with one hand while the other flew straight to my purse.

The creature spun around mid-run and darted down the stairs as if it were headed to the underworld where it belonged.

I gasped. Loud, theatrical, when I saw a trickle of blood run down and settle under the strap of my heel. I yanked a tissue and a mini bottle of hand sanitizer from my purse, squeezing a quarter of it into my palm like it was holy water. I scrubbed at my ankle as if I'd been branded, dabbing it off with Kleenex.

"Ugh. Filthy little thing. It could have fleas. Or mange. Or rabies," I said to myself.

I looked up and saw her. Maddie stepped into the doorway. Barefoot. She crouched, slow and unbothered, and held out her hand.

"Come on, Leech," she whispered to the cat.

The creature skidded to a halt at the bottom of the porch steps, tail twitching, turned around and trotted back toward the door as soon as Maddie called to it.

The cat obeyed without hesitation, slinking back into her arms like it belonged there. She scooped it up and stroked its back with two fingers, as if I wasn't still standing there mid-disinfect.

Finally, her eyes met mine. Calm. Cold. And laced with something just shy of smug.

"Well," she said, her voice like honey on the edge of a blade, "Hello to you too, Imogen."

CHAPTER 12

Madison

Leech was purring, loud and content, his body curled into mine like he was mine. Like this wreck of a house and this mess of a life were good enough for him.
I held him close. Too close, probably. But I needed something solid. Something breathing.

I ran my fingers through his fur, felt the way his heart ticked steady under the pads of my fingers.
Good. At least one of us was calm.

When I opened the door, the last person I was expecting was Imogen, but there she stood. My stomach tightened the second I saw her. That old, familiar twist. The one I thought I'd grown out of. But I guess not.

She looked like she'd just stepped out of a Banana Republic catalog. Flawless. Untouchable. Lipstick perfect. Not a hair out of place. Sunglasses still on like she was too good to look me in the eye.

Her perfume hung in the air, stuck on the humidity, wrapping me up in a cloud.

Miss Dior Parfum. The new one. I recognized the orange and amber notes immediately. Sally made us all wear it to a shoot in Milan last year and made the assistant write it into the credits.

Of course, Imogen would be wearing it now. She always had to have the best. Be the best.

Here she was, still the queen bee and here I was feeling just as out of place as the young girl I used to be. The new me, withdrawing into the shadows.

I cursed my ineptness to stand strong in Imogen's presence. I swallowed hard, trying to keep my face expressionless, as she fervently wiped herself down like Leech had rolled her in sewage. Gasping and muttering, as she lathered herself in hand sanitizer.

Of course this was her reintroduction into my life.

I should've laughed.
Or said something sharp. Something cutting.
But all I could think was...
Why was she here?

Out of all the people in the world, there she was.
The very last human on earth I wanted to see standing on the porch of this albatross of a house.

Uninvited. Unannounced. Like she had every right to show up here and pretend we weren't standing on the shadow of a grave.

I adjusted Leech in my arms. He let out a tiny meow like he was just as annoyed as I was.
Good cat.

Imogen turned, as if she didn't miss a beat.
She smoothed her blouse, adjusted the strap of her designer bag, and

smiled...tight and deliberate. Positioning the bag so I'd see the designer logo. LV.

Did she really think that would impress me?

"Well, aren't you a sight," she said, her voice just sweet enough to sting.

Her eyes trailed over my body, evaluating me in my wide leg cropped jeans and faded band tee, my hair pulled up in the elastic band I always wore on my wrist. Gathered half up, twisted with loose ends falling.

I couldn't believe how quickly she had the ability to take back the power. And just like that...make me feel small.

She tilted her chin toward Leech, who was glaring at her as hard as I was.

"So... is that animal yours?"

I blinked. Hesitated.
Leech breathed deeply, as his warm body pressed against mine.

I hadn't thought of it before.
Not really.

But standing here, with Imogen on my porch and this feral little thing clinging to me like I was home, something clicked.

He'd followed me into the house without hesitation. Trailed behind me around the house like I was someone worth following.

And yeah, maybe he was just a cat.
But he was the first thing in a long time that felt like family.

Something stirred in my chest, and I adjusted my grip on him.

"Yes," I said, slow and steady, letting it settle like a truth. "Yes," I said slowly, the word blooming like a decision.

"He is. And apparently, he's got a good sense of character."

Imogen laughed...sharp and hollow, like it was a punchline in a joke she didn't quite get.

 But I knew she picked up on the jab. She just didn't care. Nothing could knock Imogen off her throne.

"Well," she said, raising an arched brow over the rim of her sunglasses. "Aren't you going to invite me in?"

Even though my heart was kicking against my ribs and my insides were screaming no, I stepped to the side and invited her in.

Imogen walked right past me, without hesitating, and sank into the middle of the couch without a word. She shoved aside the mountain of open Amazon boxes that still hadn't made it to the donation pile.

More junk. Trinkets.

I didn't address the obvious. I didn't trust my voice not to crack or betray the ache blooming in my chest. Instead, I turned and walked briskly toward the kitchen, calling over my shoulder with a faux sense of ease.

"Let me get us something to drink," I said, my voice sounding too even, too clean, like it had been rinsed of everything real before it reached the air.

BETWEEN FRIENDS

The kitchen was cold. Not from the air conditioning, but from the way memory clung to the walls...thin and sharp like frost. Nothing in this room had ever felt warm. Not since the laughter of a little girl went quiet.

Now it was just tile, and silence, and air that pressed too tightly against my ribs.

I didn't linger in the emotion. Didn't let myself feel too much. Instead, my eyes scanned the counter for the only comfort that had ever worked. The wine.

I grabbed it without thinking, my hand moving faster than my thoughts.
The bottle was open already. The glass close by.
I was halfway through the pour when my gaze caught the microwave clock.
11:02 a.m.

I froze.

What would Imogen think?

Not that it mattered.
Not really.
But still… eleven a.m.

I stared down at the glass, the wine glinting in the light.
My mouth was already dry.
My fingers already curled around the stem.
If I had orange juice and champagne,
I could've spun it as a brunch indulgence.
Something playful. Harmless.

Somehow brunch drinking was charming.
This?
This just looked like a problem.

I reached for a coffee mug instead.
The one with the faded flower etched along the side.

I poured the wine in and let it settle.

There.

No questions would be asked.

"Peppermint tea?" I called out, already boiling the water for her mug.

"That's fine," Imogen answered, her voice drifting in like a memory.

By the time I stepped back into the living room, she had removed her sunglasses and was lounging with one leg crossed over the other, scrolling on her phone like she had just been here yesterday.

The light hit her face just right. The cheekbones. The exact way her fingers curved when she held the phone. She looked older, sure. But still unmistakenly Imogen. Still beautiful. Still powerful.

For a second, I froze. Unable to move, staring right at her.

And just like that...my chest tightened. My throat closed. My fingers tightened around the ceramic mug, and for a moment I closed my eyes to escape the rush of feelings.

Just a second. Just to breathe.

The memory slid in without warning.

That morning after the party in the woods...after Olivia...it blurred my vision. It came racing in to remind me of who we were and what we had done.

BETWEEN FRIENDS

I'd woken up in my bed, head splitting, throat raw. Not knowing how I'd gotten home.
The room was too bright...sunlight blazing through my blinds like punishment.

There was dried blood on my hands, arms. My shirt clung to me, stiff and cold.

I'd prayed...God, please...
Let it be my period, somehow.

But then her face flashed behind my eyelids.
Olivia. The weight of her body in our hands. The memory surged.

Me and Imogen, dragging her through the brush.

Olivia's face flashed. The woods slid in.

And the hollow swallowed her like she never existed.

"Maddie!" Imogen's voice cracked through the room like a whip.

She snapped her fingers. "What's wrong with you?"

My eyes shot open, as the wine in the coffee mug sloshed against the sides. Dark red liquid slipping down the white ceramic like blood, glaringly obvious. But still I hoped she didn't notice.

I handed her the teacup, steam rising, the smell of peppermint filling the room. She took the mug without a thank you.

I discreetly wiped the wine drips against my thigh.
Hiding the truth. Again.

Leech twirled around my ankles, purring, as I took a seat across the room.

Imogen sipped her tea with the kind of elegance that didn't belong in this house.
She looked too polished, too poised for this place.

It was strange, seeing her there.
The same living room we used to build blanket forts in. Where we made friendship bracelets and painted our nails and swore, we'd be famous one day.

She looked around, her gaze catching on every surface.

"It seems smaller than I remember," she said lightly, like it was just an observation and not a judgment.

But I knew better.
Her fingers brushed along the arm of the sofa, nudging an empty Amazon box aside like it offended her.

"We used to think this house was a mansion."

I didn't respond. I sat across from her, Leech asleep in my lap, cradling my mug of wine like it was a life raft.

"Remember your thirteenth birthday?" she said, a glimmer in her eye.
"We slept right here in this living room. My mom brought the cake from that bakery in town you were obsessed with. What was it called?"

"Don't remember," I lied.

But of course, I remembered.
The name still sat at the tip of my tongue like a stone.
Sweet Cakes. Where all the girls' moms got their cakes. But mine had forgotten it was even my birthday. Just saying the name would've

cracked something open. A sliver of power given back. And I refused to let her have that hold on me. Not even an inch.

I wouldn't do it.

Not with her watching me so closely.
Not with the weight of Olivia's ghost hovering between us.

Imogen's eyes sparked and she laughed, clearly remembering more than just the cake.

"That was the night we played spin the bottle. You wanted to kiss Andy so badly."

She leaned back, a smirk tugging at her lips.
"You were such an awkward girl back then. If it weren't for me, no one would've even known your name."

My eyes narrowed as I sat up straighter.

"And yet somehow," I said slowly, voice sweet as poison, "I'm the one who made it out to LA. I'm rubbing shoulders with celebrities, while you're still here in small-town America playing house."

I tilted my head. "At least one of us did something with her life."

Imogen blinked. For a moment, I thought she might say something to match the venom I'd just spit. But instead, she looked down at her tea and smiled faintly.

"I was kidding, Maddie," she said, her voice lowered. "I don't want to fight with you."
Her eyes met mine again. This time, they weren't quite so sharp.
"I missed you."

I didn't answer.

She cleared her throat and tucked a loose strand of hair behind her ear. "So… what's it like?" she asked. "LA. The job. The magazine. I want to hear it all."

I gave her the bare bones.
Photoshoots, travel, long hours. Models who don't eat. Designers who don't smile.
Nothing too glamorous. Nothing too deep. Just enough to fill the space between us.

I turned it back to her. Away from me.
"What about you? How's life now?"

She launched into it like a practiced monologue.
The boys were growing too fast. Chris had gotten a multi-billion-dollar client. She was on a new committee at the country club. They were planning a fundraiser for the local animal shelter.
Her voice was smooth, cheerful. Like she'd told this version of her life a hundred times.

As she continued, my phone buzzed.

I glanced down.

It was a text from Andy.

    Dinner? Please :)

I turned the phone over before Imogen saw the text, but a tiny smile tugged at the corner of my mouth before I could stop it.

Imogen stopped talking mid-sentence. She'd caught it.

"Boyfriend?" she asked, suddenly all sparky. "Some hot shot from LA? I want to hear it all."

I took a slow sip from the mug.
I let the heat of the wine settle over my tongue before answering.

"It's nothing serious," I said, my mind still tracing the words he'd sent.

———————•◆◆•———————

For a very long, very strained two hours, Imogen and I made small talk. I breathed a quiet sigh of relief when she finally stood, brushing something imaginary off her slacks, and said she needed to go pick up her boys.

Logan and Aaron. Or maybe she said Landon and Aiden. I couldn't remember.

The names were something overly polished and matching. I'd seen a picture of them once. A Facebook post from a mutual friend's page. Imogen's children. Perfectly parted hair, wearing bow ties at a garden party.

She hesitated before walking to the door, one manicured hand resting lightly on the back of the sofa like she wasn't quite finished.
Like she wanted to say something.

Something I didn't want her to.

I held her gaze.
Willed her to let the past stay buried.

And she did.

Without a word, she walked out.
Gone in a swish of perfume and heels.

I stayed in the foyer long after the door shut.
Sat down on the floor, back against the wall, hands in my hair.

The air felt thinner without her here, but not in a way that brought relief.
Just a kind of emptiness.
The kind that echoed.

I'd spent years perfecting the illusion...
the California sunshine, the curated life, the smile that never quite reached my eyes.
But all of it felt paper-thin now.
Like the edges were disappearing, as if it never existed.

Imogen had always known how to poke holes in the version of myself I tried to become.
And now, just being in the same room with her again, everything I'd buried started crawling to the surface.
Too much pain.
Too many memories woven into these walls.
Into the town. Into *me*.

The truth was, I'd never really left that version of me behind. Not as much as I'd convinced myself.

And sitting here...knees drawn in, breath shaking...I felt it all pressing down, reminding me that no amount of distance could undo who I was or what we'd done.

I swiped open my phone and opened Andy's text, thumb hovering.
For a moment, I hesitated...then tapped out a single thumbs-up and hit send.

It wasn't eloquent.
But it was a yes.

I stared at the screen long after I hit send, wishing I could somehow pull it back.

Did I really want to see him again?

Andy didn't know who I was now.
Not really. He just smiled that same easy smile he always had.
The one that made me feel safe, even when I knew better.

I remembered his eyes...clear, steady, too kind.

And maybe that's why I said yes.

Maybe I needed someone to look at me like that.

Even if it was all a lie.

CHAPTER 13

Madison

After Imogen left, I poured out the rest of the wine I'd opened earlier and rinsed the glass thinking, *maybe I should stop drinking so much.* Water rushed over my fingers, warm and grounding. For a moment, I just stood there, watching it slip down the drain.

My phone buzzed across the counter. Again, another unknown number.

I stared at the screen, pulse ticking up just slightly. Another unknown caller with a local area code. I didn't move at first. Just let it ring once. Then twice. My thumb hovered over the decline button before finally pressing *accept* instead.

"Hello?"

"Hi, is this Madison Andrews?"

A man's voice. Calm, almost too calm.

"Yes," I said, sharply.

"This is Logan Harper, from Harper Funeral Home. I apologize for calling you from my personal number. I just wanted to reach out and make sure my assistant had already called you. I wanted to check in and see when you might be able to come pick up your mother's remains. I know most families prefer to have them back home as soon as they're able."

I gripped the edge of the counter, felt its cool surface steadying my hand.

"I can come today," I said, my voice catching slightly.

"We'll be here until six," he said. "Whenever works for you."

That was it. No small talk. No drawn-out sympathy. Just a flat line after he hung up.

I stood there, phone still in hand, the quiet pressing in.

Logan Harper.

The name rang a faint bell, but I couldn't place it. Just the vague sense of something old brushing against the edges of my memory, slipping away before I could grab it.

And I went to find the keys.

CHAPTER 14

Imogen

Cat hair clung to the hem of my Dior trousers, threaded into the weave like some small act of sabotage. I hadn't noticed until I sat down in the car, but once I saw it...bright, unmistakable...I couldn't unsee it.

I plucked at it sharply, one strand at a time, my breath catching in my throat. That filthy cat had brushed against me when I sat down, tail high, full of entitlement, as if it owned the house. The audacity of Maddie to let that thing near me after it attacked me on the porch. But Madison didn't apologize. Just let it happen, and I didn't make a scene. I should have.

I swallowed hard and flipped down the visor, revealing the lighted mirror. I touched my hair, checked my lipstick in the reflection. Both were perfect. I looked composed. No one would guess how tight my throat felt.

I turned the key and let the car idle, the AC blowing against my skin, cold and indifferent. Seeing Maddie was supposed to make me feel better. Instead, I felt worse and now my pants were soiled too.

Honestly, I was glad to be out of there. The whole house felt like a time capsule. That hallway, those baseboards, the creak in the floorboard near the fireplace...I knew them all. I spent half my childhood in that living room. Her mother made cinnamon toast on Sunday mornings. We used to fight over the red bowl when we made popcorn. I remember sleeping on that very couch during a storm when we were twelve. We stayed up all night whispering about boys and ghosts. Falling asleep pretending that we weren't scared.

I wanted Maddie to say Olivia's name. I needed her to.

But Maddie had already buried that part of herself. And somehow, she looked freer for it.

She looked so *comfortable.* That smug smile on her face. Standing in that kitchen with her bare feet and a Bon Jovi t-shirt. Like she was hip, cool, whatever she thought she was. Sneaking around, pouring herself wine at 11 in the morning like it was some great act of secrecy. She thought she could hide that. Not from me. Not much slipped past me. I was the queen of hiding things.

I held the steering wheel tighter, my grip stiff at ten and two. I'd come in good faith. And she couldn't even serve me a proper tea. That mug, chipped at the rim. It wasn't charming. It was careless.

She didn't even ask about me. Not really. She casually asked an obligatory question about my life, but I saw her eyes glaze over when I answered.

And what did she offer instead? A handful of vague comments about light and art and some celebrity she photographed in Milan. As if the rest of us here in Fairfield were just a bunch of hometown hillbillies she left behind.

She's rebranded herself as some kind of coastal empress...photographer to the stars, hipster wardrobe, pride as an aesthetic. And I'm supposed to sit there and sip my tea and act like she didn't vanish and leave me behind. Like I never mattered.

She moved away and found a personality.

I stayed and carried the burden of this. What thanks do I get? What loyalty did it earn me?

None.

I reached over and turned the AC down a notch. The cold was beginning to bite.

For a moment, I considered going back...knocking on the door and demanding she say it. That she say Olivia's name. That she admit what we did. *What she did.*

That she'd stop playing amnesia.

But I didn't.
Because if she said it out loud, I might break.

And Imogen Warner-Smith doesn't break. Not in Dior.

My eyes drifted toward the line of hedges that separated the Andrews' house from the next property. Old, overgrown boxwoods with thick woody trunks and gaps at the base where weeds had overtaken the mulch.

That's when I saw her.

A much older, Miss Colleen.

Standing still, just inside the break in the hedge line.
Almost hidden...but not quite.

Her arms were folded, and her posture was too still, too focused. Watching me.

How long had she been there? I wondered.

A jolt of unease threaded through my spine.

Colleen had always been in the background. When we were kids, she was the one peering out from behind her blinds as we rode bikes up and down the street. Sitting on her porch swing while we played tag on the lawns, always just *watching*. Not in a warm, neighborly way. More like a quiet archivist. Taking mental notes. Keeping a record.

She never missed anything. That was the thing about her. You'd forget she was there until you realized she'd been there all along.

I shifted slightly in my seat, unsure whether to wave, to look away, or pretend I hadn't noticed her.

She didn't move.

Her eyes were fixed on me...dark, unwavering. Her expression unreadable.

The longer I stared, the more certain I became that she knew something. Or at least she *thought* she did.

And the problem was…
She might.

I didn't wait to see what she'd do next. My hand flew to the gearshift. I jerked the car into reverse, tires bumping over the uneven edge of the driveway. I put it in drive and kept my eyes on the road ahead, refusing to glance toward the bushes.

I shot down the street, pavement spinning under the tires as I straightened out. The houses blurred past. I didn't look back. I couldn't.

I didn't slow down until I hit the main road, where the pavement evened out and the trees thinned. My hands stayed clenched around the steering wheel, nails pressing half-moons into my palms. The AC rattled through the vents, but I couldn't feel it. My whole body was burning.

BETWEEN FRIENDS

At the stoplight, I finally exhaled. The red glow cast itself across the hood of the vehicle in front of me...an old pickup with peeling paint and a crooked faded bumper sticker I couldn't read.

I adjusted my grip on the wheel. My palms were slick, and my heart wouldn't slow down.

Cracking the silence, my ringtone sounded. Sharp and jarring. I flinched and grabbed for my phone, nearly dropping it between the seat and the console.

Andy's name displayed across the screen and my chest tightened.
I stared at the screen at his name and a photo of the lake from last summer. Sunlight, water, laughter. Another life.

My heart tilted with a rhythmic ache.

We hadn't spoken in a year. Not since that quiet, unspoken weekend when everything blurred.

It began at Walmart, of all places.

Chris was out of town on business. The boys were at sleepaway camp. The house was still, and I had too much free time.

Andy stood in the outdoor aisle holding a bag of charcoal and a lantern. "Going camping," he said with a lazy grin. "Want to come?"

He was joking ...and I almost laughed.

Me. In the woods.
I hated dirt. Hated bugs. I didn't even own a pair of sneakers that weren't designer.

I'd spent years cultivating something polished, restrained, feminine without ever appearing fragile.

But something in me cracked. Quietly.

Much to his surprise, I said yes.

We drove out to the river and pitched a small tent beside the bank. The air smelled of pine and fire smoke. My hair frizzed in the humidity. I slept on uneven ground, swatted mosquitoes off my ankles, and wore the same t-shirt two days in a row.

And I was *happier* than I'd been in years.

We didn't talk about the past. Or the future.
We just *were.*

We lay side by side in the sun, letting the water lap at our feet, letting the world fall away. At night, we tangled together in the sleeping bag, limbs sliding, breath mingling, his hands on my skin, bringing me back to life.

He made me forget myself.
That was the most dangerous part.

On the last night, the fire had burned down low, just glowing embers and the occasional crack of a branch collapsing in on itself. The air smelled like smoke and pine sap and the last sip of bourbon from Andy's flask.

I sat with my legs curled under me, pretending to watch the flames. But really, I was watching him. The way his eyes stayed on the night sky, quiet. Wondering why he hadn't touched me at all since last night.

I waited a few more seconds, and said it, lightly, like it didn't matter.

"I want to see you again."

His jaw tightened.

"Imogen…" His voice was soft, but it hit me hard. "I can't."

I laughed. Or tried to. "Can't or won't?"

"This wasn't right," he said, looking at me now. His eyes weren't cold, but they were clear.

"Your married. And although I know you're not happy. Doing this isn't going to fix your problems."

My lips pursed together, watching his face, the firelight shadowing his eyes.

This was so Andy. Always trying to do the right thing. And it was annoying.

"There's one more thing," he said, cutting into my thoughts.

"And I don't know how to tell you this without hurting you. But I have to be honest."

I braced myself, something inside me knowing I didn't want to hear it.

"My heart belongs to Maddie," he said. "It always has."

He didn't say it with cruelty. That almost made it worse.

"I can't forget her," he went on, his voice barely above a whisper. "And being with you this weekend… it's only brought those feelings back stronger."

I blinked at him, stunned. The words felt like static. Like something breaking just behind my ears.

Madison Andrews. He was still pining for her. After all these years. And she wasn't even here.

I turned my face away so he wouldn't see what was rising up inside me. The heat. The disbelief. The quiet, violent *fury.*

I wanted to scream. Throw something. Grab him by the collar and shake some sense into him.

Instead, I smiled.

"I see," I said. My voice was too even. Too sweet.

But in my head…

I wanted to strangle him.

Right there on the forest floor.
And walk away like none of this ever happened.

When the weekend ended, we didn't say goodbye. Just a long hug before I got in my car and drove away.

We didn't speak again. Except for a brief moment at last year's Christmas parade. He was in uniform, hat slightly crooked like he'd put it on in a rush.

I blushed when I saw him, my boys teetering on the curb, cheeks flushed with cold, holding sticky candy canes.

Andy knelt down, smiling as he handed each of them a plastic police badge.

"Deputy for the day," he said, tapping their shoulders with a wink.

They beamed. No one knew how much my heart was racing. I stood there frozen, pretending not to notice how gently he spoke to them, how his voice softened like he belonged in our life. Pretending I didn't feel anything when he looked up at me. Not even a flicker.

But I did.

I could tell myself a thousand different ways that Andy wasn't for me. That he was too unmotivated, too blue collar, and too tied to the old version of me that I was trying to forget.

But inside, there was still a part of me, quiet and hidden and stupid, that *wanted* him.

Now he was calling me.
Then the phone lit up again.
And I let it ring and ring. I couldn't answer it.

At the next light, I glanced over at my phone. He'd sent a text too.

I picked it up, the weight of my wedding ring catching a sharp glint of sunlight as I tilted the screen toward me. Four carats of cold sparkle, a promise that meant nothing.

One new message blinked back at me.

Andy: Have you seen her yet?

My throat tightened.

I stared at the screen for a moment, thumb hovering just above the keyboard.

I typed slowly, deliberately.

Me: By "her," you mean Maddie?

Three dots appeared. Then vanished.
And appeared again.

>   **Andy:** Of course I mean Maddie.

I let the phone rest against my thigh, screen still glowing. Even *he* was asking me about her. Even now. Even after everything.

It never ends, I thought.

I typed without thinking.

>   **Me:** Why do you care, Deputy?
>   She break a nail again? Need you to kiss it and tell her she's brave? Ready to confess your love?

I didn't hit send.
But how I wanted to.

Truth be told, he was never really mine. Even back in high school.

Whenever Maddie cried…over a grade, a boy, a bad haircut, he'd drop everything to go to her. The night her dog died, I waited outside the gymnastics for twenty minutes for him to pick me up, while he sat on her porch with his arm around her shoulders.

I was always the second priority.

She got his softness. I got his schedule. I don't even know why he dated me in the first place.

I locked the phone and placed it gently in the cup holder, my teeth grinding.

BETWEEN FRIENDS

The second Maddie slinks back into town, barefoot and broken and dripping in second chances...now he finds the time to message me.

I picked it up again, my fingers shaking just enough to make me madder.

> **Me:** Haven't heard from you in months, but Maddie shows up and suddenly I'm on your mind. That's cute.

The dots appeared. Then vanished.
Coward.

My thumb hovered over the keyboard. I didn't send what I really wanted to.

I'd typed out:

> If you really knew me.
> Knew what I was capable of...
> Maybe you'd treat me a little better.

I stared at the words.
Then erased them.
One by one.

CHAPTER 15

Madison

The funeral home sat just beyond the last traffic light in town, where the cracked sidewalks gave way to fields and two-lane quiet. It didn't match the scenery. Sharp-edged, silver-gray stone rising in clean angles. Tall windows stretched across the front, tinted so dark they reflected the sky instead of revealing what was inside. The metal lettering above the doors gleamed in the sun... Harper Funeral Home...newer than anything else for miles.

Even the air felt different here. The grass had been trimmed to exact measurements, edged so carefully it formed a perfect border along the sidewalk. Polished river stones lined the base of each hedge. Not a flower out of place. Everything about it was composed, intentional, rehearsed.

The parking lot was half-empty, pavement still smooth and dark from a recent repaving. No cracks. No weeds sprouting up at the corners. A single black SUV sat in the far row, windows up tight. A darkened windowed hearse idled near the side entrance, engine low and steady, the hum just barely perceivable beneath the hush.

I pulled into one of the front spaces and stepped out of the car, closing the door with an unsteady hand. The sun felt too bold here. Too loud against the muted colors of the walls and glass. The hearse's exhaust curled into the stillness, vanishing before it reached the sidewalk.

When I opened the entrance door to the building, a cold wave of air brushed against my face.

The smell hit me first...white lilies, and new carpet. Muted piano notes spilled from overhead speakers. They barely broke through the silence, just floated there, suspended. Too soft to distract me from the pressure in my chest.

Inside the foyer, everything was grey and cream. Walls smooth and blank. Furniture untouched. No fingerprints. No scuffs. A sleek wooden counter stood near the entrance with a silver bell that didn't belong in a place like this. A bowl of mints sat beside it, untouched.

It was if they were trying to cover the grief in the air. But the place was rife with it.

Beyond the front desk, a hallway extended toward the back of the building...narrow and dim, even in the midday light. The walls there were darker, soft gray with a faint shimmer in the paint.

Several doors lined the hall, all closed. Not one with a plaque or a sign. Just black grainy wood and brushed metal handles, identical and unwelcoming. Each one a question I didn't want the answer to.

I stayed near the entrance for a moment, unsure of where to stand. My fingers brushed the hem of my shirt, restless. I fought the urge to turn around and leave. I didn't want to be here. But still, I walked toward the desk.

Each step felt strangely loud against the polished tile, though I couldn't really hear my own footsteps over the thudding in my ears.

I reached the counter, unsure whether to wait or announce myself. My fingers hovered over the small silver bell. Just as I touched the edge, barely grazing it...

A voice came from behind me...soft, measured. Male.

"Can I help you?"

I gasped when I saw him standing just beyond the edge of the front desk, half in shadow, framed by the hallway's dimness. He hadn't been there a moment ago. Or if he had, I hadn't noticed.

His suit was dark, tailored, his dark hair neatly combed back. But it was his eyes that struck me first. There was something familiar about them, though I couldn't place what. Or when.

"I am so sorry. I didn't hear you come up," I stuttered.

"That's alright, Maddie," he said gently, as if he was trying to coax me into something.

I took a half-step back, not out of fear exactly, but feeling more like instinct.

My brow furrowed.

"How do you know my name?"

He offered a small smile that didn't quite settle on his face.

"You don't remember me, do you?"

I didn't answer. Because I didn't.

"Logan Harper," he said, folding his hands in front of him. "We went to school together."

And just like that, the name came into focus. Not a full memory...just the edge of one. A moment. A hallway. Sophomore year. Olivia and I standing near her locker, swapping notes before second period. The air smelled like cafeteria pizza and cheap perfume. The crowd had thinned, and we were laughing at something when he passed us. Silent. Slow. He didn't say a word to us. Just walked by eyes fixed a little too long on Olivia...like he was absorbing her.

Once he disappeared around the corner, Olivia leaned in close.

"That guy gives me the creeps," she whispered. "I swear he watches me. Always just stares and doesn't blink. Serial killer energy."

We'd both laughed then.

But clearly her opinion changed at some point, because the last time I saw Logan was right before graduation, and Olivia was locking lips with him.

He gestured toward the hallway, waiting for me to follow.

I hesitated for just a breath, and stepped into stride beside him, keeping a small distance between us.

"You look different," he said after a moment. "Older, obviously, but... I don't know. Happier maybe. Must be that California life."

His tone was casual, but there was something stiff about it, like the words had been practiced in his head before they came out.

I didn't respond, just kept walking. The carpet in the hallway muffled everything but the sound in my ears.

"Death rates are lower out there, you know. In California. Warmer weather, fewer seasonal spikes. Less heart failure in the winter. Less frost-related mortality overall."

I blinked.
He said it without any trace of irony, as if we were discussing gas prices.

I hugged my arms to my chest, the cold penetrating or it was my nerves, I wasn't sure which.

"You talked to Olivia lately?" he asked.

My stomach flipped. The question landed so casually, like she was just another name on a list.

At that moment, we passed a room with the door cracked open. I glanced in for anything to anchor myself to. To escape the swell rising inside me.

A velvet armchair sat in the center, pale blue and sun-faded, facing a stained-glass window. A box of tissues rested on the armrest, beside a worn Bible. On the floor, a child's drawing had been half-tucked beneath the leg of a coffee table. Crayon colors, bright, unbothered, drawn into the shape of a sun.

I turned my gaze back to him, cold and indifferent.

"I'm not really up to conversation, Logan. I'm just here to pick up the ashes," I said, sharper than I intended.

He nodded, unfazed. "Of course. She's ready."

Logan said nothing else, as we reached the door at the very end. He paused, hand on the handle, and turned it without a word. He stepped aside to let me in first.

The room was small. Windowless. Pale gray walls and one framed print of a generic landscape...mountains blurred by fog, trees stripped of their leaves. A low table sat at the center, flanked by two chairs. One chair had a clipboard resting on the seat, a pen tethered to it by a thin silver chain. So much more sterile than the room we had passed. On the table, a single object waited.

A polished wooden urn, dark and rounded, sealed shut. It was simple, expensive looking. And I was surprised. I was expecting a box.

Logan stepped in behind me and gently closed the door. The click echoed louder than it should have. I stood still. My eyes on the urn.

"You can sit," he said softly, gesturing toward the empty chair.

I sat, my knees stiff, the vinyl cushion cold beneath me. He watched me for a moment too long before lowering himself into the chair across from me.

"I upgraded it," he said, motioning to the urn. "No charge. Figured you'd want something nice. We're old friends, after all."

I blinked.
Old friends?

We weren't friends. I barely remembered him. Olivia's voice echoed again in my mind...*that guy gives me the creeps.*

I shifted in my seat.

He leaned forward, putting his thumb to his chin, "I saw that you had opted for the standard container with your online order. This one is from our Heritage Collection, heirloom quality."

"I didn't need heirloom quality," I said, my voice cold.

He nodded, as if I'd asked him a question.

"Of course you didn't," he said, rising. "I'm sorry if I overstepped."

He moved to the table, fingers brushing over the top of the urn with a strange delicacy. He turned and held it out toward me.

I stood. And everything started to spin. The moment I took it from his hands, the weight hit me...dense and final. Heavier than I expected. Not metaphorically. Physically. My arms tensed. My heart kicked up.

It was her.
My mother.
In a container. In my arms.
I couldn't breathe.

The walls shrank in. The overhead lights pulsed too bright. The air grew too thin, or maybe too much. I couldn't tell which. I just needed to get out.

"I... uh...thank you," I managed, barely, the words scraping out on a whisper.

I didn't wait for him to open the door. I did it myself. My hands shook.

Down the hallway. Past the closed doors. Past the front desk and the bowl of untouched mints. I kept walking.

Out into the sun, the urn pressed to my chest.

Only when I reached the car did I realize I was crying.

———— ·•◆•· ————

The door of my childhood home closed behind me with a soft click. I stood in the entryway holding the urn, the shape of it foreign and too heavy in my arms. It didn't seem possible that something so small could carry what was left of my mother.

Leech weaved between my legs, meowing insistently, his tail brushing my ankle. I didn't move. Couldn't. I just stood there, blinking in the stillness.

The house smelled stale...leftover candle wax and something faintly floral. The scent of a life that had already faded. Her shoes were still by the door. Her jacket still on the hook. And now she was back inside the house. Just not the way she left it.

My knees buckled and I sank to the floor, as if my body no longer belonged to me, the urn still clutched tight to my chest.

The first sob hit hard...ugly, gasping. My body curled around the urn like I could protect it. Like I could protect *her*. But she was already gone.

"Mom," I whispered.
The word caught in my throat, sharp and childish.

Leech climbed into my lap, pawing at the urn like he recognized it. Like he knew.

I rocked slightly, the way you rock when you're trying to calm a baby or a wound. My fingers gripped the smooth surface of the urn, and for the first time since she died, I let it take me under. I let the grief pull me down. Drown me.

My mother and I were in the house together again.
But nothing about it felt whole.

I pressed my forehead to the urn, tears soaking into the sleeves of my sweater, and whispered the things I should've said months ago. The things I thought I'd have time for.

"I'm sorry."
"I should've done better."

The house was the only one listening and said nothing back.
Only the sound was Leech's soft purring, and my own broken breathing, filled the space between us.

The urn was warm from where I'd held it so close. I loosened my grip, just slightly, and stared down at it, willing it to speak. To say something. To fight back. To apologize for everything, she didn't do right.

But there was just silence.

I held the urn tighter, but my mind was already slipping somewhere else…somewhere far away.

Paris.

The last time she called, I was in a bar with colleagues. A place off Rue Saint-Denis with pressed-tin ceilings and red leather booths, the kind of place where everyone pretended to care about the wine and not the salary gap. Altruistic, at best.

My phone buzzed in my coat pocket. I pulled it out and saw her name.

Mom.

I stepped outside to answer, heels clicking across the tiled floor, coat still draped over one shoulder. The air smelled of cigarette smoke and old stone. Glasses clinked behind me. Laughter. Forks against plates. Sally called after me, "Madison, don't disappear…your drink is on the way!" I waved her off.

"Hi, Mom," I said into the phone, pressing a finger to my ear to block the noise.

"Oh…hi sweetheart. I wasn't sure if I should call. I know you're probably busy."

Her voice was faint, fuzzy on the line. She sounded smaller than usual. Unsure.

"It's okay," I said, though my eyes were already scanning the street. "Everything alright?"

"I just…" she hesitated. "I hadn't heard from you in a while. Thought I'd check in."

I shifted the phone, already calculating the social cost of standing outside too long. "I'm out with work people. Can we talk later?"

There was a pause.

"Of course," she said. "Of course we can."

I never did call her back.
And she didn't try again.

Now, in the stillness of the house, I would've given anything to hear her voice again. Even if she was rambling about some man she met.

"I'm sorry," I whispered, voice cracking. "I should've listened."

The urn didn't respond.
It just sat there in my lap, heavy and still.
Just like her memory.

Eventually, I stood. My knees were stiff. My face wet. I didn't remember when I stopped crying.

The urn was still in my arms. I looked around the living room...her books, her blankets, the empty space on the mantle. I couldn't put it there. I couldn't make her a centerpiece. So, I carried her down the hallway and stepped into her office.

I placed the urn on the desk. Gently. Like she might feel the jostle.

As, I turned to leave, something caught my eye.

A box.
Plain. Brown. Pushed beneath the window bench like it had been tucked there intentionally. I didn't remember seeing it before.

I don't know what made me stop and pull it out right then.
Curiosity. Or maybe something deeper. A pull I couldn't name.

I sat cross-legged on the floor, the cardboard cool under my fingertips.

When I opened the lid, I wasn't sure what I expected.
But it wasn't this.

Albums. Four of them. Fat and worn at the edges.

I opened the first.

Photos of me.
Not just birthdays or holidays...but *everything*.

Blurry snapshots of me holding up my first camera, feet in the ocean, glitter on my cheeks. Scribbled captions in her handwriting: *Maddie, age 9...wouldn't stop taking photos of the dog.*

I flipped faster.

School photos. A ballet recital I'd forgotten about. Newspaper clippings from the high school yearbook committee. My name under the photo credits, circled in pink ink.

And then... Muse.

Page after page of cut-outs.
Every cover I'd ever shot. Every spread. Every editorial.
She'd saved them all.

My breath caught fire. My fingers hovered above the page like it might burn me.

She'd been watching.
All this time.

She *saw me.*

I closed the album, clutching it to my chest like it might stitch something back together.
And that's when the real sobs broke through...loud and shattering.

It was the kind of cry that came from the center of me. The kind I hadn't made room for. The kind I thought I was too composed, too grown, *too far away* to ever make again.

"I didn't know you really cared," I choked, rocking slightly.
But she had. In her own quiet way. Not in words or actions.
But in clippings. In albums. In the pages she'd kept when I hadn't even kept copies for myself.

She knew.

I closed the album, clutching it to my chest like it might stitch something back together.

Tears were falling again. But it wasn't grief this time.
Not really.
It was something else. Something warmer.

It came from the center of me, the part that had waited *years* for this proof. That all the silence, all the distance, hadn't meant she didn't love me. Maybe she just didn't know how to show it.

The missed meals, the quiet nights, the feeling that I was never enough for her...none of that was reflective of the whole truth.

Because this...these albums, these pages...this *was* love.

Not loud. Not perfect. But real.

"I didn't know," I whispered, rocking gently. "I didn't know you loved me."

And maybe she hadn't said it. Maybe she never would have.

But she'd kept all of this.
Every piece of me.
Every photo I thought no one had cared about.
She kept them all.

I wiped my eyes on the sleeve of my shirt and stood; the album still pressed to my chest. My legs felt shaky, but lighter somehow. Like I'd set something down I didn't even know I'd been carrying.

I glanced at the urn on the desk. It looked different now.
Less like a reminder of loss.
More like something whole. Something returned.

"I love you too," I said softly.

I turned and left the room, leaving the door slightly ajar behind me.

In the kitchen, I reached for a new bottle of wine, hands steadier now. The cork gave with a soft *pop,* and I didn't bother with a glass. I drank straight from the bottle, the way I used to on the balcony in Paris when the nights felt too long.

But this time, I wasn't running.
I wasn't numbing.

I was toasting her.

And maybe...finally...letting her in.

CHAPTER 16

Madison

My phone buzzed just after sunset.

> **Andy:** Pick you up at 7?

I stared at the message a beat too long, thumb hovering.

> **Me:** I'm sorry Andy, can I have a raincheck? I just don't feel like going out.

There was a short pause before he responded.

> **Andy:** I'll bring dinner to you then.

Twenty-five minutes later, he was standing on my porch with a white pizza box and a six-pack of Coors Light. I opened the door slowly, still blotchy from crying, but trying to hide it.

"Dinner delivery, as promised!" he said with a wide smile.

His eyes scanned my face before I even said a word. "Are you okay?"

I didn't answer right away. I just stepped back so he could come in, the box warm and familiar in his hands, the beer bottles clinking softly like some nostalgic soundtrack.

After he stepped inside, I crossed my arms, hugging myself.

"I picked up my mom's ashes today," I told him.

"I'm so sorry, Maddie." I gave him a half shrug, eyes fixed on a crack in the kitchen tile.

He let a beat pass before adding, "You didn't drop her, did you?"

My head shot up. "What?"

"My cousin did once. Not your mom, obviously…his mom. Knocked the urn off the shelf dusting, and poof. Like a human glitter bomb."

I blinked at him, a laugh bubbling up without permission.

"They used a shop vac to clean her up," he said, completely straight-faced. "Swore she'd have appreciated the efficiency."

I snorted. "Stop. That's awful!"

He grinned. "Yeah, well. Sometimes awful makes things feel a little less awful."

He set the pizza and beer on the counter like we were still in someone's basement on a Friday night in 2011.

"You sure you don't want some company?"

"I didn't say that."

He smiled, small and crooked. The kind that made everything feel less sharp.

He popped open a bottle and handed it to me.

"Wow. Coors Light? We're really going retro here," I said, taking a big swig.

He opened his own with a soft hiss. "What can I say? I like a theme."

I studied him for a moment, quiet behind the low kitchen light. I'd always thought he was handsome...boyish in that small-town way, with the kind of charm that made girls laugh too loud and pass notes in class just to hear their names on his lips.

But this was different. He wasn't boyish anymore. The softness was gone. In its place was something sharper, more grounded. His jaw was more defined now, a hint of scruff catching in the shadows, and the way he carried himself...still casual, but steadier...felt heavier somehow. Like he'd lived more than he let on.

Even the way his shirt clung to him under the jacket, the way his jeans sat low on his hips...it stirred something unfamiliar in me. Something warmer. Slower. Less nostalgic and more... now. God, he was sexy.

It startled me, a little. That after everything, after the time and the silence and the damage...we could still sit here and make space for new things. New wants, sliding in behind old wants.

He glanced up and caught me looking, gave me that same half-smile that used to melt every resolve I had. But now it awoke a part of me that I'd forgotten.

Something real. Something primal, deep.

I hadn't dated much over the years. Honestly, it was almost nonexistent. There were even rumors at work...whispers behind wine glasses and breakroom coffee pots...that maybe I was a lesbian and needed to come out.

Because surely, there had to be some *reason* why I was always alone.

The truth is, I didn't know what I was. I just knew it was hard for me to connect with anyone.

167

Love never felt simple. For some people, it just happens...effortless, natural, like breathing.

But for me, it always felt like reaching through glass. Always a barrier in between.

I wanted to be held, but I didn't know how to *let* myself be held.

I clung to the wrong people. Pushed away the ones who might've stayed. Even when my heart was in the right place.

Maybe especially then.

And now, the first guy I ever loved and the only person who'd ever made me feel *anything* real, was back.

I opened the pizza box. Inside was gooey cheese, pepperoni and jalapeño peppers. The same kind we used to eat late at night after the ballgames. My favorite.

"How did you remember?" I asked.

"I don't forget things about you," he said simply.

Then he smiled, that same crooked grin that used to make me nervous for no good reason. "You remember when my brother used to buy us beer?"

I nodded, sinking onto the couch. "He'd make us call him 'sir' in exchange."

"We took that twelve-pack down into the woods and passed it around like we were kings."

"And Imogen puked behind a tree!"

He laughed. "Swore she was dying."

I sat on the couch and took a bite of the pizza, letting the silence settle. Letting the house feel full for the first time since I arrived.

"You, feeling any better?" he asked again, quieter this time.

"No," I said. "But this helps."

He nodded and sat beside me, close enough that I could feel the heat of him, smell the familiar thread of his cologne.

We didn't speak for a while. Just sat there...two kids from the woods, drinking cheap beer in an aging house, pretending we hadn't let a decade pass.

We moved to the porch without saying much. The screen door creaked behind us, hinges catching like they always had. Andy took the old wooden rocker, and I sank into the swing, the same one my mother used to sit in on warm nights with a glass of sweet tea and her silent thoughts.

The crickets were in full swing, their chorus loud and relentless, pulsing through the air like a rhythm the town still moved to. I had forgotten how much I missed that sound.

"I didn't remember how loud they were," I said, a half-smile tugging at the edge of my mouth. "It used to drive me crazy. Now it just… feels right."

Andy glanced at me, and out into the dark. "It's the kind of thing you don't know you'll miss until it's gone."

He took a sip of his beer, the bottle catching the moonlight.

"So," he said. "California. What's that like?"

"Expensive," I said with a dry laugh. "Loud. Rushed. Kind of lonely, if I'm being honest."

He nodded, like he already knew that.

"Do you miss home?" he asked.

I hesitated. "Parts of it. Not all of it."

He turned to me. His voice softer now. "Do you miss me?"

The question hung there, dangling between us. I looked at him...at the way his shoulders folded in slightly like he was bracing for something...and nodded. "Yeah," I said. "I do."

He looked down, thumb tapping gently against the bottle's label.

"I think about you all the time, Maddie. You're the only person who ever really understood me."

My heart caught in my throat.

"Imogen just... used me. Just like she used you. We were both just pieces on her little board. Still are, maybe. But you...you've never been like her. You're different. In the best way possible."

His words settled over me slowly. I felt warmth bloom through my chest, spreading through my limbs, humming beneath my skin.

Was it Andy?
Or the alcohol?

I didn't know. I didn't care.

I watched him as he talked...his fingers curled around the beer bottle, the glass slick with humidity, water slipping down the side and dripping onto the porch floor.

He didn't even seem to notice.
But I did.
I was noticing *everything* now.

He went quiet for a while after that.
So did I.

The crickets kept singing. A soft breeze stirred the hem of my shirt. And without a word, Andy stood from the rocker and walked over to the swing.

He didn't ask. He just sat beside me. The porch swing shifted with his weight, creaking gently as it adjusted. Our feet dragged lightly across the worn wooden boards, toes brushing against peeling paint. I could feel the heat of him beside me. The nearness of his shoulder. His thigh. His breath.

I took another sip of my beer, eyes scanning the yard, even though there was nothing to see but shadows. The swing moved gently beneath us, boards creaking under the drag of our feet.

"Can I ask you something?" I asked.

Andy turned slightly, the porch light catching the edge of his jaw. "Yeah, of course."

"Why aren't you with someone?" I asked. "I mean... you're not bad looking. You're decent company."

He let out a short breath of a laugh. "Decent company. High praise."

I smiled, waiting.

He shrugged, reaching down to roll the bottle between his palms. "I've had a few... things. Here and there. Nothing that stuck."

I glanced at him.

"They always start out fine," he said. "Then somewhere along the line, it just... falls apart. I do better on my own."

He looked out at the night, the quiet stretching between us.

"Like I said, you're the only person who got me," His voice was low. Steady. "Back then, and maybe even now. I don't know why. You just… do."

Warmth spread through my body...unexpected and unsteady.
I didn't respond right away.

Something about him in that moment felt both familiar and impossibly far away.

But he was right, I still understood him.
I always had.

He set his beer down beside the swing.

Without a word, he reached for mine and took it gently from my hand. His fingers brushed mine, warm and steady. He leaned forward and his hands came up...slow, careful...settling behind my neck.
One breath.
Two.

And just before his mouth met mine, a flicker of a memory rose from the dark:

Spin the Bottle on my birthday.
I was mortified when on my turn, it landed on Andy Marson.
He kissed me, quick and awkward, with the whole circle giggling.
I made a big show of wiping my mouth and gagging like it was disgusting.

But it wasn't.
It just wasn't real.

This one was.
Even compared to the other times he'd kissed me recently.
This one upended gravity.

He pulled me in gently, and our lips met again and again...not with hunger, but with something deeper. Something quiet and claiming. Like he'd waited for this moment long enough to know not to rush it.

His kiss encompassed me.
Not just my lips.
All of me.

I sank into it, into him, into the space that had once been ours and somehow still was.

It wasn't a first kiss. It was the *real* one.
The one we never got right.
Until now.

We didn't speak for a while after the kiss.
There was nothing left to say.
Only the creak of the swing, the hum of crickets, and the quiet thrum beneath my skin that hadn't been there in years.

At some point, he reached for my hand.
And we went inside.

The house felt different with him in it. Warmer. Closer. Like it felt something too.

NATALIE BANKS

In the quiet of my bedroom, he stood in front of me, brushing a strand of hair from my face like it was instinct. His fingers lingered at my jaw. Neither of us rushed. There was no urgency...just a slow unraveling.

He kissed me again, deeper this time. His hands moved to my waist, mine to the back of his neck. We moved together like we still knew each other, even if we didn't know who we'd become.

Clothes fell away softly. The air, warm between us.

We made love slowly. And again, breathless. Then slower still.

There were long stretches of quiet.
Whispers.
Hands tracing old stories into bare skin.
A laugh muffled against my shoulder. A tear I didn't expect to fall.

Passion and innocence collided in the dark, over and over, like something we both discovered and remembered.

And sometime before dawn, I fell asleep curled against his chest, his breath steady in my hair, his arm heavy across my waist like he never meant to let go.

But when I woke in the early morning light, the bed was still warm, but he was gone.

No note. No footsteps. No sound.

Just the shape of him in the sheets.
And the memory of his kiss, still soft against my lips.

CHAPTER 17

Madison

I could still taste him. That was the first thought I had when I opened my eyes, bare skin tangled in sheets that smelled faintly of beer and sweat and something sweeter underneath. *Andy.*

The way he'd looked at me last night...like I was still worth something. Like I hadn't disappeared beneath the guilt and the dust and the years. The way his hands had moved across me, careful but wanting, like he wasn't sure if it was real. Neither was I.

I wanted to hold onto the feeling. Let it bloom. But something in me was too stubborn. Or maybe just too cynical. We'd shared a night, not a future. The truth of what I'd done still lay between us. And it wasn't something we could get past. You can work through a lot of things in a relationship but when you're dating a cop, murder wasn't one of them.

I pulled on an old hoodie and an old pair of Soffee shorts and padded barefoot through the hallway, the floorboards creaking beneath me. Leech trailed behind like a shadow, tail flicking low.

The junk haulers would be here this morning, and I'd barely made a dent in getting ready for them.

————————··◆◆··————————

I was moving the last of the boxes closer to the open garage door when I saw it...Olivia's rain jacket. Still hanging on the peg by the door, next to a basket of tangled umbrellas and mismatched winter hats. Bright yellow, the kind she said made her feel like a lighthouse. It had been here all these years, untouched.

A rush of air caught in my throat, and I stared at it like it might speak. But it didn't.

If only I could remember what happened to Olivia, maybe I could move on.

That night always played in flashes...like static between stations. Olivia's voice echoing in the dark, my own hands covered in blood, Imogen's sharp whisper telling me to get it together. And then silence. So much silence.

I should've asked Imogen. Pressed her. She was the only other person who really knew what happened that night. The only one who was there with me.

But I hadn't asked her. Not once. And now it felt too far gone.

I wanted to say something when she was standing in the doorway before she left. But the words wouldn't form.

How do you even say something like that?

Hey, I can't remember. Did you or I kill Olivia? Could you refresh my memory, perhaps?

I let out a bitter laugh...dry, joyless. Even Leech looked up like I was nuts. And maybe I was.

I reached out and touched the sleeve of the yellow sleeve, cool under my fingers, and turned away.

Inside, the coffee maker gurgled to life as I leaned on the counter, watching the slow drip fill the pot. Leech curled around my ankles, impatient for me to sit. We stepped out onto the porch together, the mug warm in my hands, the morning already thick with humidity. The sun hung low and sharp through the trees, and the cicadas had started their endless thrum.

I settled into the chair with a slow exhale. The mug said *The Grand Canyon, take the leap.* I didn't know where the mug had come from. It had been in the cabinet since I was a little girl.

I sighed. I wanted to feel happy about last night. I really did. Andy had been sweet. Thoughtful. Maybe even exactly what I needed. But deep down, I knew he was just a soft place to land on the way out. Nostalgia taking the form as a second chance. A second chance that didn't exist.

I was leaving. No matter how many beers or how many times he looked at me like that.

And the truth was, I didn't deserve peace. Not yet.

The sound of an engine rolled up the drive...loud and rattling...and I looked up as the *1-800-GOT-JUNK?* truck pulled in. Two guys in matching blue shirts stepped out, already sweating under the early sun.

I waved half-heartedly and pointed them toward the garage. They nodded and got to work, loading up the stacks I'd left for them...boxes full of old junk, picture frames, and dishes. A few chairs, a dusty bookshelf.

I'd kept most of the furniture off the pick-up list. The realtor said houses showed better staged. "Just enough to make it feel lived in," she told me, as if anyone lived here anymore.

They began hauling the boxes into the sunlight, piece by piece, carrying off the remnants of a girl who no longer existed.

I sipped my coffee, even though it had gone cold.

My phone buzzed against the porch railing, screen lighting up with a message from him.

> **Andy:** Last night was kind of amazing. Like old times. Well, actually a lot better than old times. Back then I didn't get to kiss you. Not like that.
>
> **Andy:** Can I see you again tonight?

I stared at the screen and my heart fluttered like a trapped bird against my chest. A flush crept onto my cheeks, slow and warm, remembering his mouth, his lips.

I bit the inside of my cheek and tried not to smile. I really tried.

But there it was, tugging at the corners of my mouth lifting from the depths…a want I hadn't pushed away as far as I thought.

Leech stretched in the sun, tail flicking. The junk men were still clattering around inside the garage, hauling off the pieces of my old life. But none of it mattered in that second. Just the warmth in my hand and the sting in my throat and the fact that he still wanted to see me.

Part of me wanted to say yes without thinking. Let it be simple. Let something feel good without consequence. But nothing was ever that easy here. Not for me.

Still, I smiled. Just a little. And I didn't answer. Not yet.

I just held the phone in my hand, thumb resting on his name, letting the weight of his words linger there a little longer than I should have. I just looked out at the trees, letting the weight of his words settle beside me like a second cup of coffee.

A few hours later, I watched the junk haulers drive away. The garage stood hollow now, echoing with absence. Just a few scraps remained...crumpled packing paper, a stray bobby pin, a lost button glinting faintly near the corner. A movie theater ticket dated 2008 lay curled on the concrete, water-stained and curling at the edges. All of it scattered like residue after a windstorm, the kind of dust grief leaves behind when it's finally done tearing through you.

Even Olivia's rain jacket was gone.

When they were almost done loading, I saw it again, just hanging there, bright and stubborn, and something in me cracked. I folded it quickly and shoved it into the top of one of the boxes just before they picked it up.

I watched it leave...yellow sleeve poking out, bobbing up and down with each step the man took down the driveway. Like one last wave goodbye.

The door to the house creaked as I stepped inside. It felt quieter than before. Not in sound, but in weight. I'd taken almost everything down. The pictures of my mother smiling in places she never really liked. The dusty blue vase she insisted had belonged to someone important. The framed cross-stitch in the hallway that said *Bless This Mess.*

It was all gone. So why did it still feel like she was everywhere? Her scent still lingered in the corners. That cocoa bean lotion. That old perfume she used to wear on her dates. That stubborn bleach cleaner she swore worked better than anything else.

I half-expected her to come around the corner, towel in hand, asking if I'd seen the remote.

It was almost over, and I felt a rush of relief. And then sadness chased it so fast, it knocked the breath out of me.

In the kitchen, I opened a bottle of wine and poured a glass. And another.

But before I could finish the second, I'd curled myself into the couch, Leech nestled against my thigh and drifted off with the television still playing some rerun in the background.

It was the kind of sleepiness that just crept in.

I didn't dream. Or if I did, I didn't remember.

For the first time in days, there was nothing.

Just sleep. And silence.

I woke up hours later. Sunlight shifted across the hardwood in lazy slats, warming the room in patches. Leech padded up and curled beside me, warm and purring. I scratched behind his ears without thinking, my fingers moving slow, rhythmic.

My eyes drifted open and shut.
For a moment, the house was quiet.

And then I heard them.

Sirens.

First one. Then another.
Then more.

A whole fleet of them.
The wail of them rising, falling, echoing down the quiet road.

I shot upright, heart lurching so hard I got dizzy.
Leech darted off the couch as I stumbled to my feet, my pulse thudding loud in my ears.

I didn't think.
Didn't grab shoes.
Just moved.

The sirens were closer now, sharp and rising.
tearing through the stillness like they were headed straight for me.

I pushed open the front door and stepped outside. Barefoot, breath caught halfway in my throat. Leech came out behind me, both of us squinting into the sharp light, as police cars swarmed the neighborhood, lights flashing red and blue like warning beacons.

They lined the curb just a few doors down, red and blue lights flashing against the houses that backed up to the trees.

My chest tightened.

They weren't here for the neighborhood.
They were here for what lay just beyond it.

The woods.

News vans rolled in right behind them and people began to drift from their homes, pulled by the sirens. They gathered in small knots along the street, whispering like children afraid to speak.

From the porch, I could see the officers moving...three in uniform, two in plain clothes.
One pointed toward the tree line.
The others followed, stepping off the curb, cutting across front yards without hesitation.

Their hands hovered near their belts, their pace steady, deliberate. They headed straight toward the woods.

I stepped off the porch, heart hammering so loud it made my ears buzz.

Miss Colleen shuffled over from her yard, walking toward me in pink slippers, robe fluttering around her like tissue paper, eyes wide and dazed.

"What's happening?" I asked her.

She stopped in front of me, breathless. "They found something out there."

For a second, the words didn't land. They just hovered there in the air between us, hollow and strange. A something, she said. Not *a person*. Not *a girl*. Just… something.

I blinked at her, not wanting to ask more.

Her voice cracked. "Back there. In the woods."

My throat tightened, as I swallowed a cough.

Colleen leaned in, her breath catching in the space between us. Her eyes wide, like she couldn't believe what she was saying.

"They say it's foul play at work. Something to do with a local girl."

I felt the blood drain from my face, slow and certain, like someone had pulled the plug inside me. My pulse stuttered.

Olivia.

I heard her name, without hearing it. Felt it crash into me like glass.

The world around me kept going. Birds still chirping, cars still passing on the street. But everything inside me stopped.

Colleen stared at me too long, eyes flicking across my face like she was taking notes.

I shifted my weight, suddenly aware of how still I'd gone. How loud my silence might sound.

"What girl?" I asked, though I already knew.

Colleen stepped in, breath sour and sweet all at once, teeth bared just slightly like the words themselves pained her.

"Why, your little friend, of course."

She reached up and adjusted the neckline of her robe, fingers trembling just enough for me to notice.
Her eyes locked on mine, heavy and emotional and said, "Olivia Mariner."

Olivia's name was still hanging in the air when I saw her. Kristen, Olivia's baby sister, pulled up in a dented black Ford Focus. She parked right in front of my house, practically on the curb. Before the engine had even fully shut off, she was out of the car and storming toward the line of police cruisers.

She didn't hesitate.
Just marched right up to them like she belonged in the middle of it all.
And when she passed me on the walkway, she turned and looked straight into my eyes.
No words. Just a glare.
Sharp and unblinking.
Like she already knew.
Like she'd been waiting for this day longer than any of us.

CHAPTER 18

Olivia

March 2013
Nine weeks until graduation

Whoever said Satan was a man has clearly never met Imogen Warner.

Seriously, though. If Hell had a queen, she'd be wearing Chanel and smirking in the mirror of the girls' bathroom at Palmetto High. And if evil had a ringtone, it'd be the one that played every time her calls came through…sharp and chirpy like fake laughter.

Because if anyone was the devil, it had to be her. A heartless teenage girl. Sure, there were perks to being in her little circle, party invites, rides in her BMW with the convertible open and our legs sticking out like we didn't have exams the next morning. But it all came at a price. And somehow, it always felt like I was the one paying the bill.

Imogen liked to remind me of where I came from. Subtly, of course. A glance at my shoes. A side comment about "dirty hair" when I showed up to school after oversleeping. One time she told me I smelled like fried food right in front of Coach Turner and laughed like it was some inside joke I just didn't get. Everyone laughed with her.

Except Madison. She gave me that look, the one that almost meant sorry, but not quite. Like maybe somewhere inside her, the real Maddie was still in there, wanting to say something but too scared of what it would cost.

That's the thing with Maddie. She's kind when no one's looking. She talks to me like we're still eleven and sneaking Cherry Cokes from her mom's fridge. But when Imogen's around, it's like I disappear. Like I'm not a person anymore, just a placeholder in the photo.

But I see it. I see *everything.*

Like how Imogen rolls her eyes when Andy talks, even when she's gripping his hand like a lifeline. Or how she once told me, drunk and loose-limbed on her white duvet, that she didn't even like him. "He's not my type," she whispered, staring at the ceiling like it bored her. "But he's... useful," Her word. *Useful.* Like he was a tool. A shield. A prop to keep her at the top.

That's how she keeps her power. With Andy on one side and Madison on the other, she's bulletproofed. And I'm just background. The girl from the trailer park. The maybe-pretty-if-she-had-a-different-zip-code girl.

But I know better.

There were moments. quiet ones, in-between spaces, when I caught glimpses of who I really was. When I'd see my reflection in a storefront window or the glint of interest in a boy's eyes and think, *No. You're not invisible. You're not nothing.*

I saw the way the boys looked at me. I wasn't stupid. And neither was Imogen. Which is why she always shoved her way into conversations the second I got a laugh. She'd lean over and flick her hair, all sugary voice and fake interest, sucking up every drop of attention like it was oxygen.

She always made sure I knew my place. Like that time at a party, the music was blasting, thudding against the windows while we danced barefoot across Maddie's hardwood floors. I was mid-laugh with Jacob Freeman...he'd just told me I had the best smile in the room, when Imogen appeared out of nowhere and wrapped herself around his arm like we were living in a slow-motion perfume ad. Within seconds, I was alone again. Maddie had just blinked at me from across the room, looked away.

We'd had lots of sleepovers, at her house, and Imogen's too. Their houses always smelled like Bath & Body Works candles and someone's mom's signature perfume. The kind that came in glass bottles and cost more than everything in my closet. Their moms were always polished. Pretty. With smooth hair and soft voices, like they belonged in magazines.

My house didn't smell like perfume. My house smelled like dust and reheated coffee. It wasn't even my house that my baby sister and I lived in. It was my grandparents' single-wide trailer, older than I was, with soft spots in the floor and floral curtains that had faded to a washed-out pink. I didn't have a car. And Imogen refused to drive all the way into the trailer park. No matter the weather…rain, sleet, snow, it didn't matter, she made me walk to the main road. I'd climb into the backseat soaked and shivering while she scrolled through her texts and said nothing.

They wore brand names like they were protective armor. I wore thrifted clothes and made it work. But Imogen noticed. She always noticed.

"Did you even try today?" she'd ask, scrunching her nose as she looked me up and down. "You really should do something with your hair."
I wanted to scream.
But instead I smiled and said, "Yeah. I overslept."

I didn't need her approval. I knew I was pretty. Maybe not the manicured kind of pretty, but the kind that had bite to it. Something untamed. Something real.

And still…I wanted her to like me.
God, I hated that. But it was true. I wanted her approval like it meant

something. Like maybe if Imogen liked me, then I *was* worth liking. Even when she was cruel. Even when I felt sick, just walking next to her.

There was a day, last semester, I was wearing this soft, faded floral blouse, a relic of the eighties. One of the only things my mom left behind. It still smelled like her. Like cheap vanilla body spray and Suave shampoo. I only wore it when I really needed comfort. That day, I'd pulled it on to anchor me.

We were in the girls' bathroom between second and third period. Imogen was fixing her eyeliner in the mirror, tilting her head like she was the star of a movie, and the mirror was the camera. Madison stood beside her, chewing bubble gum and scrolling her phone.

I was standing by the sinks, pretending to be interested in my hair.

And then Imogen turned to me and said, "Are you seriously wearing *that?*"

I froze.

"Were you aiming for tragic fashion, Olivia? Or just landed there?"

She laughed and ripped the blouse right at the seam on my shoulder. Like it was hers to ruin.

I just stood there.

I didn't cry. I didn't yell. I didn't say a word. My throat burned like fire, and I kept blinking really fast, willing the tears not to spill.

Madison looked up for a second. Met my eyes. And looked back down at her phone like she hadn't seen anything at all.

I laughed, too.

Or tried to.

"That thing was ugly anyway," I said. My voice cracked, just slightly.

Imogen smiled wide and said, "Exactly."

And just like that, it was over. Like it never happened.

Most girls at our school would kill to be in our circle. And I was already in. I wasn't about to fight back and lose my place. I knew what happened to girls who stepped out of line...Imogen made sure of it. They got iced out, forgotten and quickly replaced.

I wasn't strong enough to be on the outside. Not yet.

So, I let her tear the only thing I had left of my mom, and I smiled though I felt like dying.
Like I didn't want to go into the nearest stall and scream into my hands until my throat gave out.

As if ripping my mother's top wasn't enough punishment, Maddie and Imogen left campus for lunch, without permission, to go get Sonic Drive-In burgers and didn't invite me.
That's how Imogen rolled. If *she* did something wrong, *you* got punished.

I sat alone at one of the sticky corner tables in the cafeteria, trying to act like it didn't bother me. The air smelled like reheated pizza, orange-scented cleaner, and too many perfume samples trapped under fluorescent lights. Someone had spilled a Sprite nearby and the floor tiles squelched every time a sneaker passed over it.

The plastic seats creaked every time you shifted your weight, and the long rectangular tables were dotted with Sharpie graffiti, names carved inside hearts, song lyrics, inside jokes that were never funny to begin with. Laughter echoed off the cinderblock walls, loud, fast, casual. Like everyone else had already figured out how to be okay.

I pretended to read my textbook, unbothered by the loneliness pressing in around me. Just another forgettable lunch hour. Just another day of acting like being left out didn't sting like hell.

My sleeve was stitched up with a safety pin, scratching my arm every time I moved. Like a physical reminder of the shame, I wasn't allowed to talk about.

I thought about how easy it was for Imogen to break something that mattered to me. How she didn't even blink. Just tore through it like it was nothing. Like *I* was nothing.

And then he walked in.

Andy.

Gray hoodie. That thick, messy hair falling into his eyes. He had this walk...quiet, like he didn't want to take up space, but also like he knew exactly where he was going. He passed my table, not fast, not slow. And he smiled. Just a little. Not huge. Just enough that I felt it in my chest.

I swear, for a second, I forgot all about how much I hated Imogen Warner.

My eyes followed him as he sat down at the table with the sports guys, all of them crowded around someone's phone, whisper-laughing about something probably stupid. But Andy...he looked back at me. Not in a creepy way. Just this soft, kind glance that made my stomach flip and my skin feel warm.

I liked him. A lot more than I ever let myself admit.

He was smart. Sweet. The kind of boy who actually listened when you talked. He didn't interrupt or look over your shoulder at someone better. He looked at *you*. And not the version of you were trying to be, but the real one. The quiet one underneath.

And just like that, the sharp edge inside me dulled. Just a little.

Just last week in biology, I'd dropped my pen and when I bent down to grab it, he went to grab it too and we knocked heads. We both laughed.

He didn't look away from me when our eyes met. He didn't stare like I was some joke or someone to fix. He looked at me like I was *already okay*.

Like I was beautiful in a way that didn't need approval.

Once, after class, he was asking me about our homework. Imogen walked up. I saw her glance at him and then at me.

So, I ran.

I didn't say anything. I didn't even smile. I just muttered something and took off down the hall like my lungs were collapsing. I knew if she looked into my eyes she would instantly know how I felt about him. I couldn't risk it. So, I pushed the feelings down.

But just now, he smiled at me again. The smile that made my legs feel like jelly. I felt it blooming again. The will to try with Andy.

A chance. A tiny window cracked open in a hallway full of locked doors. A chance to choose *for me,* instead of for stupid old Imogen.

That night, a fire ignited inside me. I lay on my bed, eyes fixed on the plastic glow-in-the-dark stars still taped to my ceiling since ninth grade, my whole-body trembling with impulse and possibility.

What if I was brave enough to want something? To take it? To let myself *be seen* without apology?

I knew if I ever had the chance with Andy, I was going to take it.

Surely, all of this has to mean something. That boy. This night. My decision. While Skyscraper by Demi LeVato plays in the background, I stared at the ceiling like I'm in a movie. Imogen can tear me down, alright, but I won't stay down.

I've been waiting my whole life for the moment when it all clicks. When I *become* whoever I'm supposed to be. But what if this is it already, at eighteen years old. What if I never get cooler or smarter or prettier than this?

My grandma keeps telling me to make good choices, and I nod like I hear her, but the truth is... I'm just trying to feel something. Not numb, not scared. Just *something*. I overthink everything. Smile. Not smiling. Eye contact. Did I say too much? Was I too much? Am I not enough? Can I hack it where I'm headed?

I feel like I'm always too much and never enough at the same time.

And I swear I'm fine. Like, *really* fine. Just don't ask me twice because I might start crying and never stop.

I've got nine weeks left in this town. Nine weeks of walking hallways that smell like bleach and broken dreams. Nine weeks of pretending I don't care when Imogen tosses me aside. And then I'm gone.

New York is waiting for me. I've been saving all the money from babysitting in a coffee can under my bed. I doodle skylines in the margins of my notebooks. I imagine the hum of city air, the blur of taxi lights outside my window, my name on some mailbox that *isn't* in a town where everybody already knows everything about me.

But just because I don't have money like Imogen or teeth as perfect as Maddie's, doesn't mean I'm less than. It just means I have to fight harder. And I'm okay with that.

Because I've got fire.

And when I leave this place, I'm taking every spark with me.

Let them keep their mascara cliques and their boyfriend power plays.

I'm going to be *something*.

And when I am, they'll remember me.

Even if they try not to.

CHAPTER 19

Madison

I slipped back inside and closed the door behind me, letting it click softly into place.
The sirens were still going outside, but in here, the sound was dulled, giving me a sort of refuge.

I didn't turn on the lights.
Didn't move.
Just stood in the foyer, hands shaking, body caught in that liminal space between dread and denial. The house was dim and still. I didn't bother with the lights. Just stood there, trying to breathe.

Sunlight spilled across the floor in sharp angles, catching the dust in the air. The wine glass on the counter was still half-drunk.

Leech was nowhere in sight. Probably hiding.

I stood there for a moment in the quiet, my back against the door.
The air pulsed with the feel of a memory I didn't want.

Then came the knock.
Soft. Measured. Like whoever it was knew why they were here.

My heart pounded out of control.

Was I being arrested already?

The thought rooted deep and fast.

My first inclination was to run. But where would I go? To the woods. To where they were probably already finding Olivia's body in the hollow.

The same hollow we had left her to rot. It wasn't far. A small enclave in the side of a mossy hill near the creek. Back then, we'd called it the fairy cave.

Imogen and I never told Andy about it.
It wasn't for boys.
It had been our secret.

Well, it *was*. The police were back there now. Searching the ground.

My hand hovered near the doorknob as my pulse pounded in my ears. The knock came again, a little more insistent this time and I finally opened the door.

Andy stood on the porch in full uniform.
His badge caught the light, jarring me.
The dark navy fabric of his shirt clung to his frame, the sleeves stiff, the collar pressed sharp.
His belt was weighed down with equipment...radio, handcuffs, something tucked just out of view.

He stepped inside and I closed the door behind him. I held my breath, waiting for what he would say. He looked taller somehow. Older. Undeniably handsome. But his face was pale, eyes rimmed red, jaw tight. He had the expression of someone holding something heavy, like grief or shock or both.

I was waiting for the hammer to drop. For him to say, *I know what you did.*

For a few seconds, he was silent. The air between us, heavy, and laden with what he wasn't saying.

"It's Olivia," he finally said, his voice barely above a choked whisper. "Something happened to her. They think somebody killed her. Her bloody clothes were found in the woods."

The words drifted, floating between us. I sucked in a breath, waiting.

Was there more? Did he know?

Suddenly, his face twisted, his breath coming in uneven waves, as tears slid down his face. His emotions, raw and uncensored. He looked to me for comfort, his eyes searching mine for warmth.

No. He didn't know.

Not with the way he was looking at me, like I was the only person in the world who could possibly understand what he was feeling.

I stood still, caught in his grief, unable to return it. My arms stayed at my sides. My body didn't know what to do.

He had to have thought I was in shock.
That I was just hearing it for the first time.

Something happened to Olivia.

But I knew that. I knew all too well why her bloody clothes were in the woods.

He stepped forward and wrapped me in his arms like he thought I might collapse.
Like I was the one who needed comfort. His grief pressed against me, hot and shaking, as he buried his face in my shoulder. I didn't move. Didn't speak.

Just stood there, hollow and still, while he cried for her.

He had no idea what I had done.

To him, I was still the girl who'd loved Olivia like a sister.
The girl who should be devastated at the news.

But inside…
there was only silence.

Andy pulled back, wiping his eyes with the back of his hand, trying to compose himself. His eyes scanned my face.

"At times like these…" he started, his voice rough, "you've got to stick close to the people who matter most."

He reached for my hand, gave it a gentle squeeze. "I still want to see you tonight. If you're up for it."

I nodded before I could stop myself.
My mouth said yes.
But inside, something was clawing and screaming, *run!*

He lingered another second, eyes glassy but sharp.

"I'm going to find out who did this to Olivia," he said, steady now. "Whoever it is… they're going to pay."

His grip tightened for just a moment...then he let go.

"I'll be back soon. Maybe an hour or two," he said.

And just like that, he was gone.
Back down the steps, back to the sirens and the uniforms and the flashing lights.

BETWEEN FRIENDS

The door clicked shut behind him, and I stood alone in the foyer, his words still clinging to my skin.

They're going to pay.

I moved without thinking.
Paced to the kitchen.
Opened the fridge, closed it.
Took the mugs from the living room. Washed them. Washed them again.

I scrubbed the counter.
Wiped down the table, even though there was nothing there.

Everywhere I looked...a memory of her.
Olivia's laugh in this room. Her pink converse by the door. The way she used to twirl her hair when she lied.

Her water bottle was still in the back of the cabinet.
Pink with a Marilyn Monroe sticker on it.
She used to drink everything from that bottle.

I could still hear her humming in the bathroom, off-key and careless, while steam curled beneath the door.

Her voice on the stairs, shouting for Imogen.
Her fingers brushing mine when we passed notes in class.
Her bare feet on the kitchen tile, dancing to a song we both pretended to hate.

It was like she hadn't left at all.

Like the air still remembered her shape.

And now...it was only a matter of time before they found her body.
Not the girl we remembered.
But the girl we left behind.

I paused in the doorway of the kitchen, my hands braced on either side of the molding. The thought of running was still tumbling around in my mind. A wild and useless idea. Where would I even go?
If I was a suspect, there was no getting away.
No escape.

The thought of being arrested. Of them showing up at my door with questions I couldn't answer, sent a wave of nausea through me.
And Andy.
What would he think when he realized what I'd done?
Would he look at me the way he used to? Or would his eyes go cold, like he didn't know me at all?
I pressed my forehead against the wood, willing myself to breathe.
Then a colder thought came. There was only one other person who could be accountable for this. The only other person in the woods with me that night.

Imogen.

Did she know yet?

Was she watching the news with a glass of wine in her manicured hand, already piecing together her version of the story?
And if I did call…could I trust her? *Could I trust* anyone?

But I had no choice. Whether I liked it or not. Imogen and I were in this together.

I pulled back from the doorframe, fingers shaking, and I reached for my phone.

Imogen's name hovered on the screen.
Just seeing it made my stomach twist.

I hesitated...thumb hovering...and tapped the call button.

She picked up on the second ring.

"Maddie," she said.
Her voice was low, clipped. Already knowing.

A few words were all I could muster. Woods. Olivia. Scared.

"Stop," she said, cutting me off before I could find the words. "Don't say another thing."

There was a pause. Then she said, "I'm coming over."

The line went dead before I could respond.
I stood there, phone still pressed to my ear, the silence humming against my skin.

She's coming here. And Andy would be back soon.

I hadn't told her about Andy.
Not a word.
Not the dates. Not the connection between us.
Nor the fact that he had just stood in this room in uniform and cried in my arms over a girl we helped bury.

What would she say if she found out?
No, what would she *do?*
Imogen didn't handle betrayal quietly.

Even though it had been a decade...whatever was Imogen's, was always Imogen's. No one knew that better than me. And if you betrayed her, you better watch out.

She'd always had a way of twisting hurt into something sharp, something dangerous.

And if she knew I'd been seeing Andy behind her back, after everything…

I sank down onto the kitchen floor, back against the cabinets, knees pulled to my chest.

What was I thinking?

Of all the secrets I'd buried, this one suddenly felt the most dangerous.

Because Imogen didn't share.

Imogen didn't *forgive.*

And now she was on her way.

CHAPTER 20

Olivia

Seven weeks until graduation

Being in a popular high school clique isn't as fun as it sounds. It's not some shiny television teen drama. It's more like survival of the fakest. Group chats that never stop buzzing. Whispered secrets in the bathroom that you pretend not to hear. Outfit approvals. Screenshot scandals. Crying in your car, then walking into class with winged eyeliner sharp enough to slice open your grief.

And in 2013, popularity comes with a dress code. Victoria Secret yoga pants, even if you've never done yoga. UGG boots in ninety-degree weather. Longchamp totes, monogrammed. North Face fleeces. Tiffany heart necklaces. Michael Kors everything. Starbucks in hand. EOS lip balm rolling loose in your purse like a personality trait.

And me? I live in Hillshire Park. My grandparents can barely afford groceries, let alone gas for our '86 Toyota Camry that sounds like it might die every time we turn the ignition. I can't even afford something new from Walmart, let alone anything with a name stitched into the tag.

My entire wardrobe is curated from thrift stores, clearance bins, and garage sales. But I have an eye for the good stuff...hidden gems buried in the piles...and a sewing machine that hums late into the night while I reshape my finds into something that passes. Something that fits *them*.

My grandparents do what they can, but they're old. Worn thin from years of just barely getting by. My granddad works nights at the factory, even though his knees are shot and he can't hear out of one ear. My grandma mostly watches TV and forgets what day it is. She's not exactly warm...never tucks my hair behind my ear or asks about my day...but she tries. She folds my clothes, leaves dinner in the oven, tells me to be careful when I leave the house.

Sometimes I wonder if it would've all been different if my mom hadn't run off. She dropped my sister and me on my grandparents' doorstep when I was fourteen and Kristen was six and we never saw her again. My grandmother always makes a point to tell me I am just like my mom. A wild cannon, set to go off at any moment. Can't contain wild things, she'd say.

I revolted against that. I didn't want to be like my mom, not really, but the truth was deep down I knew I had that rebel bone too.

I made it just fine without a proper mother. I learned how to take care of myself. Learned how to survive. How to fit in.

But of course, I knew it was just smoke and mirrors. All of it. But I played the part well. They let me into the group because I'm pretty. That's the truth no one says out loud. Pretty enough to stand next to them. Pretty enough to borrow from, copy, envy. But I'm not one of them. Not really. Just the girl they like to keep close enough to feel charitable.

Still...I stay. I smile. I laugh at the right jokes. I let Imogen call me "Liv," even though it makes my skin crawl. Because outside the circle is worse. Outside the circle is nothing.
And I know what nothing feels like.

Today was no different. I walked up to the front entrance of Palmetto High with my bag slung over one shoulder and the silence pressing against my ears. The courtyard was empty. First period had started ten minutes ago, which meant everyone was already tucked into their desks, pretending to pay attention, scrolling through their phones under the table.

I adjusted my jacket, a black cropped blazer I'd scored for four dollars from a thrift store bin. It still had the shoulder pads when I found it, but I ripped them out and replaced the buttons with gold ones I'd scavenged from a worn-out blouse. Underneath, a vintage Blondie tee with a tiny hole near the hem, and my favorite pair of skinny jeans that used to be flared before I took a seam ripper to them. My boots were scuffed but real leather. I had an eye for that. And I knew how to fake the rest.

The only sound was the slap of my heels against the pavement. Imogen had forgotten to pick me up again.

But truthfully, she never *forgot* anything. It was just her way of reminding me where I stood. I was disposable and she wouldn't let me forget it. A little charity project with a pretty face and sad eyes.

I had to wake my grandfather up to take me, even though he'd just gotten home from working the third shift. His knuckles were raw, his shoulders heavy. He didn't say much...just sighed, grabbed his keys, and motioned for me to follow.

I offered to drive, but he waved me off. Too tired to argue, too stubborn to let me take the car.

He didn't say a word the whole drive. When we pulled into the school parking lot, I thanked him, soft and quiet, and he just nodded. His eyes already half-closed. I watched him pull away, the Camry rattling down the road, and pictured him kicking off his boots and collapsing on top of the covers without ever making it to the pillow. Guilt sat heavy in my throat, even though none of this was my fault.

I walked slower than I needed to up to the school steps. Letting the silence of the courtyard wrap around me for a moment longer. Letting myself breathe. And I pushed through the glass doors and braced for whatever version of hell waited on the other side.

When I pushed open the classroom door, every head turned.
Mr. Raley paused his lecture, "Nice of you to join us, Olivia."

My cheeks burned, heat creeping up my neck. I gave a tight-lipped smile...the kind that wasn't a smile at all...and slid into the only empty desk in the back row.

Imogen snickered under her breath, loud enough to be heard, quiet enough to be ignored.

As I dropped my bag onto the floor, she leaned over, her breath sticky sweet with cinnamon gum.

"Nice of you to join us, loser."

I didn't flinch. Just turned my head slowly and stared at her, long enough to let her know I heard. Long enough to let her feel the heat of my glare without saying a word.

She blinked, still smiling, and turned back to her notebook like nothing happened.

I pulled out my textbook, heart beating faster than it should've been. My fingers trembled slightly as I flipped to the right page. Page 147. *American History: Reconstruction to Present.*

Everything felt heavier than it should.

I didn't say a word.

Because I knew better.

Because if you speak, they win.

Because silence is the only real weapon they don't know how to use.

When the bell rang, I slipped out of my desk as fast as I could, keeping my eyes low, my steps sharp. I didn't want to give Imogen the chance to say anything else.

She called after me, voice high and syrupy. "Livvv...wait up!"

I pretended not to hear.

In the hallway, I passed Maddie. She gave me a small wave and a smile, like that made her different. Like a silent apology from twenty feet away meant something. And maybe she *did* feel bad when Imogen pulled this kind of crap...ditching me, mocking me, making me feel two inches tall in front of everyone. But she never felt bad enough to stop her.

I stopped in the bathroom between classes to reapply my lip gloss. The lighting was trash, but I tilted my chin toward the mirror and touched up the shimmer just enough to catch the hallway light. My hair still looked decent...long and blonde, curled at the ends, the way Imogen said made me look "effortlessly seductive," which was her polite way of saying I tried too hard.

I didn't care.

I had Biology next.

Which meant I'd get to sit next to Andy.

I passed him in the hallway when the bell rang. Headed to meet Imogen. His eyes searching the crowd for her. But my heart still fluttered when

I saw him. He looked so cute, I could hardly stand it. He was wearing a faded black t-shirt that stretched across his broad shoulders and jeans that rode low on his hips with his hair, messy in the kind of way that only looked good if you didn't try.

I swiped the gloss across my lips, thinking about how sweet he was. Always offering me the better specimen, the good tweezers, ripping out pages from his own notebook when I forgot mine. And he helped me with the assignments, even though I could've figured them out myself.

Of course, I didn't need the extra help. Biology was simple for me. But I liked hearing him explain things to me. The way he leaned in, just close enough that our arms touched. The way he pointed at the diagrams, his fingers brushing the edge of my paper like it was a secret only we shared. I breathed him in when he got that close. Just enough to make my chest ache.

I really wanted to keep the promise I made to myself.
To take my shot with him and see where it landed.
But who was I kidding anyway? He belonged to Imogen.
And that burned. Worse than I liked to admit.

They didn't even make sense together. She was all gloss and cruelty and curated moments. He was steady, kind, almost too good for this school.

But she was a cheerleader. And he was the star wide receiver. That's how it worked.

Imogen didn't have to be kind to get what she wanted.
She just took it.

From behind me, I heard the bathroom door creak open, and Maddie stepped in, wearing that too-sweet smile she always used when she didn't know what else to say.

"I'm sorry Imogen forgot to pick you up," she said, her voice barely audible.

I tilted my head, slowly. "Forgot?"

She looked down, not answering.

I turned back to the mirror and unscrewed my mascara, brushing it carefully through my lashes.

My reflection didn't flinch. "It's fine. I'm used to it."

A pause stretched between us.

I capped the tube, smoothed my fingers under each eye, and let the words come out low but clear.

"I can't wait to get out of this town and get to New York."

Maddie gave a small laugh, almost nervous. "You're still planning on New York? How will you survive?"

I met her eyes through the glass. "I'll get a job. Waiting tables or selling knockoff perfume on the sidewalk...I don't care. I'll do whatever it takes to get away from here."

I looked over just in time to catch Maddie rolling her eyes.

My voice tightened. "Graduation day, I'm out. And I'm not looking back."

The bathroom door slammed open, the sound sharp against the tile, and the air shifted, thick and immediate. I didn't have to turn around to know it was her. Imogen's presence always carried a certain weight, like the temperature dropped the moment she entered a room. Her heels echoed across the tile as she made her entrance, slow and deliberate...like she owned the place. Like she owned *us*. Her heels clicked sharply across the tile as she walked in, tossing her hair like she was entering a stage.

"Aww, Liv. That's adorable," she said, her voice curling around the bathroom, like a snake.

She never asked if she could shorten my name. She just did it. Claimed it, like everything else.
And I let her. Because that's what you do when someone like Imogen decides you're hers.

I froze, mascara still in hand.

She stepped beside Maddie and crossed her arms.

"New York, huh? What are you going to do? Smile at people until they give you rent money?"

"Leave her alone," Maddie said, barely above a whisper.
But Imogen ignored her. Her eyes were locked on me, glittering with cruelty.

"You're not going anywhere. You'll chicken out like you always do. End up stuck here, thirty years old, waiting tables at Shoney's, crying about how no one ever gave you a chance."

Something in me quietly rose up.

"I don't need a chance," I said, turning fully toward her. "I'll make my own way."

Her smile didn't falter. It just sharpened.

"You're not built for that kind of life, Liv. You're good at being beautiful, and let's just be real, you're not even that pretty. You will never make it in New York. And if we are having real talk, you will never even make it to the airport to go. I promise you that."

"I'm taking the bus," I snapped back.

"Of course you are," she said, laughing.

She looked straight at Maddie, her voice dripping with mock sincerity as she repeated my words.

"She's taking the bus."

They both burst out laughing, loud, unfiltered, like it was the funniest thing they'd ever heard.
Like I wasn't even standing there.

For a second, I couldn't breathe.
Maybe they were right. Maybe I wouldn't make it.
New York felt farther away than ever. Just a foolish dream cooked up in the back of a cheap notebook.

I blinked hard, willing the sting in my eyes to disappear.
Not here. Not in front of them.
They'd already taken enough.

Imogen turned back to the mirror, smoothing a piece of hair behind her ear like none of it had mattered. I shoved my mascara back into my bag, heart pounding in my chest, and walked out before either of them could see that they had gotten to me.

The hallway blurred as I moved.

But I didn't stop walking.

CHAPTER 21

Olivia

Six weeks until graduation

After the bathroom confrontation, things between Imogen and me shifted. Not in any obvious way...she still smiled at me in the halls, still tagged me in group photos, still tossed me bites of gum like we were best friends...but underneath it, something had cracked.

And I could feel it.

I stood up to her and now she didn't want me there anymore. I could see it in the way she glanced past me when I spoke, how her compliments felt sharp-edged, how her laughter never quite reached her eyes when I was the one talking.

Maddie didn't notice. Or pretended not to. She still passed me notes during class, tagged me in photos when Imogen didn't, and offered to buy me Starbucks when we were in drive thru. She always made sure I was included in the plans that they made. But there was no heart in what she did. Not really.

That was the thing about Maddie. She liked to act like the nicer one. The gentler one. The girl who felt bad when things went too far. But in the end, she was just as caught up in it. Just as obsessed with Imogen, as Imogen was with herself.

She'd never risk being on the outside. Not for me. Not for anyone.

And once I saw that clearly, it was hard not to start questioning everything else.

Imogen was keeping me around for a reason. What that reason was, I didn't know.

But it wasn't real friendship. Not anymore.
Maybe it never was.

Having me around made Imogen feel important. I was her contrast...her proof. Someone to show off in front of. To dangle things in front of...bags, clothes, plans...just to remind me I'd never really have them. I made her feel exclusive. Untouchable. Better.

And the worst part?

I wanted them to like me. I wanted to belong. I told myself the social status was enough...that the way the other girls looked at me with envy when Imogen looped her arm through mine in the hallway was worth it.

Like we were queens of the school.
And we kind of were.

But I was never wearing the crown. I was just close enough to catch the light.

———————•◆◆•·———————

I stayed a few minutes after the final bell because Mrs. Langley flagged me down outside the auditorium. Something about the spring dance...decorations, theme colors, floral centerpieces from the PTA. She talked with her hands and her heart, all soft curls and enthusiasm, but I kept checking the clock over her shoulder.

"I just thought you'd have a good eye for this," she said, flipping through fabric swatches like we were planning a wedding instead of a high school gym transformation. "You've got that vintage thing, Olivia."

I smiled. "Yeah...totally. Love that. I was thinking maybe... paper lanterns?"

"Oh, that's cute!" she beamed. "Like a magical nights themed soiree."

"Exactly," I cut in, already gathering my bag. "I'll sketch some ideas and drop them off tomorrow?"

She blinked, seemingly caught off guard by how quickly I wrapped it up, but recovered with a smile.

"Of course, sweetheart. Thank you!"

I jogged down the hallway, already knowing I was late. With the way things had been the last few days, probably much too late. My shoes echoed off the empty linoleum, every step faster than the last. I pushed through the double doors, out into the afternoon light, eyes scanning the lot. And I was right. The car was gone.

Imogen's white BMW convertible, the one she never let anyone eat in, the one with the pink rhinestone license plate frame...was nowhere in sight.

They'd left without me.

I stood at the top of the steps, chest tight, staring at where the car should've been.

My hands clenched around my bag strap. I looked down at the concrete. Willed the sting in my throat to disappear before it reached my eyes.

Because this is what it meant to be *included,* right?

You get the ride when it's convenient.
You get left when you're not.

I stood there for a second, staring out at the lot, willing the BMW to just… appear.

For once, I wanted to see Imogen's face.
Wanted her to come back for me.
Even if it was just to pretend, she cared. I squeezed my eyes shut and when I opened them again, the car still wasn't there. Not that I believed it would be.

What was I going to do now?

It wasn't like I had a phone to call anyone with. I never had. Imogen used to tease me about it...asked if I communicated by smoke signal or handwritten letter.

So now I'd have to go back inside, use the office phone like a lost kid in a movie.

The thought made my stomach turn.

But what choice did I have?

I turned around, pushed open the heavy front doors again, and walked the long stretch back to the front office. Miss Keller, the school secretary, was already shutting down her computer, her floral tote perched precariously on the edge of the desk. Her thin, over-plucked brows arched with exhaustion, and the faint clack of her acrylic nails against the keyboard marked the last of her patience for the day.

"Miss Keller?" I asked, trying to keep my voice steady. "Can I use the phone? My ride left without me."

She pursed her lips but didn't argue. Just slid the receiver toward me and turned her back to me.

I dialed Maddie's number first. Straight to voicemail.

Of course.

I paused, and dialed home. My granddad's landline. The one with the cord that always tangled and the buttons that stuck if you didn't press just right.

It rang. And rang.

No answer.

He was probably still asleep. He usually didn't wake up until around 4pm.

I set the phone down gently, even though I wanted to slam it.

"Thanks," I said, more out of habit than anything.

Miss Keller didn't look up.

I exited the school. Again. Out the doors, down the steps, into the sharp afternoon wind.

I had four miles between me and Hillshire Park, and no one coming for me.

So, I started walking.
Because that's what you do when no one's coming.

The heat pressed down on me before I even got across the grass. Summer had arrived early, thick with humidity and the kind of gnats that hover near your ears no matter how fast you walk.

My shirt clung to my back before I even hit the sidewalk, and my hair was already sticking to the sides of my neck. I cut across the student parking lot, head down. Most of the cars were gone. This morning it had been packed...every kid's beat-up hand-me-down crammed into the lot, mostly minivans and sedans passed down from moms who'd upgraded to SUVs once the last kid hit middle school.

Now just a few cars were left, scattered in the sun, like forgotten toys.

Logan Harper's dented old Chevy pickup sat crooked in a corner space, the tailgate down. He and his brother Daniel...both in my Art and Design class...were perched on it, smoking and talking low. Their heads turned when they saw me crossing.

They went quiet.

Logan nudged Daniel, who grinned and looked me over like I was some kind of joke they'd been waiting to tell.

"Where's your royal court?" Logan called out, voice lazy and loud.

Daniel snorted. "What, did they leave you behind?"

I kept walking, fast but not too fast to make it obvious I was trying to avoid them.

"I had an afternoon meeting. They had to go," I said, glancing around, hoping someone would appear. But no one did.

The heat rose up my neck like it was trying to choke me.

218

"So much for loyalty, huh?" Logan flicked ash from his cigarette, still watching me.

"We could give you a ride," he added, a slow smirk pulling at his mouth.

"Yeah," Daniel echoed, laughing. "We could definitely give you a ride," He elbowed Logan, almost knocking him off the tailgate.

Logan punched Daniel in the arm.

I didn't stop. Didn't blink. Just shot them both a look sharp enough to cut and picked up my pace.

"Suit yourself," Logan called after me. "Must be nice...too good to ride with the peasants."

I didn't respond, I just kept moving.

A block later, sweat was running down my back and gathering at my temples. My shirt was soaked. Mosquitos circled my ankles every time I stopped to shift my bag, and something bit the soft underside of my arm.

I passed into the historic part of town, where the cracked sidewalk wove through old oak trees and spilled into driveways made of brick and shell. The kind of houses that didn't just sit...they *stood*. Proud. Timeless.

White picket fences lined the edges of wide, manicured lawns. Wrought iron gates curled in elegant patterns, framing the houses beyond like flourishes on a signature. Grand, deliberate, and meant to be remembered. Some had wraparound porches with wicker swings, others had second-story balconies framed in ivy and flower boxes blooming with colors that took my breath away.

The air changed here...thicker, slower. It smelled like jasmine and damp moss and something older than I could explain. The homes were grand.

Not in the way Imogen and Maddie's were. Theirs were new construction, sharp-edged and spotless, like someone tried too hard.

These were quiet giants. Full of creaking floors and stories. Magic in the bones.

I couldn't imagine stepping inside one. Much less living in it. The closest I'd ever come was walking past, trying not to stare too long, as if someone might notice I didn't belong here.

I kept walking, the houses offering little distraction from the heat or the steady ache in my legs. Every so often, the breeze would stir, merciful, but thin. Barely brushing my skin before vanishing again. Wind chimes clinked from an unseen porch, a delicate scatter of sound, high and hollow.

I slowed when I reached my favorite. A gothic Victorian set back from the street, shadowed by trees that looked like they belonged in a fairytale. The paint was chipped in places, but it only made the pale blue trim, and the black gables feel more like something out of a dream. Pink flowers spilled over the walkway, blooming wild and soft. The porch wrapped all the way around, with a swing drifting gently at the far end. Moving on its own, slow and rhythmic, like something remembered in a dream. And stained-glass windows that caught the sunlight and scattered streaks of colored light across the cracked sidewalk like confetti.

I stopped, despite my misery.
Just for a second.
I imagined walking up the steps, turning the knob.
Hearing creaky floors and old pipes. Breathing in wood polish and history and quiet.

I imagined someone waiting for me inside, someone kind. A room that smelled like roses and worn linen. Sunlight slanting across the floor in long, golden strips. A soft chair in the corner with a book left open, a glass of water on the nightstand, beads of condensation still clinging to the side. A bed I didn't want to leave. Pillows fluffed just right, the covers tucked around me like I mattered to someone.

I stepped a little closer to the fence, fingers grazing the iron.

And then... a snarl echoed across the grass.
Fast. Too loud. And violent.

A massive Doberman came charging from the side yard, its body a blur of muscle and rage. It slammed into the fence so hard the gate rattled, barking with its whole chest. Spit flew from its teeth. Its collar was black leather, studded with silver spikes, thick like it had to hold back something feral.

I stumbled back, my heart thundering. The sting of shock moved through like I'd been struck by lightning. The dog barked again, throwing its weight against the gate like it *knew* I didn't belong. Like it had been waiting for me to get too close.

I turned fast, swallowing the lump in my throat, and started walking again...faster this time.

That's what I got for pretending.

I'd barely caught my breath, still trying to shake off the image of that dog's teeth, when I heard a sharp honk behind me.

I turned, bracing for more embarrassment.

But it was Andy. He was slowing to a stop in his little red Ford Ranger pickup, one arm resting on the open window, his hair wind-tossed and soft, like he'd just run his hand through it. The sunlight hit the hood in a dull shimmer, and for a second, I thought I might actually pass out.

"Olivia?" he called out, brow furrowed. "You walking home?"

I blinked. Couldn't even think of a lie fast enough.

"Yeah," I said, voice small. "Just heading back."

He looked me over, and how I wished he wouldn't have. My face was flushed; I could feel the heat rising all the way to my ears. Sweat slid down my spine, slow and humiliating. Bug bites dotted my calves, red and angry. I was flushed and frizzy and exactly the kind of mess Imogen would've rolled her eyes at.

But he didn't laugh.
He leaned toward the passenger seat. "You want a ride?"

I hesitated...only for a second...but everything in me screamed *yes*.
"Yes. God, yes. Thank you."

I jogged over and climbed in, sinking into the seat like it might swallow me whole. The air conditioning hit me instantly, cold and clean, and I swear I could've cried.

He glanced over. "You, okay?"

"Just overheated," I said, brushing sweat off my forehead. "Well, and being slowly devoured by mosquitos."

He laughed, that quiet little chuckle that started low in his chest. "Well... lucky for you, I showed up when I did."

I smiled, before I could stop it.

"Yeah," I said softly. "Lucky me."

The silence settled for a minute, broken only by the hum of the A/C and the soft rattling of something in his glove compartment.

I risked a glance over at him. I knew this was my chance. The one I'd been waiting on.

"You know," I said, trying to sound casual, "I like that shirt on you."

He looked down at it...just a simple gray t-shirt, a little worn at the collar, sleeves rolled slightly.

"Really?" he said, glancing at me. "Imogen hates this one. Says it makes me look 'too basic."

I snorted. "God forbid you look like an actual person."

He smiled, but I didn't stop there.

"I see how she treats you, you know."

His smile faltered, just a little.

"I don't know why you stay."

I swallowed and kept my eyes out the window. "She's so different from you."

Still no answer.

"I just don't get it. You're... better than that. Better than *her.*"

His fingers tapped the wheel once, thoughtful. And quiet as a breath, he said, "I could say the same about you."

I turned just enough to meet his eyes.

We didn't say anything else for a second.
We didn't have to.

We rode in silence for the last few minutes, but it wasn't the awkward kind. It was charged. Like there were too many words hovering between us and neither of us knew which one would tip the whole thing over.

When we pulled up to the entrance of Hillshire Park, I shifted in my seat.

"Stop here," I said quickly, already reaching for the handle.

He slowed to a stop but didn't put the truck in park.

"You don't have to be weird about it," he said, glancing over at me. "I don't care where you live."

I looked at him, really looked at him...and for a second, I was ready to take my shot. I almost said something. Something real. Something stupid.

And then I almost did something even worse.

I almost leaned over and kissed him.

My heart was pounding so loud it drowned out everything else. His face was right there, all soft and open, and the A/C was still blowing that clean, warm smell around the cab and...

I pulled back.

Fast.

"Thanks for the ride," I said instead, already opening the door.

He gave me a little smile, the kind that tugged at one side of his mouth. "Anytime."

Then he pulled away, tires crunching on gravel, and I was left standing in the sun like an idiot.

I couldn't believe I almost kissed him.

I shook my head at my own stupidity. If anyone found out, it would be social suicide. Imogen would kill me. Like, actually buried-my-body-behind-the-school kill me.

I adjusted my bag on my shoulder and started walking toward my trailer, trying to shake it off.

But the truth was, my heart wouldn't slow down.

Not even close.

It just kept quickening with every step.

All because of Andy Marson.

CHAPTER 22

Imogen

It was late afternoon, and I hadn't sat down once since Chris had called and told me the news about the police's discovery in the woods. He thought I would want to know since Olivia was a friend of mine. If only he knew *who* he was calling.

I folded the same pair of leggings three times and still couldn't make my hands stop shaking. I pressed my palms flat against the marble countertop. The coolness anchored me for a second. Just long enough to keep from screaming.

Outside, the cicadas were already buzzing, and it wasn't even summer yet. They were out early.
It wasn't the season for them to be here and for some reason that rubbed me the wrong way.

But everything felt wrong right now. Even the feel of my own skin on my body was offensive.

I wanted to scream.
I want to run.
I wanted to…
Smoke. That's what I wanted. A cigarette.

It was a risk to step out...especially with the kids home...but they were curled up on the couch, hypnotized by some YouTuber with fake nails and bright hair squishing neon goo into a microphone. They wouldn't notice if the roof caved in. Their little mouths hung open, eyes glazed over. A priceless babysitter named Internet.

I slipped through the side door and shut it quietly behind me.

The sun had moved just low enough to cast long, lazy shadows across the lawn, slicing the grass into strips of gold and green. The garden was supposed to be my sanctuary. I'd paid extra for the landscaping, even sketched out the layout on hotel stationary during our beach trip last spring. But now the hydrangeas were scorched, from the early heat. The boxwoods had gone patchy and brown, and the neighbor's cat had used the herb bed as a litter box again. Everything was starting to fall apart. Even here.

Behind the glass door, the boys' voices rose suddenly in unison...loud, sharp, that chaotic pitch only children could reach when something disgusting happened on YouTube.

"Ew! Broooo, look at that slime!"

"She's gonna pop it...she's gonna...!"

"Yesss! She popped it! It's in her hair!"

I flinched. Closed my eyes.

Took a breath.

Their laughter scraped across my nerves. I wanted to snap. Tell them to use their inside voices even though they weren't doing anything wrong. I hated the sound of it...joy unbridled. Joy when I could barely stand.

The laughter kept going. On and on.

I counted to three. Then five. Then seven. Just to keep my hands from shaking.

It was nothing. Just kids being kids.
But today, everything was too loud.
Too bright.

I stepped farther onto the stone pavers, letting the sun hit my face, let it sear into my closed eyelids. The air was thick, damp with the weight of impending rain. Somewhere, a neighbor's wind chimes started up, thin metallic tings echoing like bells in a funeral procession. I wanted to find them and rip them down.

I lit the cigarette with stiff fingers and took a long drag. I leaned against the stucco wall and exhaled.

I closed my eyes. Only for a moment.

And there she was.

Not a memory. Not at first.
A flash...blood on her temple, eyes wide, startled. Her mouth opened like she was about to scream.

But when I blinked, it was gone.

I took another long drag, remembering.

She was just standing there.
Next to the lockers.
Ribbons in her hair.
A faded denim mini skirt that didn't fit right, probably from Goodwill. Trying too hard. Always trying too hard. In my head, she was always seventeen. Always standing a little too close. Always smiling like she didn't know what it meant.

God, she was *so* annoying.
Trying to be one of us in all the ways that made your skin crawl.
Like she wanted to be noticed but hadn't figured out how to earn it.

And Andy?
Of course she liked Andy.

She tried to hide it, but I saw it.
She looked at him like he was air. Like she couldn't breathe without him.

She was subtle the way a house fire is subtle.
But I didn't blame her. Everyone wanted him.

He was mine.

I made sure of it.

I crushed the cigarette out and flicked the butt into the flowerbed. It landed near a wilting peony and a half-buried Hot Wheels car.

I didn't even bother to try to hide it. If Chris asked, I would tell him the pool guy left it.

My phone buzzed inside.
It was Maddie on the line.

Her voice shaking. Panic thick in her throat, stammering something about the news, about the police all over the neighborhood. I could barely understand her. And I knew damn well she wasn't going to hold up under pressure.

I didn't even remember getting in the car. One minute I was in the backyard, flicking ash into the hydrangeas. The next, the sitter was sitting on the couch with the boys, and I was behind the wheel with the AC blasting the scent of my Bath and Body Works air freshener.

I gripped the steering wheel too tight. My knuckles blanched. The streets of Fairfield hadn't changed, not really. Same sagging power lines. Same cracked sidewalks buckling under roots. Same girls pushing baby strollers with cigarettes hanging from their lips. I rolled through a yellow light that turned red too fast and kept going.

I didn't want to stop.

As I passed Hillshire trailer park, I felt it again...that familiar knot in my throat.

The roofs were patched with tarp. Lawnmowers rusted beside plastic flamingos. Someone had tied a bedsheet across the front of one trailer, spray-painted with *Happy Birthday, Tucker* in loopy letters. The paint dripped down the fabric like tears.

I swallowed.

These people weren't living.
They were surviving.
Born here, raised here. Most of them never left.
Like the tide washed them up young and just… never pulled back out.

They built lives on the same streets their parents did, married each other, had kids who'd do the same. Escaping was a story people told themselves. An empty promise.

This town was a prison dressed up as a zip code.
And some of us were serving life sentences.

I used to tell myself I was different.
That I'd really get out. That I *deserved* to get out.

But I didn't.
I was still here.
Still circling the same blocks, still passing the same rusted mailbox with the dented flag.

Still heading toward the same girl, I used to whisper secrets to in the dark and now couldn't even trust with silence.

Maddie. I should've cut her loose back in middle school.
She was too soft. Too *emotional.*

But I didn't. I kept her close. Maybe out of loyalty. Maybe out of habit.

I turned left onto her street and eased off the gas.

I could feel it coming...the thing inside me I didn't want to name. My stomach clenched, and for a second, my vision blurred. It wasn't tears. I wouldn't let it be.

I blinked hard and sat up straighter. Adjusted the mirror.

Tucked a loose strand of hair behind my ear.

I was fine.
I was always fine.

Even if I was unraveling, no one would see it.

Maddie was the weak link.
She always had been.

I had to get over there.
I had to look her in the eye, make her *remember* how much she owed me.
How far we were both in this.

We needed to get on the same page before Maddie opened her mouth to the wrong person.

Because I wasn't going down for this.
Not after everything I'd already done to survive.

The police finding Olivia's clothes hadn't changed anything. It wasn't my fault she was dead. Other people were to blame here. I was just one piece of a bigger puzzle.

"I am innocent," I said it out loud. Soft, but certain.

I wasn't going down for this. I was sure of that.
Let Maddie fall apart. Let the whole town light up with whispers and old secrets.
I would survive this.

I always do.

And just because they found something, doesn't mean they know what happened.

All they really have are guesses...fragments of a story no one can tell in full.

The woods don't keep records.

There were no cameras. No one was watching that night.

No one was there at all.

Except... me. And Maddie.

CHAPTER 23

Madison

Imogen knocked...the echo, sharp and urgent. Like I hadn't been sitting on the other side of the door this whole time, listening for the rush of her tires.

I didn't get up right away.

I just sat there, elbows on my knees, pressing the heels of my hands into my eyes, hoping that when I opened them, I'd know what to say. Because whatever came next...It wouldn't be small. It wouldn't be forgettable. Some things, once spoken, can't be taken back.

I'd spent years convincing myself it was better left untouched. That what happened to Olivia was final. That digging it back up wouldn't change anything.

But I've never really let it go.

I don't remember that night...not all of it. Just flashes of fear.
And blood.

So much blood.

On my skin. In my hair. On the clothes I threw away before anyone could see.

People say blackout like it's just a blank spot. A blip.
But it isn't. It's a hole you carry around with you. A silence you have to fill with guesses.

And no matter how much time passes, there's always a part of me that can't stop asking what I did that night.

Or what I let happen.

Because I was there.
That much I know.

And that kind of knowing doesn't fade. It festers.

When Imogen stepped inside, the whole house shifted. Her energy filled the space...restless and frantic. She didn't even wait for me to say hello before the words started spilling out.

"They found evidence in the woods. But there's no footage. No one was around. There's nothing that ties us to it, Maddie. They can't prove anything. No one saw..."

"Will you shut up and let me speak?" I snapped.

She flinched. Actually flinched.

Her eyes cut into me...rage and disbelief, tangled together.

My mouth opened, but no sound came out.
And suddenly, I couldn't speak. No words would form.

"What the hell, Maddie?" she hissed. "We need to focus here."
I swallowed hard, forcing a few words. "I need to ask you something."

"No," she said quickly, already shaking her head. "What we *need* is to get our story straight. To be smart. You know what could happen if they find out we were there? If they find out, *we* were involved?" Her voice cracked on that last word.

I stood there, pulse pounding, the question about what happened, still lodged in my throat like it had nowhere to go. Imogen stepped closer, heels clicking against the tile with military precision. Everything about her was too composed...lipstick perfect, her clothes neatly pressed. But her eyes... her eyes were wild.

"You're spiraling," she said coldly. "And I'm not going to let you blow this up because you're feeling emotional all of a sudden."

"I'm not emotional," I whispered, even though we both knew I was.

She ignored me, or maybe just didn't care.

"You say nothing. Do you understand me? Not to the cops. Not to your creepy neighbor. Not to *anyone.*"

I shook my head. "I don't know what I'd say since I don't remember much."

Imogen laughed. Short. Bitter. "That's rich, Maddie. That's *so* convenient."

"I don't know what I'd say," she said mocking me.

Imogen's posture stiffened, her chin lifting like a blade. "You don't *need* to remember. You need to keep your mouth shut."

"I'm trying," I said. "But I have questions."

"No. Absolutely not!" She raised a finger, pointed it toward me like she was scolding a child. "This is not the time for soul-searching, Maddie. This is the time for strategy."

I blinked. "But what if I remembered something important? What if..."

She cut me off again.

"*Important* to who? To the cops? To your conscience?" Her voice dripped with disdain. "That's how people get caught, you know. They get emotional. They start thinking truth equals justice, and the next thing you know, you're giving interviews and wearing handcuffs."

I stared at her. "So, we just keep pretending that we are innocent?"

Imogen crossed her arms, exhaling hard through her nose. "We don't *pretend*. We preserve."

I swallowed. "That's not the same thing."

"It is now."

I opened my mouth, but she beat me to it again.

"You think I haven't spent the last decade years waking up in a cold sweat? You think I don't see her face every time I close my eyes?" Her voice wavered, just for a second, then steadied. "You want answers, Maddie? So do I. But answers don't keep you out of prison. Discipline does. If one of us goes down… we both go down. Don't you get that?"

She didn't blink. "We are both guilty."

I looked away. My throat burned. "I blacked out."

"No," she said, voice dropping to a hiss. "You *checked out*. There's a difference."

That made me look at her. Really look. And for a second, I didn't see the girl I used to sneak into the basement with, stealing sips of her mother's vodka and refilling the bottle with water like a couple of criminal masterminds. I didn't see the friend who used to write my name on the bathroom mirror in heart-shaped lipstick.

The one I used to laugh with until our stomachs hurt, our mascara smudged, and neither of us remembered what was so funny in the first place.

Instead, I saw someone I didn't recognize.

Someone who would do anything to keep her world from cracking.

"You're scared," I said.

238

Her jaw twitched. "No. I'm prepared. There's a difference."

She turned away from me, pacing now, fingers tugging at the sleeves of her blouse like she couldn't stand being still. "They can't prove anything," she muttered, more to herself than to me. "There's no weapon. No witnesses. We're fine. We have to be."

I stayed quiet, watching her spiral beneath that polished exterior. She was unraveling. Maybe not all at once...but thread by thread.

And yet... she still scared me. She always had.

"I need to understand what happened," I said softly.

Imogen froze.
And turned.
"Don't," she warned. "Don't do this now."

"Why not?" My voice rose before I could stop it. "Why *not* now? She's dead, Imogen. She's been dead for more than ten years."

"Exactly," she snapped. "She's gone. And if we don't keep our shit together, we'll go down with her."

There was a pause.

We stared at each other, both of us breathing hard.

And somewhere behind it all, behind the fear and guilt and desperation...I felt it again.

The hole.
The blackout.
The part of me that would never be sure.

That's when Leech padded into the kitchen.

He stopped at the edge of the tile, tail twitching, eyes locked on her. His ears flattened.

"Ugh," Imogen groaned. "Not that disgusting thing again."

She took a step back as Leech let out a shriek...pure, primal, guttural.

"Keep that thing *away* from me," she shrieked.

I stood there, watching him scream at her like he was trying to protect me.

Her lip curled in disgust, eyes wild. Her fingers twitched toward her neck like she wanted to pull her skin off.

And that's when I really saw it.

The cracks in Imogen's perfect image.

The way her face twisted when she was angry. The way her mascara had started to smudge, sinking into the creases under her eyes. The way her voice was starting to rise and fall without rhythm. She wasn't the teen queen I used to follow around like a shadow.

Back then I thought she was as pretty as a movie star...untouchable, flawless.

But now? She looked like a washed-up lunatic with a fading spray tan and too much eyeliner.

She always needed someone to control. Someone to blame.

And I always let her.

I glanced down at Leech, still stiff-legged beside me, his eyes never leaving her.

And then it hit me...this twist of truth I'd been ignoring for years.

She hated anything she couldn't control. And she definitely couldn't control Olivia.

It was all so clear now. She hated Olivia. Hated the way people looked at her. The way she didn't have to try so hard to be liked. She was beautiful in a way money couldn't fake. Graceful in a way you couldn't buy at a boutique. Olivia had something natural, something effortless, and Imogen couldn't stand that. Couldn't *stand* that someone from a trailer park could walk into a room and pull the spotlight without even trying.

She was jealous.
She *despised* her.

And yet somehow... I'd spent the last ten years believing it could be *me*.

Believing I was the one who went too far.

But now, standing here, watching Imogen unravel in front of me...

I had to ask myself something I never had the courage to say out loud:

If Imogen hated Olivia so much...
Then why did I ever believe I could be the one to kill her? What reason would I have? Though the thought rooted, something still itched at the back of my mind. Something I had forgotten, knocking quietly.

Imogen started pacing again, heels echoing against the tile like a metronome ticking down the end of the world.

"They'll twist everything," she muttered. "They always do. We were kids. We didn't know what we were doing. But none of it matters because if we don't stay ahead of it, it's all going to come back on *us.*"

She kept going, spiraling. Words tumbling out in half-sentences, frantic, breathless.

My ears were buzzing. My chest felt hollow.

"Nothing ties us to her death, Maddie. Unless someone *talks,*" she snapped, flinging the word like a weapon. "So, if you're thinking of getting sentimental or brave or whatever the hell this is, I suggest you rethink it."

I didn't respond.

I stood in front of her, frozen halfway between the sink and the table, arms limp at my sides.

Her voice had started to sound like static. That high, panicked pitch people get when they're trying to seem in control but aren't. It bounced off the tile and the cabinets and the inside of my skull.

But her eyes…

Her eyes didn't blink.

They were wide and glassy, too still for how fast her words were moving. Focused on something behind me. Or maybe inside herself. She looked insane.

It hit me then...not just fear, but something colder and I swallowed hard. There were things about that night I still didn't remember.
But suddenly, the part I did...the part I had buried the deepest...wasn't what scared me most.

It was Imogen. *And she was terrifying.*

I glanced at her as she stopped pacing, now checking her reflection in the microwave door, tilting her head slightly, smoothing her hair with the flat of her palm.

"I have to go," she said, like it had just occurred to her, like it was some revelation even to her own ears.

She was halfway out the door when she paused, one hand gripping the frame.

"We should've just thrown her down that old well," she muttered.

Her voice was dry. Casual. Like she was commenting on the weather. "No one would've found her there. That contractor, the one building the neighborhood, he is planning to fill it with concrete in a few days. We would've gotten away with this if we had common sense to hide the body better."

The door clicked shut behind her.

And just like that, I was alone again. Her words dangling in the air. *We should've thrown her down that old well.* Like Olivia was a piece of garbage we forgot to throw out.

I stood there for a minute, trying to breathe.

I went upstairs.
Each step heavier than the last.

I peeled off my clothes, slid into bed, and pulled the covers up to my chin. My head hurt. My heart wouldn't stop racing.

Outside, the birds had gone silent.

I texted Andy and told him I didn't feel like hanging out.

And I closed my eyes.

And all I could see was Imogen...her voice still ringing in my ears, her hands trembling, her smile twisted. There was something in her eyes I couldn't unsee now. Something cold. Unfeeling.

I used to think she'd do anything to protect me.

Now I wasn't sure what she'd do to protect *herself.*

Maybe I didn't want to remember what happened that night.
Maybe the part of me that forgot was trying to survive.
Maybe the truth was too much to bear.

———◆◆———

Sometime in the night, the phone rang, jarring me. I jolted up, hands fumbling for it in the dark. The screen was blank. No caller ID. Just a local number.

"Hello?" I whispered.

There was silence.

Then breathing.

Then… a voice.
Distorted. Mechanical.

"I know what you did."

The line went dead.

CHAPTER 24

Olivia

Five weeks until graduation

I sat on the edge of Imogen's bed, trying not to sink too far into the plush mattress. The sheets were some kind of Egyptian cotton. Imogen had bragged once that they were fifteen hundred thread count, and they felt softer than anything I'd ever slept on. Pillows fluffed to perfection were stacked behind me, satin and velvet, pale rose and bone white.

The canopy above me fluttered slightly from the ceiling fan, casting shadows over the room like lace. I looked around slowly, careful not to seem too interested, even though I was taking in every detail like it was a museum exhibit of someone else's life.

Posters were taped to the back of her closet door...Chad Michael Murray, Jesse McCartney, and some shirtless guy from *Laguna Beach*. Her cheerleading jacket hung from the bedpost, the sleeves stiff with old glitter hairspray. Gold and burgundy pompoms spilled from the corner of the room in a tangled heap, as if she'd tossed them there mid-meltdown and forgotten.

Her vanity looked like something from a movie...covered in glass bottles and expensive tubes. Chanel lipsticks lined up in a row beside YSL compacts, Dior foundation, and that Viktor & Rolf perfume in the crystal grenade bottle. It was a world of high gloss and designer names, and none of it felt real to me.

Maddie and Imogen stood by the mirror in their bras and panties, trying on dresses like it was a competition. Lace and satin floated in the air as they spun and judged and yanked things over their hips.

"This one makes my butt look weird," Imogen said, wrinkling her nose as she turned sideways in the mirror. "Ugh. I'm throwing it out."

"You're insane," Maddie laughed, adjusting the strap of her own dress. "That's the one from your birthday that you got at Saks."

Imogen rolled her eyes. "Exactly. I've already worn it once. What am I, a peasant?"

They both burst into laughter.

I didn't say anything. I just ran my fingers along the embroidery on the pillow beside me and tried to look interested in something far away. I didn't belong in this room. I knew it. They knew it. But they liked having me here sometimes...like a stray they fed when they felt generous.

Imogen flung the dress onto the floor.

"I'm buying something new for Spring Fling this weekend anyway. Maybe red this time. Something tighter. Something nobody forgets."

Maddie raised her eyebrows. "Going to seduce your way into a college acceptance letter?"

Imogen smirked. "If that's what it takes."

The laughter started again...louder this time. I smiled faintly, not because I thought it was funny, but because I didn't want to be the only one who didn't.

Imogen turned toward me suddenly, eyes sharp with mock curiosity.

"What are *you* going to wear to the dance, Liv?"

Before I could answer, she glanced at Maddie and smirked.

"Goodwill clearance rack, probably."

Heat rushed to my face. Maddie's gaze flicked from the pile of discarded dresses on the floor to the wide-open walk-in closet behind us...racks of clothes spilling over, designer labels pressed shoulder to shoulder in pristine plastic sleeves.

"Why don't you let her wear one of yours?" Maddie asked, a little too casually.

Imogen made a noise in her throat. "Eww. No. I would *never* let that freak wear one of my dresses."

Maddie raised an eyebrow. "You're giving them away anyway."

"I'd rather see them burned than on her."

"Oh my God, Imogen," Maddie said, covering her mouth, laughing.

I cut in before it could go any further, swallowing the knot in my throat. "I have a dress."

They both turned to look at me, clearly surprised I'd spoken at all.

"I got it a while ago," I added quickly. "It's a vintage Marchesa."

I didn't mention that I'd found it at the Goodwill on Rivers Avenue. That I'd nearly dropped it when I saw the tag, right there between a polyester bridesmaid gown and a ripped prom dress from 1998.
The style was dated, but it was real. And it was mine.

Marchesa.
Not a knockoff. Not a junior label. Real Marchesa.

I'd been sewing on it every night after my grandparents went to bed, hemming and reshaping it into something new. Something worthy.

Maddie's mouth fell open. "Where did you get a Marchesa?"

"I thrifted it."

They both burst out laughing.

"Of course you did," Imogen said, flipping her hair over one shoulder.

"That's so… Olivia."

I mumbled something about needing to grab something from my backpack that I left downstairs.

Neither of them looked up, as I slipped out of Imogen's bedroom and padded down the stairs, the laughter still echoing behind me, muffled through thick walls and privilege.

Outside, the air was sharp with the smell of jasmine and cut grass. I stepped onto the back porch and sat on the top step, curling my arms around my knees. The warm sun pressed through my jeans, grounding me.

And then I cried.

Quietly. The kind of crying that sneaks out slow...like your body can't hold it in anymore. My fingers clenched around the fabric of my sleeves, trying to keep it together. Trying to pretend I still had dignity.

They didn't care about me at all.

Not really.

I was their charity case. Their background friend. Good for jokes and borrowed notes and being the audience to their beautiful, sparkling lives.

I wiped at my cheeks quickly, trying to regain control.

I didn't want them to come looking for me and see me crying like this. Over them and their designer world. Not that they would.

Everything comes so easy for them. And for me? Everything is a struggle. Why can't something...just one thing...be easy?

The door creaked open behind me, as footsteps crossed the landing. I swiped at my cheeks, quick and quiet, and glance back.

It was Imogen's dad. He paused on the stoop, and said, "Got room for one more?"

I nodded. He eased down beside me, carefully like he didn't want to scare me off. There was a softness in his expression...not pity exactly, but close.

"Hi, Mr. Warner," I mumbled.

He smiled, faintly. "Why don't you call me Jason?"

I nodded.

"Rough day?" he asked.

I shrugged. "Kind of."

"Anything I can help with?"

I shook my head, not trusting my voice. I refused to cry in front of him.

The air was warm, almost too still. A faint breeze stirred the trees, but the porch stayed quiet.

Somewhere out in the yard, a bee buzzed past. The kind of midday silence that made everything feel louder.

He sat with that for a second and then leaned in just slightly.

"Why don't you talk to me? I'm a good listener, you know."

I gave a half-laugh. But it sounded in-authentic. "It's nothing serious. Just stupid, really."

He tipped his head. "Is it Imogen? Did she upset you? She can be kind of bossy, I know."

"No," I said quickly. "No, it's not that. It's just... the Spring Fling dance is coming up. Last one before we graduate."

I glanced down at my hands, nails bitten, fingers tugging at the hem of my shirt.

"My grandparents... they can't afford to buy me a dress. Not the kind Imogen and Maddie are going to wear."

There was a pause. And he said, gently, "You know... I could help with that."

I looked up, startled. "No... I couldn't. I couldn't ask you to."

"You're not asking," he said with a soft smile. "I'm offering. Imogen's never let me take her shopping before. I embarrass her, apparently."

He lowered his voice, "Wouldn't it be kind of nice? Just you and me. We'd keep it our little secret. You don't have to tell the girls where the dress came from."

I felt my throat tighten. There was something too easy in his tone, too confident. But also... the idea of walking into that dance and not standing out for the wrong reasons... it pressed hard against all my pride.

"I... I don't know," I said.

He leaned back just a bit, like he didn't want to scare me off. "Just think about it. That's all I'm saying."

The offer hung between us.

I wondered what it would even feel like...to walk into a store and not glance at the price tags first? To try on something because it's beautiful, not because it's on clearance. To stand in front of a mirror and twirl and feel pretty...without worrying if I could afford to keep the dress on my body a moment longer. The wish hit like a wave. Not because I believed it would happen, but because I wanted it to. So badly it hurt.

I'd tagged along with Maddie and Imogen plenty of times. Watched them sweep through racks of dresses with their moms trailing behind, arms full of shopping bags. They'd hold things up to each other, laugh, twirl in the mirror with iced coffees in hand. I stayed a few steps behind, clutching my sleeves, pretending not to care. One time...just once...Maddie's mom offered to buy me a pair of jean shorts. "They'd look adorable on you," she said, already walking to the register. And I let her. I said thank you. I even smiled. But Maddie... she didn't speak to me for the rest of the day.

He shifted beside me, just slightly, and before I could react, his hand came up. Fingertips brushed against my temple and tucked a strand of hair behind my ear.

I stilled.

"You don't need a fancy dress to look beautiful, Olivia," he said softly. "But a little silk and satin never hurt."

I felt my breath catch.

"Just say yes," he said, his eyes never leaving mine.

For a moment, I forgot he was Mr. Warner. Imogen's dad. The man who always stood a little too close in the kitchen or laughed too hard at his own jokes. For a moment, none of that mattered. I was just a girl being treated like a lady. Even though I knew he was much older than me, there was something about him...something polished and attentive, the kind of man who made you feel like the only person in the room when he looked at you. There was something attractive about him. About Mr. Warner. About Jason. And in that moment, I wanted to say yes. So why shouldn't I?

———————⋅◆⋅◆⋅⋅———————

He drove us to Raleigh.

Said it would be better that way...quieter, more private.

"So, you can feel comfortable," he told me, one hand on the wheel. "No risk of bumping into someone you know."

I nodded, grateful. Or maybe just relieved. Maybe both.

He didn't just buy me a dress. He bought me a pair of silver earrings that shimmered when I moved, heels that matched the color of the dress exactly, and a soft clutch...pale champagne, with delicate embroidery that caught the light. It felt like a dream. Like I'd stepped into someone else's life.

We didn't talk much on the drive back. By the time we pulled into my driveway, the sky had turned heavy. Rain beat softly against the windshield in slow, metronome taps. The soft hum of the engine was the only sound between us. I moved to open the door.

"Wait," he said, his voice low. "Don't go yet."

I paused. My fingers tightened around the handles of the shopping bags.

He hesitated. Like he was gathering something inside himself, something too big for the silence.

"I've always had a thing for you, Olivia." His voice was a little rough, like he'd been holding it in too long.

I blinked, caught off guard. The bags shifted in my arms. Too much. Too fast.

"It upsets me," he continued, "seeing the way those girls treat you. Like you're less than them. You're not. You deserve better. You deserve to be seen for who you are."

He looked at me, and I felt it...that intensity, that heat behind his words. It made my stomach flip, uncertain and unsteady.

"But I see you," he said.

I clutched the bags tighter. There could be benefits to being seen this way… right? That's what I told myself. That's what I needed to believe.

"I mean it," he pressed, leaning just slightly toward me. His gaze didn't waver.

"I'd do anything for you. Anything." He reached out, his fingers brushing against mine. Warmth spilled from his touch into my skin like it meant something. Like it had always been there, waiting. He leaned in closer...closer than anyone had in a long time...and whispered near my ear. "It's the truth."

My mouth gaped slightly, startled by the closeness. Part of me wanted to laugh it off, to change the subject. But something in his eyes stopped me. Something raw. Hungry. I never thought of him that way. But I'd always found him handsome. All the girls joked about how Imogen's dad was hot. Those soft, messy waves that always fell just right. Those sea-green eyes that looked like they held stories no one had dared to listen to. And now they were looking only at me.

The next week he passed me a white gift bag. No tag. No card. Just tissue paper and a note written in neat, slanted script.

For emergencies, just in case.
-J

I pulled the phone out slowly. A brand-new iPhone, already in a limited-edition floral *Wildflowers d*esigner case. A case that every girl at school had been fiending for and it was mine.
I stared at it, not quite believing it was real.

My grandparents couldn't afford extras like this. I hadn't had a phone of my own since freshman year, when my old flip phone stopped working and we couldn't pay to replace it. I'd gotten used to borrowing Maddie's or messaging through school computers.

But this… this was mine.

I turned it over in my hands, feeling equal parts thrilled and sick.

He said it was for safety. Said he wanted to make sure I could call him if I ever needed a ride, if something ever happened.

Said it didn't mean anything.

But phones mean something.

Phones are *connection.* And ownership. And access.

I didn't tell Maddie or Imogen. I didn't tell *anyone.*

I just slid it into my backpack and kept playing the part. Innocent and sweet. And Jason loved it.

———————•◆◦•———————

The next couple of weeks were filled with quiet rendezvous. Secret shopping trips. Dinners out. Always in Raleigh. Always far from the eyes that might recognize us. Up until now, he'd been a perfect gentleman...hadn't even tried to kiss me. It almost felt innocent. Like he wasn't after anything except a little company. Someone to talk to. Someone who looked at him like he mattered.

He told me how Imogen and his wife, Deborah, took him for granted. That at home, he was just a token piece...someone to open jars or fill the gas tank, not a man with feelings. Not a man who wanted to be heard. And I listened. I nodded. I cared about Jason. I did. But not like that. Still, as time went on, it became clear...he was attracted to me. There was something in the way he looked at me. I knew he wanted more. But he didn't dare cross that line. Not yet. But it was pressing.

After one of our shopping trips...new perfume, a satin skirt, another purse I didn't need...he didn't drive toward home. Instead, he pulled into the circular drive of the Hyatt Hotel in Raleigh.

"What are we doing here?" I asked, my voice barely more than breath. Something in my chest tightened and squeezed.

He didn't answer right away. Just put the car in park, turned down the music. He looked at me with that same soft smile, the one I used to think was kind.

"Do you want to go up?" he asked.

"Up where?"

He motioned to the hotel.

"To the room. I booked one for us. Somewhere we could be… a little cozier than we usually are." His hand slid across the console, and he took mine...lightly, deliberately. His thumb rubbed the back of my hand in slow, circular strokes.

I knew exactly what he meant. He wanted something, alright. Not company. Not conversation. Something else. Something more. I felt a wave of heat rush up my neck...embarrassment, fear, confusion. And something else, too. Revulsion. The urge to pull my hand away was so strong I could feel it in my spine. But I didn't move.

After everything he's done for me, I told myself, I couldn't just pull away.

The dresses. The shoes. The dinners. The way he made me feel special. How could I say no? But the truth sat cold and unmoving in my chest. No part of me wanted to say yes.

My stomach turned. My fingers twitched to pull away from his hand still on mine. But I stayed still. Silent.

Finally, I said, "I'm actually… feeling really tired. I want to go home."

He didn't let go. His smile stayed, but it tightened. Shifted. Just enough to notice.

"Are you sure?" he asked gently. "Don't you like what we have going on? The fun, the freedom? The way I take care of you?"

He rubbed his thumb more slowly across my skin.

"I just… I don't want to go up tonight," I said.

My voice sounded small, even to me. He leaned in a little, still smiling.

"It's worth it, Olivia. All of this… it's worth it. You deserve nice things. You deserve to feel wanted. Seen."

I said nothing.

"I promise," he added, voice low now. "I won't hurt you. I'd never do anything you wouldn't like."

Something cold unfurled in my chest. A strange ache...part shame, part fear. And still, I didn't move. His thumb kept tracing the back of my hand...slow and expectant.

I felt it in my throat. That rising tide of panic. And...suddenly, without thinking...I yanked my hand away.

"You know I appreciate everything you've done," I said quickly.

My voice wavered, but I held his gaze. "It means everything to me. You've treated me better than anyone ever has."

He didn't speak.

"But tonight…" I exhaled. "Tonight, I'm just really tired. Could you please take me home?"

A beat passed. And he smiled again, but it didn't quite reach his eyes.

"Of course," he said. "Whatever you want."

But I felt it...the shift. The way his knuckles tightened slightly on the wheel. He was pretending to be okay with it. But I could tell he was mad. The drive home was silent. No music this time. Just rain and headlights and a growing knot in my stomach.

He didn't take the usual turn into the entrance. Instead, he slowed near the front of the trailer park, headlights dimming as he pulled onto the shoulder of the road, just shy of the entrance sign.

I didn't move for a second, as the rain pattered against the windshield. I swallowed.

"Why are you stopping here?"

Jason kept his eyes on the road. "I can't risk being seen dropping you off."

My stomach tightened. "You've dropped me off *so* many times before."

He didn't answer. Just made a face. His jaw clenched. A flicker of something ugly passed across his features...and I knew.

He was really mad.
About the hotel. About me saying no.
Silence filled the car like a noxious gas, and I couldn't breathe.

"Next time," he said quietly, dangerously, "we *are* going up to the room. Got it?"

I turned to him, heat flaring in my cheeks. "I don't think we should see each other anymore, Mr. Warner."

His head snapped toward me.

"Oh, I'm *Mr. Warner* now?" His voice was sharp, like broken glass.

"Now that I've spent money on you. Now that I've *invested* in you?"

I recoiled slightly. "It wasn't like that."

"Wasn't it?" he cut in. "You really think you can play innocent after everything I've done for you?"

"I didn't ask for any of it," I whispered.

His hand shot out, grabbing my wrist.
Tight. Controlling. Just enough to make me freeze.

"Let go of me," I said, breath hitching. "I'll tell!"

His eyes darkened.
"You're not going to say a word."

"I mean it," I snapped, voice cracking.

He leaned in just enough to make the air between us choke.
"You think anyone's going to believe *you* over *me?*"

I yanked my arm away, trembling now. "Let go of me."

He did...but not gently. My wrist stung where his fingers had been.

I shoved the car door open and climbed out, heart slamming, hands shaking. I didn't care that it was muddy, that the streetlight above barely worked, that the air was thick with rain, humidity, and shame. I just wanted out.

"You forgot something," he called, his voice like poison.

And he threw the bags out after me.

The skirt. The purse. The shoes. Everything spilled onto the wet shoulder of the road. White shopping bags hit the ground, burst open, and tumbled into the dirt like trash. Rain poured down soaking everything.

Drops ran down my face, warm and relentless, mixing with the tears I hadn't meant to cry. My new cream-colored skirt landed face-down in the mud.

He peeled off a second later, tires screeching, his taillights reflecting on the wet street, as he disappeared into the dark.

I stood there shaking.

The road was empty now. Just me, the crushed purse box, my rainwater-soaked outfit, and the realization that whatever *this* had been... it was over.

CHAPTER 25

Madison

I woke up with my heart pounding. For a second, I couldn't remember why.

Then the phone call came rushing back.

The breathing.
The voice saying, *"I know what you did."*

It echoed in my head like it had been whispered directly into my skull.

I sat up slowly, pushing the covers off, my skin damp with sweat. The phone was still on the nightstand, screen dark. I'd checked it three times in the middle of the night, half-expecting a follow-up text or a voicemail.

Nothing had come through.

This morning, there was a text, but it was from Andy saying he'd be here at 6:30 p.m. to pick me up. Nothing from the unknown caller.

I opened my contacts and scrolled down until I found Adrienne, my friend from the magazine. She picked up on the second ring.

"Mads?" Her voice was bright, still morning raspy. "You, okay?"

"Not really. I need a favor."

She was quiet for a beat. "What kind of favor?"

"Can you run a number for me? Figure out who it belongs to?"

A pause came first and then, "You know I can't do that."

"Adrienne," I said, trying to keep my voice even, "You're the same person who figured out J. Lo's vacation boyfriend *before* *TMZ* even posted the first grainy yacht pic."

She sighed. "That's a different kind of technology. But listen, I might not be able to. But the new girl we just hired. Sydney Perry. Her boyfriend works for the police department. She's been dying to prove herself. Get in Sally's good graces."

I sat up straighter.
"You think she'd help?"

"I am sure she would *love* to help. And if we frame it like we're vetting a source or something... maybe we can get her to ask the boyfriend without it being a whole thing."

"Adrienne," I exhaled. "You're a lifesaver."

"No. I'm a gossip. But I'm *your* gossip."

———— ◆ ————

I leaned over the hall bathroom sink, the faucet dripping slow and steady. The wallpaper was still the same from when I was a child...tiny, faded flowers climbing toward the ceiling, their once-burgundy petals now dulled to something closer to rust. A chipped ceramic dish sat by the sink, still holding my mother's favorite lipstick. Dust clinging to the cap.

The air smelled faintly of powder and something older. Like the past had been sealed in here, waiting. For a moment, I saw us again. Me,

Imogen, and Olivia, fifteen years old, elbow to elbow in front of this very mirror. All of us talking over each other, laughing too loud, swiping mascara and smudging liner like it was life or death. Getting ready for the Kings of Leon concert in Raleigh, all three of us trying to look older, cooler, like we had something figured out.

Imogen had worn her hair up in that sleek ponytail she thought made her look "mature." Olivia had drawn a tiny heart on her wrist in eyeliner, whispering that she hoped the lead singer would notice.

Now, the only sound in the bathroom was the drip. And the flicker of the light above me, twitching in and out, as I stared into the mirror.

I barely recognized the reflection. There was something different in my face now, something softer, plainer. The LA glow had long faded, and what remained was just... me.

I looked a little sallow, eyes dulled like someone who was ready to give up. And for just a second. For just a blink. I could see my mother's reflection staring back. Same warm hazel eyes. Same perfect cupid's bow, soft and pink, shaped just like hers.

I blinked again, and her reflection was gone.
All that was left was just me now. Tired, stretched thin, and wearing every bit of it on my face.
Sally wouldn't approve.

I could see her now, snapping her fingers in my face, saying, "Get with it, girl. Slap some mascara and lipstick on that face and remember who the hell you are."

The problem was, I wasn't so sure anymore.
The girl that Sally thought she knew so well, felt long gone.
And all that was left was this. *Whoever she is.*

The light above me blinked again. Once. Twice.
Like a message I couldn't quite catch.

"I'm leaving," I said quietly.

There was a long pause. Then the bulb steadied, warm and low.
I reached up and ran my fingers along the edge of the mirror. "You remember, don't you?"

There was one final flicker.
Then stillness.

———————◆◆◆———————

At 6:31 the doorbell rang echoing through the house.

And there he was.

Andy stood on the porch, his truck idling behind him. A light blue button-up rolled at the sleeves, jeans that fit too well, boots scuffed just enough to still count as clean. His brown eyes landed on me, sharp and steady, cutting straight through the nerves I'd tried to quiet.

God, he was handsome.
Too handsome.
And all I could think about was how his hands felt on me.

I swallowed, hard, as my gaze caught on a thin scar tracing his chin, one I'd never seen before. It jarred me more than it should have. There were parts of him now I didn't know. Moments and injuries I hadn't been there for. Whole years of stories I'd never heard.

A dull ache opened in my chest.
I used to know everything. Every secret. Every dream.
Now… we were practically strangers.
Twelve years without him.

A chill traced down my spine. I wasn't sure how I'd survived the last decade without him,
and I had no idea how I'd survive the days after this one.

He smiled a little. "You ready, *Tiger?*"

That word.
Tiger.

He used to call me that when we were kids…after the time I jumped off the playground swings and tackled a boy who pushed Imogen. I had scrapes all over my knees and a scab on my chin for a week. He said I pounced like a tiger and wouldn't let go.

I stood in the doorway, watching him.

Longer than I should've. The air between us felt stretched thin, like it might snap if I moved the wrong way. Something tugged deep in my chest, tight and sharp. Panic. The kind that rises without warning.

The kind that said run.

Run fast.
Run far.
Leave this place, this man, this memory.

They found Olivia's clothes. It wouldn't be long now before they found the rest.

Before they found her.

Andy stood waiting in the glow of the afternoon sun, one hand shoved in his pocket, the other scratching the back of his neck.

I opened my mouth, but no sound came.

I wanted to tell him to leave. To get in his truck and disappear.

That I couldn't do this. Not now. Not ever.

My chest ached. But it wasn't just anxiety. It was the guilt. Thick and creeping.
A shadow that had followed me everywhere I went.

And once Andy knew what I'd done. He would never look at me with that warm, penetrating gaze again. He'd only see a criminal. The kind he lived his whole life to put behind bars.

Andy hadn't done anything wrong.
He was kind. He was real. He was exactly who he'd always been.
But I couldn't look at him without remembering that the bill was coming due for what Imogen and I had done.

I really wanted to run.
But somehow, I didn't.
I swallowed the panic.
Pressed it down where it couldn't reach my throat.

"Yeah," I said, stepping out onto the porch. "I'm ready. Let's go."

BETWEEN FRIENDS

I climbed into his truck without a word. The cab door gave a groan, and I settled into the seat and for a second, I felt like I was suffocating. I almost got out and ran back to the house.

But he put the truck in gear, and the spell of fear broke. I could breathe again.

Andy's hand gripped the wheel, a soft smile on his face. The windows were down, wind rushing in and tugging at his hair, wild and weightless.

He didn't look at me. Just kept driving, eyes locked on the road.

But I felt it. The way everything between us snapped back into place.

Effortless and familiar.

And still, despite everything, when I looked at him now, really looked, all I could feel was everything I'd carried for him. All those feelings I thought I'd outgrown.
Years of it.

Pressed down deep, showing up in every silence, every time I thought I'd finally let him go.

And no matter how scared I was of the consequences that were coming due, being here with Andy, right now, was all that mattered.

For the moment I let myself just be Madison. Not the Maddie of the past, the girl whose truth was buried in secrets, but the Maddie of the moment, free…and in love with the boy next door.

The past was calling, louder by the hour.
But tonight…
Tonight, there was just me and him.

Andy reached for the dial and turned the radio down, the noise fading into quiet.

He glanced over at me, eyes catching mine, twinkling with something soft, something almost boyish.

"Figured we could grab food. There's still that place off Highway 9 with the giant barbeque sandwiches. You remember it?" he asked, a wide grin spreading.

I nodded without speaking. Andy reached across and took my hands in his, the heat of his palms spreading from my fingers all the way to my chest. A warmth that didn't stop at skin, something deeper. Steadier.

We pulled off the main road and into a gravel lot packed with sun-faded trucks and dented sedans. The BBQ place wasn't much to look at...just a rusted-out trailer with a crooked awning and two cut-out windows, one for ordering, one for pickup. A faded plywood sign nailed to the roof read *Briggs Bar-B-Q* in peeling red paint. No frills. No menu boards. Just the kind of place where you ordered what they had and hoped they hadn't run out of ribs.

Smoke poured steady from the tin vent above the trailer, curling into the air like it had somewhere to be. The smell of meat and hickory and grease hung thick, sweet and sharp, coating everything in reach.

I rolled down the window and let the scent hit me. It brought back this one afternoon...me and Mom, pulling in for sandwiches one lazy Sunday. She'd worn a yellow dress and let her hair down for once. No man in the car. No one to impress. She'd laughed at something I said and bought us both Cheerwine in glass bottles.

That was rare.

A day that felt like it belonged just to us.

Didn't last long, of course. But long enough that I remembered it.

Andy pulled into a spot near the edge of the lot, tires crunching loud against gravel. He shifted into park and cut the engine. The hum of the vent fan, voices ordering, the shuffle of feet across rock...it all felt exactly the same. Nothing had changed.

I waited in the truck and Andy came back with two warm paper bundles and a grease-stained brown bag of hushpuppies. The smell filled the cab in seconds...smoke, salt, and sweet vinegar. My stomach growled, but the hunger was hollow.

He handed me the food as he climbed inside.

"Figured we'd take it somewhere quieter," he said. "Like Town Lake Park."

I gave a small nod and looked out the window.

Town Lake Park.
We'd been there together. A long time ago.

With a whole group of friends. We skipped afternoon classes.
Most of them were behind the bathroom building, smoking and pretending to be cool.
Andy and I wandered off, peeling away from the noise, not saying much.
He pushed me on the swings, slow and steady, like we had all the time in the world.

I remembered the way the light slanted through the trees. The way my stomach fluttered every time he pushed the swing. I soared through the air, suspended for just a moment, then rushed back down, into his arms, and he'd push me again.

It was like we were the only two people in the whole world.

And then Imogen appeared, out of nowhere, screaming like she'd been stung.
She said a bee flew down her shirt, started tearing at her clothes in front of everyone. But I knew there was no bee. She'd seen us. Andy and me. She had to create a scene to get Andy's attention back on her. Because that was Imogen.

And of course, Andy ran to her, leaving me behind on the swing.
It kept moving without him, slow, uneven, until it finally came to a stop.
I kept my hands on the chains, kept my feet from touching the ground.
Just waiting.

He looked back once, just before he disappeared into the crowd.
And mouthed *I'm sorry.*

And I believed him.
Because he was Andy.

A few minutes later, we pulled into the park. It was quiet. Still warm, but the kind of warmth that came with a breeze...soft and slow, brushing past my cheek like a soft embrace.

We passed the main path entrance, and Andy slowed the truck.

"Is that...?" he started, narrowing his eyes.

I saw him too.

Logan.

He was standing near the old picnic shelter, half-shadowed under one of the oak trees. Not moving. Not talking to anyone. Just... watching the lake. One hand in his pocket. The other holding a cigarette, its orange ember glowing in the low light of early evening.

I shifted in my seat, trying not to stare. But something about the way he stood there made my stomach twist.

"What's he doing?" I asked, more to myself than to Andy.

"Who knows," Andy muttered, his eyes fixed on Logan's back. "He gives me the creeps. Always has."

A hush fell between us. Somewhere in the distance, a hawk high in the sky, called out, long and low like a warning.

"Stay away from him," Andy said, his voice low.

"Why?" I asked, as my eyes flicked to Logan, shadows folding over him until his face was nearly lost.

Andy lowered his voice and leaned in, like whatever he was about to say wasn't meant to carry far.

"He was weird in school, but now? There's something off. Honestly…" he said, pausing.

His eyes flicked toward the shadows beyond the parked cars. The kind of look that said he knew something he couldn't quite name.

"Between you and me? I am wondering if he had something to do with Olivia."

"You're serious?" I asked, feeling like the cab of the truck was shrinking.

"No evidence. Just a feeling. The way he looked at her. He was obsessed."

I didn't respond. Just kept my eyes on the trees.

Didn't trust them to not to betray me.
Didn't trust him not to see it.

Andy pulled forward and turned the truck away from the main loop, circling us around to the back of the park. Farther from the benches. Farther from Logan.

Back here, the trees pressed closer to the edge of the asphalt. Spanish moss hung lower, heavier, brushing the top of the windshield as we parked. The lake curved just beyond the hill, water catching what little bit of light that was left.

Andy put the truck in park and rolled down the windows. Crickets were singing from somewhere deep in the pines...loud, rhythmic, endless. A red-winged blackbird flitted from one branch to another, chirping sharp between the chorus like it had something important to say. Above us, the oaks bowed inward, their limbs heavy and gnarled, casting a lattice of dark patterns across the dashboard.

Andy handed me one of the sandwiches, the paper still warm in my lap. I unwrapped it and took a bite, just enough to taste the smoke and sauce. I set it down on the dash, not able to eat.

He watched me for a second, and asked quietly, "You, feeling, okay?"

I nodded once, slow.

"Just… got a lot on my mind."

"That's understandable. With finding out that something happened to Olivia."

His voice caught for a breath before he kept going.

"It's bringing up a lot of emotions for me too. I didn't sleep at all last night. I just kept thinking about how innocent she was. How sweet. She didn't deserve…"

The words hit me sideways.
Sweet.
Innocent.

My fingers curled tighter around the fountain drink in my hand. I didn't say anything. Just kept my eyes on the lake like it might offer a way out.

Andy looked over at me, and back down at the hushpuppies he hadn't touched.

"I shouldn't have brought it up. I'm sorry."

"It's fine," I said. Too quickly.
But it wasn't fine. Was it?

She didn't deserve it. That's what he said. And he was right. I just didn't know if he meant the death or the way we erased her long before she disappeared. The truth sat thick in my throat.
Not the whole truth. Not even half of it. Just pieces of a memory I still couldn't grasp.

Blood. Laughter that turned too sharp. Imogen's voice saying we'd figure it out.
My own silence.

I stared at the lake, watching the water barely move.
It looked like ink. Dark and still, shadows swallowing it in slow, soft ripples. A swan floated near the edge, its feathers glowing pale against the dark surface. For a second, I watched it just to have something to focus on. Something that didn't look back. That didn't care what I'd done.

Andy sat beside me, chewing slowly on his sandwich, completely unaware.

Somewhere further in the park, a dog barked once. Short. Alarmed. Then nothing.

The sun set quickly, turning the soft glow of the evening into darkness.

With the loss of sunlight, the air suddenly shifted, and cold breeze cut through the cab of the truck, and I shivered.

Without a word, Andy reached behind his seat, the leather creaking under the shift of his weight. He pulled his police jacket from the back. The one with his name stitched above the chest. And draped it over my shoulders.

"Here," he said, voice soft. "You're freezing."

I didn't say thank you. Didn't have to. He knew by the way I smiled.

The fabric smelled like Andy. Warm and comforting. I pulled it tighter around me, fingers brushing the embroidered letters of his name. His presence still lingering in the seams.

I reached for my sandwich again but stopped when I saw headlights. A car, pulling into the far end of the lot. Slow. Too slow. And parked directly across from us.

Andy turned toward the windshield, his whole body going still.
The lights cut off.
And no one got out.

Andy leaned forward, squinting toward the dark silhouette. "That's weird."

My breath caught in my throat. "Do you think it's Logan?"

He didn't answer.
Seconds passed. The car didn't move.

"Maybe it's just some teenagers coming to make out," Andy said, though his voice was tight.

I snorted. "Does anyone even do that anymore?"

He didn't laugh. Didn't take his eyes off the car.

"I think we should go."

There was something in his voice I hadn't heard before. Not fear exactly. Something deeper. Worn. The kind of instinct you don't question.

I straightened, heart ticking up as I watched the motionless car.

He started the engine, and I kept my eyes on the dark shape of the car as we pulled away.

Still no movement. Just sitting there, engine off, lights dead.

But I swore...I swore I saw someone watching us.

Just past the glass.
Still.
Waiting.

And for a split second,
I thought...*what if it's Imogen?*

She still doesn't know I've been seeing Andy.

The thought came so fast I couldn't stop it. Couldn't even trace where it came from.
She had no reason to be there. No way to know.

But still.

That's where my mind went.

Straight to her.

And maybe that was the scariest part of all.

CHAPTER 26

Olivia

One and a half weeks until graduation

I sat behind the science wing, knees pulled up to my chest, back pressed against the bricks that still held the morning's chill. The bell had already rung for lunch, but I couldn't make myself go in. I'd barely eaten all day. My stomach twisted too tight to hold anything but air and dread.

Every time I closed my eyes, I saw his face. Jason. His hand gripping my wrist too hard. The way he smiled like I was some secret to be kept.

I hated him now.
And worse, I hated myself for not stopping it sooner.

For ever letting it happen in the first place.

I'd been avoiding Imogen's house all week. Pretending I had a dentist appointment, a group project, a migraine. Anything to not sit in that perfect kitchen with her perfect mother and pretend I hadn't crossed a line that couldn't be uncrossed.

The weight of it pressed into me. Made my skin feel too tight, too filthy.

I hadn't told anyone. Not even Maddie.
Because saying it out loud made it real.

And if Imogen ever found out…

I dropped my forehead to my knees, willing the breeze to blow harder, cold enough to freeze everything inside me solid. At least then, maybe I wouldn't feel so sick. Tears slipped down my cheeks, and I wiped them away. I didn't want to cry. I didn't want to feel anything.

Sudden footsteps sounded on the walkway behind me. And I stiffened. Then the scent hit me...burnt tobacco and cheap cologne. I looked up just enough to see the lit end of a cigarette glowing near the edge.

"Geez," a voice muttered. "You scared the shit out of me. I didn't think anyone was out here."

It was Logan.

He stopped short when he saw my face.

"Shouldn't you be in the cafeteria with your royal court?" he asked, flicking ash off the end of his smoke.

I didn't answer.

He squinted. "Wait... you crying?"

I wiped at my cheeks quickly, but it was useless.

He exhaled and looked away like he suddenly felt too visible, too close to something raw.

"Didn't mean to intrude," he said after a second. "I just come out here to smoke sometimes. Not, like... following you or anything."

I didn't respond, just stared down at the concrete.

He shifted his weight and stubbed the cigarette out against the wall.

"Look," he said, voice quieter now. "You, okay?"

278

I shrugged, still not meeting his eyes.

"I didn't mean to be a jerk," he added. "Back in the parking lot the other day. I was just messing around."

I nodded slowly.

But even now, even with that voice in my head reminding me not to trust him, I could see it...
The way his shoulders were slouched, how his voice dropped low. The quiet nervousness as he spoke. He wasn't as sure of himself as he wanted everyone to think.
That whole cool guy routine...
It was a costume. One he wore because he didn't know how to be anything else.

He hesitated and sat a few feet away from me on the same low stone ledge, picking at the hole in the knee of his jeans.

We sat in silence. His leg bounced restlessly. He pulled out another cigarette, held it between two fingers, but didn't light it.

"I don't like seeing girls cry," he said eventually. "Makes me feel like I did something wrong."

I didn't know what to say to that. It felt honest. Messy, but honest.

"I'm fine," I whispered.

He glanced at me sideways. "Yeah. Well... if you ever need a smoke or something, I'm around."

I almost laughed at that but didn't.
He stood and dusted off his hands.

Then a serious look came over his face.

"Hey. If anyone's messing with you...like, for real...I don't mind helping out. You know? Just say the word."

He walked off before I could answer.

I stayed there for a moment longer, heart still raw.

Logan was strange. Unsettling in a way I couldn't quite name. But he stopped. He'd seen my face, streaked and hollow, and he hadn't laughed. Hadn't made a joke. He just tried to comfort me in the only way he knew how. That counted for something.

Logan certainly wasn't as bad as I thought.
Not perfect. But solid.
Maybe even… protective.

And right now, that was more than I had from anyone else.

If I could have Andy, I would.

But Andy doesn't see me. Not like that. He doesn't look at me the way he looks at Imogen.

But Logan does.

And maybe that's enough. Or at least… enough for now.

The hallway buzzed with noise...lockers slamming, sneakers squeaking across tile, someone's laughter echoing too loud. I was at my locker, pretending to dig for a pencil I didn't need, when Shane Stone walked up beside me.

Shane freaking Stone.

Varsity jacket. Blonde curls. Stupid-perfect smile. Every girl's bad boy crush.

He leaned against the locker next to mine like we were in a scene from a movie.

"You coming to my party next Friday night?" he asked, smirking.

I blinked. "What?"

"My house," he said, tilting his chin up. "Music. Beer. Starts at sunset."

I could barely find my voice. "Oh. Um. Maybe."

Shane grinned like that was enough. "Cool. You should come."

He walked off, and I just… stood there. Heart pounding. Brain short-circuiting.

Was that real? Did that just happen?

I spotted Maddie across the hall and practically sprinted toward her.

"You are *not* going to believe what just happened."

She raised her brows. "What?"

"Shane Stone just invited me to his party."

She laughed. "We've been invited. Didn't Imogen tell you?"

The words hit like ice water. Of course she didn't. *Of course,* Imogen didn't tell me.

"She is *such* a bitch," I muttered.

Maddie's eyes widened like I'd just slapped someone.

"What did you just say?"

Before I could answer, a ringtone started blaring from my bag, sharp and chirpy. I jumped, scrambling for it and realized Maddie was watching. So, I just let it ring and ring.

Maddie tilted her head. "Are you going to answer that?"

She reached into my open bag before I could stop her and pulled it out...my *Wildflowers* case, shining like new.

Her jaw dropped. "When did you get a *phone?*"

"I...uh...it was a gift."

She turned it over in her hand. "Wait a minute. Is this the newest Wildflowers case?! Oh my God, even Imogen doesn't have this one yet. She is going to be so jealous."

I grabbed it back from her, fingers fumbling.

"Who gave it to you?" she asked, more curious than accusing.

I didn't answer.

The screen rang again. Bold and glowing.
J calling.

My thumb hovered over the decline button.

Maddie squinted. "Who's *J?*"

My pulse jumped. "Just... some guy I met."

Her brows lifted, but before she could press, a voice cut through the hallway behind us.

"Maddie!"

We both turned to see Imogen strutting down the hall in her low-rise jeans and that smug little half-smile. Hair curled, lip gloss shiny, attention magnetized to her like it always was.

Maddie immediately forgot about the phone.

"Oh my God, I have to tell her what happened in AP Chem," she said, already waving.

I slipped the phone into my pocket before either of them could look again. The screen dimmed to black.

"Olivia," Imogen said coolly as she reached us, barely acknowledging me.

"Maddie," she went on, "did you hear what Haley said about your cheer skirt? I'm dying."

They linked arms, walking down the hallway like they'd rehearsed it.

I followed a few steps behind, heart still hammering.

Just some guy I met.
Even I didn't believe it.

Imogen glanced over her shoulder, eyes sweeping past me like I was roadkill on the shoulder of her perfect life. She slowed and turned around. And looked at me full-on...eyes narrowed, nose slightly wrinkled. Like she was trying to figure out what she was smelling.

"Why haven't you been coming over like you used to?" she asked, voice coated in faux concern.

I froze.

My heart twisted in my chest. She was watching my face too closely. Looking for something. Some crack in my expression. I tried to swallow it all down. Tried to stay still.

Don't let her see. Don't let her know. Just say something...anything.

But before I could answer, Maddie cut in, nudging my side with her elbow.

"Ooh, she's got some *new guy* she's been spending time with. Right, Olivia?"

I turned to her, startled. She was grinning, eyes teasing like this was some kind of game.

Maddie held up her hand in a fake whisper gesture. "His name's *J.*"

My stomach dropped.
Imogen's head tilted.

"*Who?*" she asked, sharp now.

I opened my mouth, but no words came out. Just a rush of heat behind my eyes, my throat locking up, pulse racing in my ears.

Just some guy I met is what I wanted to say. That's what I said before to Maddie. But now... now it didn't feel like enough.

"Who *is* J, Liv?" she asked, voice syrupy and sharp at the same time. "Come on. Spill it."

BETWEEN FRIENDS

The fake laugh in her tone cut like razors.

I could feel Maddie's eyes flick between us, waiting to be let in on the joke.

My throat tightened.

Imogen never asked things twice. She wasn't going to let it go.

Her gaze pinned me like a thumbtack...cold and glittering. Like she could peel the truth straight off my skin if I didn't hand it over myself.

I opened my mouth.

Nothing came out.

My eyes burned.

Don't cry.
Not here.
Not in front of *her*.

"What's the big deal?" Imogen pressed. "Is he some freak from the gas station? Or is it that substitute teacher who smiled at you once?"

Her voice got louder.

"Tell us, Liv," she snapped. "Or is it one of your creepy little secrets like *everything else?*"

I flinched. Her voice was slicing through the hallway now, drawing attention. Heads were turning. People were slowing down to listen. And I was frozen.

Suddenly the fire alarms shrieked to life above our heads. Lights flashed red. Screams rang out. The hallway exploded in motion. Kids shouted, teachers swore, doors slammed open as the building sprang into chaos.

I turned with the crowd, startled, and just before I moved with them, I caught a glimpse...down the hall, just past the lockers...

Logan.

Leaning against the wall beside the fire alarm panel. One hand still resting casually on the red lever. He looked straight at me. Smirked. And winked.

He turned and disappeared into the surge of bodies and crimson-colored strobes.

I stood frozen for a second longer, blinking in disbelief.

He did that... *for me.*

Maddie grabbed my sleeve. "Let's go!"

I nodded, forcing myself into motion, even though my heart was still cracked wide open.

The courtyard was chaos...students scattered in little knots, some laughing, some annoyed, a few pretending it was a real emergency just to skip fifth period.

I stood near the edge of the crowd, still half in the fog of the hallway, when I saw him.

Jason.

He was leaning against the stone column by the admin building, arms folded across his chest, one foot hooked behind the other like he'd been there a while. He wasn't scanning the crowd. He wasn't looking for Imogen.

He was staring directly at *me.*

Just standing there.
Watching.

Before I could react, I heard her voice.

"Dad?" Imogen said, surprised. "What are you doing here?"

Jason didn't flinch. Just straightened and slid a mask over his face like it was second nature.

"I was in the office," he said smoothly. "Guidance counselor had some paperwork for me to sign."

A lie.
I *knew* it was a lie.

Imogen blinked, uninterested. "Okay, well, I have to go."

She turned on her heel, already pulling out her phone.

He didn't move. Didn't follow. He just watched her walk away... and shifted his gaze *back to me.* His jaw clenched.

He started forward...just one step, like he was about to call my name.

I felt my entire body lock up. I had nowhere to run.

But just then the heavy double doors behind me banged open.

Logan burst out, his jacket flapping behind him, his curls wet with sweat and mist, a half-eaten sucker in his mouth.

"Mrs. Lenner's gonna crucify me," he laughed, breathless. "She *knows* I pulled it...swear to God, she has freakin' psychic powers."

He glanced around once, and said, "I'm getting out of here before she finds me."

He paused just long enough to register me standing there, frozen.

I blinked. Shook my head. "Wait...wait. I'm coming with you."

He turned fully toward me, his eyebrows raised, "Seriously?"

I nodded, quick. "Yeah. Seriously."

Behind me, I felt the weight of Jason's stare, pressing into my back like a shove.

"Come on then," Logan said, flashing a crooked grin. "We're hitting the woods behind the tennis courts. Nobody goes there but band kids and feral squirrels."

He started walking fast, and I caught up beside him, breath shallow.

"You know, I thought you hated me," he said, glancing at me sideways.

"I don't," I whispered.

He shrugged. "Cool. I mean, I get it if you did."

"Thanks for saving me," I said. "I just… couldn't breathe back there."

Logan nodded like he understood something I didn't even say.

We ducked around the side of the building, past the dumpsters and out toward the rusted fence line that backed up to the woods. No one followed. No one looked twice.

The moment we stepped past the trees, the noise of the school dropped away.

BETWEEN FRIENDS

Just wind. Leaves. Our footsteps over wet pine needles.

I didn't look back.

But I knew Jason had come for me.
Not for his daughter.
Not for paperwork.

He came to talk to me.
To make me remember what I owed him.
What he'd *given*. What he *expected* in return.
Like kindness came with a receipt.

And this time, I could see it in his eyes...
He was not going to let this go.

CHAPTER 27

Olivia

2 days until graduation

Maddie and I sat cross-legged on the floor, surrounded by curling irons, open eyeshadow palettes, and a pile of outfits we'd both vetoed. The radio played some throwback Top 40 hit low in the background.

Maddie's room wasn't big, but it was warm.

The walls were covered in magazine clippings and polaroids curled from too much sunlight. A crooked corkboard above her desk held cheer schedules, a poem she'd written, and a faded concert ticket from a band we both pretended to like sophomore year.

Her bed was unmade, her floor was half laundry and half glitter, and there was a mug with dried mac and cheese in it on the nightstand.

I felt more comfortable here than I ever had at Imogen's.

Maddie's house was way more relaxed.
I didn't feel like I had to take off my shoes at the door or remember every little rule.
I could just be.

No one cared if I said *please* or *thank you* or left a dish in the sink. Maddie's mom was cool, too...barefoot in the kitchen, humming to herself, letting us come and go without interrogation. If she was even home. Which most times she wasn't.

I still can't believe Shane Stone invited us," Maddie said, grinning sliding on hoop earrings.

I smiled, twisting a piece of hair around my finger. "Do you know why Imogen decided not to come?"

I tried to sound casual. Like I hadn't been thinking about it since Maddie told me.

"She's not mad at me, is she?" I asked quickly, before Maddie could answer. "Because if this is some weird punishment thing."

"No," Maddie cut in. "Oh my God, Olivia... you don't know?"

I turned toward her. "Know what?"

She stared at me. "Her dad. He... tried to kill himself. Two nights ago. He's in the ICU in a coma."

The air in the room shifted.

I didn't move. Just stood there with one hand still in my hair, fingers frozen mid-curl. "Wait, what?"

"Carbon monoxide," she said quietly. "In the garage. Her mom found him."

I sat down. My knees just sort of buckled, and I landed on the edge of her bed, staring at nothing.

"I didn't know," My voice sounded too small, too far away. "I thought, he always seemed fine. Like, nice," I said, knowing full well that was a lie. Jason was definitely not classified as nice.

"He was," Maddie said. But there was a strange tightness in her tone, like she didn't really believe it.

I pressed my thumb into the inside of my wrist. The bracelet Jason had given me two weeks ago shifted. A handcrafted designer piece, with a tiny glass globe holding a flower. He said it reminded him of me, beautiful and delicate.

I didn't look at her.
I didn't want to see whatever might be written across her face.

"Why would he…?" I asked.

Maddie hesitated. And said, "Apparently, he was having an affair or something and his wife found out. She threatened to leave him. And apparently all the money, the house, and everything is hers. He'd be left pretty much penniless if she follows through."

The words hit harder than I was ready for. Like a guilty sentence.

I didn't say anything. Just tucked my right arm behind my back, letting the bracelet slide out of view.

I hadn't thought about Jason in days. Not really. Not since the day in the courtyard at school. But now, sitting here in Maddie's room, with hot air curling through the half-cracked window and the sound of her hair dryer still lingering like static in the walls, I felt responsible.

The weight.
Like maybe this was my fault.

The silence between us stretched long, wrapping around my throat.

Maddie turned back to the mirror putting on lipstick, her mouth forming a long oval.

Outside, I could hear the faint hum of cicadas.

"Anyway, we will still have fun," I said, trying to keep my voice light and believable. The truth was, I was glad she wasn't coming. No matter what the reason. I was glad to go to this party without being under her thumb.

Maddie flopped back on her bed, watching me take my turn in the mirror.

"You look good, Liv."

I stopped and blinked.
Did she just call me Liv?

I hesitated, brushing mascara onto my lashes. "I'm leaving in two days."

Maddie sat up. "Wait...what?"

"I mean after graduation is over. Like, right after."

Maddie's eyes widened. "What?"

"I've got a place lined up with my second cousin's ex-girlfriend. She's cool. She's letting me crash on her couch until I figure stuff out."

Maddie blinked. "What do your grandparents think about that?"

"They don't know yet."

"Are you serious?"

"They'd never let me go, so... I'm just gonna leave. I'll call them after I get settled."

"That's kind of messed up. What about your sister?" she said, staring at her nails.

"They'll all be fine," I said, sharper than I meant to. "I was going to leave anyway, it's easier this way. No arguing."

Maddie didn't respond. She stood up, adjusted her dress again and checked her reflection.

I looked at her for a long time.

Something about the way she moved disturbed me. She wasn't Imogen. But she was trying.

And I was just trying to disappear without anyone noticing I was gone.

Finally, Maddie smiled. "Well... you're not going to the big senior party, then?"

I shook my head. "No. I'm getting out of here."

She nodded slowly, tugging her hair into a ponytail. "Fair enough. But you better at least dance tonight. Shane Stone's gonna be looking for you."

I laughed. "I highly doubt that."

She winked. "You never know. He did invite you."

We finished getting ready, slipping into heels and spraying perfume in clouds that caught the bedroom light. Maddie's mom yelled something about not staying out too late, and we shouted back promises we wouldn't keep.

As we stepped out into the dusk, the night air was warm against my skin. Heavy with the smell of jasmine and potential. The kind of air that made you feel like something was about to happen, even if you didn't know what. And I let myself believe...for just a second...that I was already that girl.

The one I always wanted to be.

Where I was free from the labels. From the trailer park. From Imogen.

———————————•◆◆•———————————

Maddie and I walked up the long drive to Shane's house. Crickets were loud in the woods nearby. The driveway curved in a perfect circle, like everything here was built to be admired. At the top of the hill, the house rose into view like it had been planted there on purpose. Too wide for the lot it sat on. Too white under the porch lights that buzzed faintly overhead. The windows all glowed gold, soft and curated, like secrets were being kept just behind the glass.

It didn't feel lived in.
It felt staged.

Perfect hedges, perfectly swept steps, a perfect brass knocker on the door that no one ever used. A house that looked like it came with rules. A code to get in. Rules to keep once you were inside.

But tonight, it pulsed. Overrun with teenage angst and the tension of an animal that had been caged too long.

Shane's black Mercedes SUV was parked crooked near the front. Blue LED running lights still on. A statement, not an accident.

"His parents are in Barbados," Maddie said, like she was bored. "They won't even be here for his graduation."

His dad was some kind of financial advisor. His mom didn't work. Not unless staying thin and tanned counted as a profession.

They left Shane alone a lot. So, he threw parties. Big ones.

BETWEEN FRIENDS

Always.

The front doors were already open. Music poured out...low and thick. I stepped inside and felt uneasy right away. My shoes clicked across cool tile. Air conditioning struggling to keep up. Voices bouncing off high ceilings.

There were kids everywhere. Upstairs, downstairs, pressed into corners, sliding around in socks. Someone had already spilled beer on the entry rug. A girl in too much eyeliner laughed too loud near the stairs.

Maddie slipped off toward the kitchen without saying anything. I didn't follow.

I just stood in the doorway a second longer.

I was trying to hold onto the shaky confidence that felt almost powerful just moments ago in the driveway.
Like if I could fake it long enough, maybe it wouldn't slip through my hands. It teetered and sputtered out.

And I almost turned around to leave.

But then I saw him.

Andy.

Standing near the back sliding doors, half-lit by the glow from the porch lights. Maddie was standing next to him, laughing. He had a drink in his hand, his baseball cap backwards, laughing at something Maddie said. The kind of laugh that leaned in close. The kind that meant something. And she was smiling in a way I hadn't seen before. Not around me. Especially not when Imogen was around. They were different together. He was different. There was something there between them. It was there in the way he looked at her, I mean he *really* looked at her. Like she mattered to him.

I stood frozen for a second too long. My hand reaching for the doorknob. The music thumped around me, the scent of weed and sweat and cologne tangling in the air.

Someone walked up and offered me a Jello shot. Sweet and sharp.

I committed. I stepped inside and took it.

Then another.

The floor shifted slightly beneath me, but I smiled anyway. It was easier that way.

Easier to blur the edges.
Easier to stop thinking.
Easier to pretend I wasn't jealous.

Even if I was. Even if I wanted him to look at me like that.

I don't remember deciding to move. One second, I was watching Maddie and Andy from the entrance, the next I was wobbling across the house, trying not to knock over someone's Solo cup tower on the coffee table.

The music was louder now. People were dancing. Shouting. The lights felt like they were too bright and too dim at the same time.

I bumped into someone near the bottom of the stairs, nearly falling.

"Whoa," a voice said, hands steadying my arms. "Easy!"

I looked up and Logan was standing there.

He smiled. "Didn't know you were going to be here tonight."

I blinked, the room tilting slightly.

"Didn't think you'd save me again," I slurred.

He grinned. "Guess I'm full of surprises."

Someone passed us with a tray of shots. Some kind of clear liquor. He grabbed two. Held one out to me.

"Cheers!"

I took it without thinking. It burned all the way down.

The music shifted. Or maybe my head did. I couldn't tell.

Logan leaned closer. His hand was still on my arm. I didn't pull away.

"Are you okay?" he asked, softer now.

I shook my head. "No."

And he kissed me. Or maybe I kissed him. Or maybe we just fell into it, because it was easier than standing still. His mouth tasted like peach schnapps and smoke.

And for one second, it worked.

For one second, I wasn't thinking about Maddie.

Or Andy.

Or *him.*

Just Logan.
And the blur.

At some point, I was outside. With Andy. Logan was gone. I don't know how I got there. The night had come apart...split into blurry pictures and flashes of color. Red Jello. Spilled drinks. Laughter that didn't sound like mine.

Andy was smiling at me.

I think I said something that made him laugh. Or maybe he was just being nice.

The porch light cast a glow across his face, and for a second, I let myself believe it was okay. That maybe this moment could mean something. That maybe I still had a chance with him.

Then the ground tilted. The music swam through my ears, too fast, too loud.

The next thing I knew, I was face-down in the bushes.

Puking.

Mascara streaked. Knees in the dirt. Hair clinging to my face.

Everything spinning.

And somewhere behind me, Andy's voice saying my name.

CHAPTER 28

Imogen

The clock on the nightstand blinked 2:47 a.m.

I couldn't sleep. Again.

The room was too still, like a hotel suite no one ever lived in. Everything was color-coordinated: pale bone walls, soft gray linens, crisp white trim. The comforter was Italian. The headboard upholstered in cream velvet. There were no books on the nightstand. No framed photos. Just a white marble lamp, a bottle of sleep spray I never used, and a charging cord that didn't quite reach the bed.

It was beautiful.
But it wasn't *comfortable.* Especially not tonight.

The sheets were too hot, the air too thick. Chris was snoring lightly, one arm flung across my back like he thought we were still cuddling teenagers.

I threw his arm off in disgust, and rolled away from him, sitting up.

"You're grinding your teeth," he mumbled, half-asleep.

"And you're breathing too loud," I snapped.

He let out a soft groan and turned over, taking all the blankets with him. And I got up.

The tile was cold beneath my bare feet, sharp against my heel where I'd torn a blister in those stupid Louboutin's earlier this week. I padded across the cool tile into the hallway in the dark and down the stairs, my hand gliding against the railing. The motion sensor lights flicked on low, casting everything in a soft gold hue meant to feel luxurious. It just felt sterile.

In the kitchen, I pulled a crystal glass from the cabinet and filled it halfway from the filtered tap. The water made no sound against the sink. The marble counters gleamed in the low light. Not a single crumb. Not a single fingerprint. The fruit bowl was full, but the bananas were fake...glossy and flawless, a photo shoot centerpiece.

I sipped the water and leaned against the counter, staring at nothing.

The house felt like a showroom. No warmth. No softness. Every space built to be photographed, not lived in. Even the scent...vanilla cedar, piped in through a smart diffuser...smelled like a catalog. Untouchable. Just the way I liked it.

I walked slowly into the living room.

The furniture was all angles and clean lines. Neutral tones with accent pillows no one was allowed to use. The fireplace was gas. The books on the shelves were color-coded hardcovers, most of them unread. The art on the walls had been chosen by a decorator. I didn't even know the names of the pieces.

I sat on the edge of the sofa and set the glass on the side table too hard. It made a sharp clink that echoed louder than it should have.

My chest felt tight.
Like something was pressing down on it.

BETWEEN FRIENDS

There was too much pressure.
Too many cracks forming all at once.

Maddie was unraveling. There was gossip going everywhere about Olivia and the cops and the suspected foul play. And to top it... the memories...God, the memories...were starting to feel less like shadows and more like spotlights.

I hadn't seen Olivia's face in years.
And yet I could still trace every detail from memory.
The gloss on her lips. The delicate shimmer at her collarbone. Her laughter filling the room.

The past was everywhere now.
Screaming through the screen and all around me.
Clawing its way to the surface.

The silence around me was deafening.

The edges of my vision were starting to blur.

My heart was pounding...too fast, too loud.
I could feel it in my throat, my ears, my fingertips.

My skin felt hot. My stomach twisted.
I pressed my palm against it like that could settle the rolling inside me.

I was sweating.
But I was freezing.

I tried to swallow, but my mouth was dry. My tongue felt like paper.

I stood up too quickly and had to grip the back of the couch until the room stopped tilting.

Maddie. She was going to crack.
I could feel it. She was going to ruin everything.

She was already breaking... Asking questions. Panicking.

And if she kept it up...

It would all come crashing down. Everything I'd built. Everything I had left. It wouldn't matter how careful I'd been. It wouldn't matter what I told myself to survive. If Maddie opened her mouth to the wrong person, we were done.

No.
I was done.

I paced the room in tight circles, one hand pressed to my sternum like I could hold my body together from the outside. I didn't know how much longer I could hold this together.

Suddenly, I stopped pacing. I just stood there in the middle of the living room, chest heaving, palms damp.

And the thought came.
Quiet.
Clear.

I know what I have to do.

I hoped I could avoid it. That Maddie would hold it together. That I wouldn't have to burn everything down to protect myself. But she was unraveling.

And I couldn't risk it anymore.

Thank God I prepared.

I'd gone over it all before, in my head, in my notes, in those late-night drives when the fear wouldn't let me sleep.
The words.
The tone.
What I'd say if it ever came to this.

It was time to confess.

On *my* terms.

With *my* version of the truth.

I turned and walked toward the stairs, the house silent behind me, save for the faint hum of the refrigerator and Chris snoring softly upstairs like a man with nothing to lose.

I knew exactly where it was.

Tucked away in the drawer of my nightstand, plugged in and ready.

I didn't need to rehearse.

I didn't need to stall.

And I'd be ready to go.

CHAPTER 29

Olivia

Graduation day

I woke up to the taste of something sour at the back of my throat.

My head was pounding. Not just from the drinking...but from the remembering.

The room spun a little when I sat up. Light slanted through the blinds, too bright, too sharp. My mouth was dry. My tongue felt thick. My body ached ferociously.

Pieces came back slowly.

The bushes.
Andy's voice.
His hand on my back, holding my hair.

The Jello shots.
The back porch.

I pressed my palms into my eyes. Hard.

I remembered him helping me. I remembered the bushes. The way he held my hair when I was sick. He sat by me for hours. He didn't leave me there alone. And I thought that meant something. That he cared.

I pulled the blankets tighter around me. Squeezed my eyes shut.

The rest of it came in pieces.

The car ride.
His hand on the wheel, jaw clenched like he was mad or trying not to be.
Me, slurring some half-thought about how good he smelled.

The streetlight flickering above us when we pulled up in front of my house.

I remembered leaning across the console.
My mouth finding his neck, too wet, too messy.
His hands pushing me back, not rough…just final.

"Don't," he said, flatly.
Just that. Nothing else.

I should've stopped after that.
But I didn't.

I reached for his face again, slower this time.
Let my lips graze his.

And that's when he really pushed me. Hands on my shoulders, firm.

"What the hell are you doing?" he snapped. His voice wasn't kind anymore.

I blinked at him, drunk and stunned and humiliated.

He stared ahead, not looking at me, like I disgusted him. Like he wished he hadn't even brought me home. The shame burned hot under my skin. It clawed up my throat, swallowed my breath.

BETWEEN FRIENDS

I laughed. That awful fake laugh I used to hide my embarrassment.

But I felt it.
That tiny splinter in my chest.
The bruise forming where pride met want.

He didn't say goodbye. Just stared straight ahead, fingers drumming on the steering wheel like he couldn't wait to drive away.

He wouldn't even look at me when I got out.

I stepped out of his truck holding onto the last bit of dignity I had. Which, at that point, was basically none.

But shame rose up to take its place. The heat rising behind my eyes. The part of me that wanted to disappear and the other part that wanted to *make him sorry*. I'd never been turned down before. Not like that.

I sat up, fast in my bed. The nausea returned instantly.

I reached for my phone. My fingers were shaking. I opened the messages. Stared at his name.

Andy Marson.

Tears burned behind my eyes as I typed.

> Me: I need to talk to you.

I hit send.
Then dropped the phone like it was poison.

CHAPTER 30

Imogen

I never went back to bed after I made my decision.
Sleep had no chance of finding me, not after that.

I drifted through the day in silence, moving from room to room like a shadow that didn't belong. Silent. Detached. Waiting for the right moment. For the house to empty. And finally, it did.

Chris packed the boys into the car and left for the ballgame in Raleigh. Some charity thing through his company...corporate box seats, hot dogs, foam fingers. The kind of all-American memory he'd call perfect.

I told him I had a headache. Pressed two fingers to my temple and winced for good measure.

He kissed my cheek and said, "Text if you need anything."

The second the front door closed behind them, I went upstairs and changed.

Cream blouse. Dark jeans. Clean makeup.

The kind of outfit that says *stable. Composed.*

I didn't even need to think about it.
I'd planned for this day more times than I could count.

I went upstairs to get my ammunition. My fingers wrapped around it. The weight of it pressing into the palm of my hand. I pulled it out slowly, tilting it toward the light. A pale pink iPhone with a floral Wildflowers limited edition case.

Olivia's phone.

I slipped it into the side pocket of my purse, right next to the packet of tissues and the bottle of headache medicine I didn't take.

Then I got in the car and started driving. The roads were mostly empty...everyone still tucked away in weekend routines. Kids' sports games. Brunch. Farmer's markets. I passed the same gas station where we used to get snacks after school. The same intersection where we all used to park during fireworks.

I didn't let myself feel anything. I just kept going. Toward the police station. Toward the story I was ready to tell.

I wasn't going down for this. I wasn't cut out for prison...God, the idea of it made my skin crawl. The cold floors. The metal toilets. The uniforms.

No, no, no.
I pressed the heels of my hands against my eyes, breathing through the panic.

Let Maddie play the martyr if she wanted. Let her pretend she was stronger than she really was.

But I knew the truth.

I wasn't built for this kind of fallout. And if someone had to take the fall...
It wasn't going to be me.

I didn't even make it out of town before I hit traffic. At first, I thought it was just a light...then I saw the flashing lights ahead. A fender bender, two sedans crumpled at the nose, hazard lights blinking like a warning. Cars were backed up for a quarter mile, snaking through the intersection with the world's slowest urgency.

I drummed my fingers against the steering wheel, and then I checked the time. A deep and unsettled sigh rose from my chest. I needed to be back before Chris and the boys got home. Before they walked through the door with popcorn bags and souvenir hats, with a gawdy mascot on it.

The minutes bled away, slow and cruel. I shifted in my seat, heartbeat beginning to pick up.

This wasn't part of the plan.

When the wreck finally cleared and traffic began to inch forward, I let out a breath...and that's when it started.

A single drop tapped against the windshield.

And another.
Then the sky opened.

A sheet of rain came down like the clouds had cracked in half.

My wipers screeched to life, working overtime but barely keeping up. The road blurred into a mess of gray and glint. Headlights shimmered through the downpour like apparitions.

I leaned forward, knuckles white against the wheel.

"Come on," I whispered, eyes locked on the road, at the traffic slowing because of the rain.

"Come on, come on," I muttered, gritting my teeth.

Because this was supposed to be simple.
Controlled. Clean. And now everything was unraveling again.

When I finally pulled into the lot, rain still coming down in heavy sheets. My headlights cut through it, but barely. Everything looked washed out. Blurred. Like the world didn't want to be seen.

I put the car in park and kept my hands on the wheel. They were shaking. Not the kind of shaking you can hide with a deep breath and a good foundation. This was bone deep. Violent.

I didn't move. I didn't even blink. I would have to calm myself before I got out.

The station sat ahead of me, quiet and square. Lights on. Doors shut. It looked exactly how it was supposed to look...ordinary. But something about it felt final.

What are you doing, Imogen? I questioned.

My throat tightened. My chest felt too small for my heart.

I wasn't supposed to end up here. I wasn't supposed to be the one falling apart. But Maddie was a mess. And if she cracked... we'd both go down. I knew that. I whispered something...maybe a prayer. I'm not even sure who I was talking to. God. Myself. Whoever was still listening.

Just let me get through this.

I'd practiced what I'd say. I had the phone. I had the story.

A version of it, at least.

One that made sense. One that made me sound scared, not guilty. Caught in the middle. Young. Confused. Trying to do the right thing.

I could sell that. I *had* to.

My hand hovered over the door handle.
Breathe.
Just breathe.

And walk in like you don't already know how this ends.

Suddenly, a sharp rap knocked against the driver's side window I flinched so hard my knee hit the steering wheel. My breath caught in my throat.

The rain blurred everything outside ... a smudged world of silver and shadow. I could barely make out the figure hunched beside the driver's side window, face hidden under the sagging hood of a poncho. Just the suggestion of him.

My fingers fumbled with the window control, and I rolled it down halfway, my breath fogging the glass.

It was Andy. My heart stuttered with fear.

He motioned for me to roll the window down all the way, and I did.

His eyes found mine through the rain, steady and unreadable. His face was soaked, water dripping from his brow, clinging to his jaw. He looked like a stranger.

"What are you doing here?" he asked, voice raised just enough to cut through the storm.

I didn't answer. I couldn't.

Water slid off the edge of his poncho and spilled into the car, soaking the leather armrest. He gripped the bottom of the window frame with both hands.

"Imogen."

My name on his lips didn't sound accusatory. But it didn't sound safe either.

"What's going on?" he asked.

"Nothing," I breathed.

"You were sitting out here in the rain," he said. "At the police station. You weren't exactly grabbing coffee."

"I was just driving," I swallowed hard, trying to steady the tremor in my voice. "I didn't even realize where I was going."

His expression didn't change, but I felt his gaze tighten, like he was narrowing in on something I hadn't said.

"You're shaking," he said after a moment.

"I'm cold," I replied, brushing my hands down the front of my coat, trying to hide the tremble.

But he didn't move. He stayed exactly where he was, eyes fixed on mine, like he was trying to read what lived behind them.

"You know," he said softly, "I've seen that look before."

"What look?"

"The one you have when you're hiding something."

A beat of silence passed between us. Thick and endless.

I whispered. "It's not what you think."

He nodded slowly, but there was doubt lingering behind his eyes.

"What *would* I think, Imogen?" he asked.

I turned my head, staring out at the glowing station doors through the sheets of rain.

And for one fractured second, I didn't know what I wanted more...absolution or escape.

CHAPTER 31

Olivia

Graduation felt like a dream I wasn't part of.

Everyone was clapping. Smiling. Tossing their stupid caps in the air.

I walked across the stage with a pounding headache and a piece of gum I found in the bottom of my bag just to keep from puking. My stomach twisted every time someone cheered. My name got called and nobody really clapped except Maddie, and even that felt fake.

I saw Andy.
Just for a second.

He was standing in a group of guys, his gown wrinkled, tie crooked. He didn't look at me. Didn't even pretend to. Just stared off toward the bleachers, like I wasn't even there. And then he was gone. Before I could catch my breath. Before I could decide if I was going to scream at him or ask him *why*.

I skipped the photos. I skipped the cupcakes. I walked to the parking lot and in my dress and flip-flops, heels in my hand, my cap stuffed in my purse. I got in my grandparents' car, as Imogen and Maddie whizzed past in the BMW with the top down. And I didn't care. That wasn't my life anymore.

By the time I got to my room, the sun was too bright, and my mouth felt like it was full of cotton.

I pulled my phone out and opened the travel site. Booked it.

One-way.
New York.

Tomorrow morning, I would be gone. Out of here for good. I leaned back, hair a mess, bags under my eyes, and took a picture. Held up my middle finger. Let the sunlight catch the fire in it.

I sent it to Imogen.
See you, never! I wrote under it.

I made the photo my screensaver.

My battle cry.

Andy still hadn't texted me back.

Loser.

I stood in the middle of my bedroom and looked at the scattered clothes, the worn shag carpet, the cracked mirror. I didn't need anything else.

Shoved everything I owned into a duffel and kicked it under the bed, just as the knock came.

"Yeah?" I said.

The door eased open, and Grandpa stepped in. His tie was crooked, and he looked like he'd been holding tears in since the ceremony. He cleared his throat.

"We're proud of you, sweetheart," he said. "Really proud."

I nodded, biting the inside of my cheek. I couldn't say anything. If I did, I'd cry, and I couldn't fall apart now.

He gave me a small smile and backed out of the room, closing the door
soft behind him.

I reached for my phone, just to check.
And there it was.

> **Andy:** What do you want, Olivia?

My chest went cold.
He was pretending.
Like nothing happened.

I stared at the screen and typed.

> **Me:** About last night.

I watched the dots bubble and disappear.
He was hesitating.

> **Andy:** What is there to say?

I wanted to scream.

> **Me:** Meet me tonight. I need to talk to you about it.
> **Andy:** I can't. I have dinner with my grandparents. Then I have to
> study for my entrance exam. It's tomorrow morning.

That's all he said.

No "how are you feeling?"
No "you okay after last night?"
No guilt. No curiosity.
Just a wall.

I chewed the inside of my cheek until I tasted metal.

I typed:

```
Me: I'm leaving for New York tomorrow.
Me: I just want to see you once before I go. Please.
```

Three dots.
Then nothing.

Anger rose up inside of me…hot, electric. That's when I heard her voice in my head. Imogen. Cutting, cold. She would do whatever it took to get her way.

So, what would Imogen do in this situation?

She wouldn't beg.
She wouldn't wait around.
She'd strike.

I picked up the phone, my fingers moving faster than my heart.

```
Me: If you don't come talk to me, you won't have a police academy
    to go to.
Me: I'll tell them that you did something to me when I was drunk
    last night.
```

I stared at it for one second too long.
Long enough to feel sick.
Then I hit send.

I couldn't take it back.

The reply came fast.

```
Andy: What the hell, Olivia?
Andy:  Fine, I'll get there as soon as I can.
```

BETWEEN FRIENDS

I stared at the screen, throat dry.
Tossed the phone onto the bed like it burned.

Something in me buzzed, low and steady.

It worked.

He was coming.

—————————◆◆◆—————————

The graduation party was in full swing when I arrived.

Laughter echoed through the trees...wild, drunk, too loud. Music pulsed from speakers dragged onto Shane's back deck, bass thumping so hard it rattled through the ground like distant thunder. There were red cups tossed in the grass, the smell of cheap weed curling through the air, and girls in cropped tops laughing like nothing could touch them.

I ducked my head and kept walking.

The trees were thicker since the last time I'd been back here. Wild. The path overgrown with vines and thorny weeds. The air turned damp, cool against my skin, and the farther I went, the harder it was to hear the party.

I made it to the tire swing. It still hung from the old sycamore, its rope frayed and sagging. The creek trickled nearby, moonlight catching on the water like slivers of glass.

I texted him.

    Me: I'm by the tire swing. At the creek.

I didn't know what I was going to say yet. Not really.

Maybe…You hurt me.
Or… tell me something that makes this make sense.

I paced in the dark, my arms wrapped around myself, fingers tucked into my elbows like that could hold me together.
Like I could keep everything from spilling out.

I regretted threatening Andy.
I did.

But the worst part?
It felt good too.

To get his attention. To know I could still pull a string and make him move.

For once, I wasn't the one left waiting.
Wasn't the one with her heart cracked open and no one bothering to look.

I hated that it worked.
And I hated how much I wanted it to.

Some part of me whispered that this was the only way to survive now. To stop being the girl they discarded and become the one they remembered.

Even if it meant becoming something I didn't recognize yet.

A bottle floated down the creek, half-submerged. Probably from some idiot upstream thinking it was funny. The wind shifted, carrying the faint sound of someone yelling back at the party, followed by a shriek of laughter and the crack of a can being opened.

Then...footsteps in the woods.

Not loud, but not careful either.

I froze.

Through the trees, just past the bend in the trail, I saw movement. A flash of someone. Tall. Hoodie. Cigarette glow flaring for a split second.

Logan.

I dropped low behind a fallen log, heart hammering in my throat. I didn't know if he'd seen me. His face was in shadow, but he looked around before moving on, deeper into the woods. I didn't want him to see me. For him to be here when Andy arrived.

I waited for what seemed like forever.

Long enough that my legs started to cramp. Long enough that I started to second-guess everything.

Why wasn't Andy here yet? How long could dinner take?

What if he never meant to come? What if he's going to leave me out here, humiliated? The thought of that caused a sudden rush of tears.

Would he do that?

A branch cracked behind me.

I stood too fast, swiping tears from my eyes, voice shaking.

"Andy?" I called out.

No one answered. Only the creek gurgling, and the wind, and the dark.

"Andy?" I called out again.

Still nothing. I took a step back.
And that's when I felt it...
Something wasn't right.
Something was very, very wrong.

The wind shifted. The air turned still.
A shadow moved between the trees. Suddenly I saw it.

A face illuminated against the moonlight. Anger pulsing.

My voice cracked as I whispered to myself, "Oh God."

CHAPTER 32

Imogen

Rain still lashed against the windshield. Andy's hands were slick with water where they gripped the window frame,

He leaned down further, eyes searching mine. "Can I get in the car? I'm getting soaked."

"No," I said it too fast. Too firm. "Stay there."

He frowned, blinking rain from his lashes. "What's going on?"

"You tell me." My voice broke. I gripped the steering wheel tighter. My hands were still shaking.

"I swear, I don't understand any of this," he said, his voice rising now. His fingers curled tighter around the edge of the window, knuckles pale. "Why won't you let me in? What are you afraid I'm going to see?"

My jaw locked. My heart pounded. He looked angry. Defensive. His shoulders tense under the poncho, his lips set in a tight line.

"This is your fault. I know about Olivia," I snapped, my voice tight and trembling.

His eyes widened like I'd slapped him. A vein pulsed hard at his temple. He stepped back from the car, the wind catching his poncho, flaring it out like wings that didn't work anymore. He looked pale. Soaked. Terrified.

"Imogen, listen to me…"

"No," I cut him off. "You listen. I kept your secrets. But I'm done…"

He slammed his palm against the roof of the car so hard it echoed above the rain. I flinched.

"Do you even know what you're doing?" he shouted. "You think you've got it all figured out?"

I reached across the console and yanked Olivia's old phone from the charger, the screen glowing blue in the dim car.

I shoved it through the window, inches from his face. "You see this? Olivia's phone. Her *actual* phone."

His whole body stilled. "Where did you get that?"

"You don't get to ask questions," I said. "Not anymore."

"Imogen…" he started, stepping closer. His mouth parted, eyes wide, something unraveling behind them. "Give me the phone."

"No! I am not giving you the phone," I said, shoving down in between the seats.

His face contorted, rain dripping off his jaw like sweat. "You're going to regret this," he said, quietly now. "You don't understand what you are doing."

"I understand enough to know that I would've done anything for you and all you did was play all of us. Olivia, me, and now Maddie. Well, I am done covering for you. I am going to tell Maddie and then the police. It's over, Andy. I am going to finish this once and for all."

I threw the car into drive before he could respond. Tires screamed against the slick pavement.

Andy's hand slipped from the window just as I peeled away. In the rearview mirror I saw him, face twisted with rage, and I hit the gas.

CHAPTER 33

Madison

Coffee in hand, I settled onto the front porch.
The wine had almost won but I'd reached for the caffeine instead.
A small choice.
But it felt like something to be proud of.

I stared out toward the horizon, where reds and oranges were just starting to bleed through the sky. It was soft and open...the kind of sky that made promises. But I didn't trust it.

Leech was curled up at the edge of the porch, tail flicking every few seconds like he was annoyed with the silence. Or with me. He hadn't left my side much lately. Not really. Just lingered nearby like he was waiting for something to happen.

Evening was settling around us.
Still cool. Still quiet.

But I could see the dark clouds gathering low in the distance, crawling across the sky like a warning. A storm was coming.
The kind that didn't ask permission.

The air had that sharp, electric weight to it...heavy and still, like it was waiting to snap. My hair had already started to frizz around my temples, strands lifting with the charge.

Leech felt it too.

He sat up straighter on the porch rail, ears twitching, eyes pinned to the horizon like he saw something I didn't. His tail thumped once against the wood, slow and deliberate.

I took a slow sip and let the heat settle into my hands. But with the feel of the warmth came that same dull pressure in my chest I'd carried for years. That same ache just beneath the skin. I couldn't name it exactly...only that it felt like something was shifting. Like something bad was coming.

I pressed the mug to my lips and thought,
I can't believe I'm leaving my fate in her hands.

Imogen.

The girl who could make you question your own reflection if she said it with enough certainty.

She'd been doing it for years.

In third grade, she convinced me to give her my Hello Kitty backpack...the pink one with the glittery straps and the silver heart zipper. The one I'd begged for.
She told me I'd promised it to her.
Said we made a deal on the swings.
Said I must've forgotten.

I handed it over at recess and walked home with my books in my arms, trying to remember when exactly I'd said yes.
But I never had.

That's how it started. Small. Easy. Just one little piece of me at a time. But that was always her gift. She could make you doubt your own memory. Your own gut. Make you believe that silence was the right thing. That doing nothing was a kind of protection.

She'd been doing it since we were kids. Because that's the kind of thing Imogen did...she made you forget what you knew. Made you question the part of yourself that wanted to say *no*.

And I'd been saying yes to her ever since.

But the truth was, one of us was guilty. That was the part I couldn't ignore.

It was hard to believe that Imogen would do it. She was a bitch, sure. Controlling. Cruel, when she wanted to be. Crazy, even. Especially lately.

But violent? A murderer?

I didn't think she had it in her. Not the way I remembered her.

She didn't have a real reason, either.
No motive. No rage. Yes, she hated Olivia. But enough to kill her? That's the part I didn't part I wasn't convinced of.

And that's what ate at me most of all.

Because if it wasn't Imogen…then who did that leave?

Me.

Because we were the only two out there that night. The only two that drug her lifeless body and discarded it like it was a used napkin.

The thought sat heavy in my chest, pulling everything down with it.

I brought the mug back to my lips, but the coffee had suddenly gone cold. My fingers tightened around the ceramic anyway.

I didn't know how it was possible that I was the one who killed Olivia.

But sometimes, in the quiet...before the sun rises and before the lies harden back into armor...I wonder if I did.

I was covered in blood.
My hands. My clothes.
It soaked through everything.

And my memory of that night?
Gone.
Just this jagged blank space where something should be.

So yeah, it *looks* like I did it. It *feels* like I did it.

But *why?*

That's the part I can't reach.
That's the part that keeps me up at night.

Because if I did it… there had to be a reason.
And if there wasn't?
Then maybe I'm more like Imogen than I ever wanted to admit.

Suddenly, the porch disappeared behind a haze in front of my eyes.
The evening, the breeze, even Leech faded into the background.
All I could hear was the sound of my own breathing...and that sickening thud of what I *couldn't* remember.

My ears buzzed, too loud to ignore. My chest felt like it was closing in on itself, like the truth had stirred and was clawing to get out. Because the memory was already blooming...pulling me backward, dragging me into a moment I'd forgotten until now.

BETWEEN FRIENDS

Shane Stone's party was already too loud.

He was notorious for throwing these kinds of ragers whenever his parents left town...cheap beer, too many bodies, and music that rattled the windows like it was trying to break free.

I didn't really want to come.
But Olivia insisted it would be social suicide if we missed it.

When we got there the house was chaos.

Someone had knocked over a vase in the hallway, shards scattered like confetti across the floor. A girl in a sequined tank top was dry heaving into a potted plant on the porch while her friend held her hair and kept saying, *You're fine, you're fine,* like that would make it true.

Couples were sneaking off into dark corners...bedrooms, closets, even the garage...hoping no one would catch them making out.

The whole place felt like it was sweating, and I couldn't breathe.

One minute I was refilling my cup in the kitchen, the next I was leaning against the hallway wall, flushed and breathless, Andy standing across from me with that crooked smile of his, the one that made it hard to think straight.

We'd been talking for ten minutes. Maybe longer. It felt like a blink and an hour all at once.

It was easy, the way it used to be.
Before everything got complicated.
Before Imogen took him like he was her prize.

He said something about our history class being full of idiots and I laughed, a real one, the kind that rose up out of my chest without asking permission.

And he looked at me, head tilted slightly.
Eyes soft.

"If we're still single when we're thirty," he said, "we'll get married."

I blinked. "What?"

He smiled. "You heard me."

I stared at him. "Why would we do that?"

Andy shrugged like it was the most obvious thing in the world. "Because if you're gonna marry someone... shouldn't it be your best friend?"

Something fluttered in my chest.
And for a second, I let myself believe it.
Believe that maybe this was how the story ended.
Just this. Him. Me. Something simple.

It sat there for a moment, soft and golden, like a dream I hadn't meant to have.

But someone shouted his name from across the room, one of his buddies, already three beers in, holding up a Solo cup like a trophy.

Andy looked over, and back at me with a crooked smile. "I'll be right back."

I nodded.

He turned and disappeared into the crowd, already laughing, already gone.

BETWEEN FRIENDS

I stood there for a beat too long, pretending I wasn't watching him go.

I followed Andy around all night like some loyal little stray, trying to time our accidental run-ins like it wasn't obvious. But somewhere between the music and the crowd surging into the kitchen for round two of shots, I lost track of him.

And the last time I saw Olivia, she was tangled up with Logan Harper in one of the back rooms.
Mouth on his. Hands in his hair. After telling me just hours earlier that she wasn't into him.

Everyone at school knew how obsessed he was with her.
But she claimed that he gave her the ick.
That she'd rather kiss a wall.

But there she was. Fully making out with him.

Not to mention she had her little secret guy friend named J who bought her a phone. No matter how innocent she tried to play, she was an attention whore just like Imogen.

I walked off grinding my teeth and wishing I was back home. I circled the house twice in fifteen minutes trying to find Andy again. He'd been right here, somewhere between the hallway and the back porch, but now he was gone, swallowed up by the music, the crowd, the blur of bodies and laughter spilling from every room.

I checked the front porch, the kitchen, even peeked into the laundry room where two people I didn't recognize were tangled up on top of the dryer. The guest bathroom door was locked, and someone was crying behind it.

I went back to check on Olivia, but she and Logan were both gone now too.

Some stoner kid had taken their place on the couch, slouched low with a glass pipe lit between his fingers. The room smelled like skunky smoke and sweat. He looked up, eyes half-lidded, and grinned at me.

"You want some?" he asked, holding the pipe out.

I shook my head and backed away. My throat burned from the smoke in the air.

I circled through the kitchen and living room again, pushing past the bodies, scanning every face. Hoping to spot Andy. Hoping he'd be alone. Hoping he'd be *looking* for me too.

But he wasn't.

A wave of dizziness washed over me.

I slipped out the side door for air.

It was cooler outside...quiet enough to think. I walked around to the backyard. It was lit only by the glow of a single string of café lights someone had half-assed across the fence. Lawn chairs laying on their side, half-full drinks, a tipped-over cooler leaking beer into the grass.

I stood near the hedges, arms crossed, hugging myself like it might make me disappear.

And that's when I saw them.

They didn't see me.
They were standing on the edge of the porch, just out of the light. But I knew those silhouettes.

Andy.

And Olivia.

She had one hand on his arm, fingers curled just so. Laughing too loud. Leaning in like she'd just said something worth hearing.

She was drunk, that much was obvious.
But the way she was looking at him….
The tilt of her head. The angle of her body was subtle enough to pass as casual, but I knew better. I'd seen that move before.

It wasn't charm.
It was bait.
And every bit of it was fake.

And Andy?

He wasn't pulling away. He was smiling. Leaning closer. Saying something in her ear that made her giggle like she'd won.

Right then something twisted inside me.

It was bad enough that Imogen had taken him first. Like he was a necklace she'd picked out just to say she had it. I'd spent *my entire life* trying to catch his attention...being subtle, waiting for my moment, thinking maybe, just maybe, if I was quiet enough, sweet enough, *good* enough, he'd see me, really see me. Not as a best friend but more. Like a girl.

But now Olivia?

Trailer park Olivia with her chipped nail polish and hand-me-down sundress?

Touching him?

Laughing with him?

I felt my face flush. My throat burned. The world blurred around the edges.

She didn't get to do that.
Not when I'd waited.

I balled my fists at my sides, fingernails digging into my palms.

I wanted to scream.
I wanted to throw something.
I wanted to grab her by those stupid fake curls and...

"I swear to God..." I muttered, so low it barely had breath. "I wish she would die!"

The words barely left my mouth.
Just a whisper.
Barely even real.
But they rose in the air like smoke from a flame.

I stood frozen.
Ashamed.
Charged.
Shaking with the kind of fury I didn't know how to carry.

And then I saw him.

Logan.

He was standing on the far side of the yard, half-shadowed by the tree line. His fists were clenched so tight I could see the tremble in his knuckles. His jaw was locked. Shoulders heaving.

And he was crying.

Not the sad, soft kind of cry.
The kind that looked dangerous.
Unhinged.

His eyes were glassy and wild, locked on the same place mine had just been.
On *her.*

Olivia.

He wasn't just upset.
He was furious.

He was madder than I was.

I swallowed hard, the feel of the cold coffee mug in my hand again. I blinked hard, the porch, the oncoming storm, and Leech came back into focus.

My hands were cold. My pulse too fast. I could still hear the music from Shane's backyard in my head, see Logan's tear-streaked face. The way he looked at Olivia like she belonged to him. Like losing her meant losing *everything.*

So many people were angry at Olivia.

She had a way of pulling people in and pushing them to the edge at the same time. Boys wanted her. Girls envied her. Teachers praised her. And some people...people like Imogen, like Logan, and even me...resented her in ways that didn't always make sense until now.

The memory slipped away, but it left something behind.
A tightness in my throat. A heat behind my eyes.

And all I could think was...
Maybe I did have motive.
After all.

CHAPTER 34

Madison

Soon, black clouds rolled low across the sky, thick and fast, dragging thunder behind them like a threat. Lightning split through the distance...sharp, white streaks that lit the horizon for half a second before vanishing again.

The rain fell hard. It came down in steady sheets, flattening the grass and pooling along the edges of the driveway.

Despite it, the realtor still came. Waved once and then jammed the metal post into the front lawn like she was planting a flag. She wrestled with a black umbrella that kept catching in the wind, flipping inside out every time she turned her back. One heel sunk into the soft ground as she bent over the sign, cursing under her breath while rain ran down the back of her neck.

She looked like she hated everything about this moment.
She wasn't alone.

I watched from the window as she slid the sign into place.

For Sale...big red and white letters, loud even through the glass.
Permanent.
Final.

Leech sat on the windowsill beside me, flicking his tail like he had something to say about it. I closed the curtains and suddenly, the house felt emptier than usual. Like it already knew I was leaving.

I went upstairs and stood in the center of my childhood bedroom, surrounded by things that no longer belonged to me.

Trinkets. Clothes. Versions of myself I didn't recognize anymore. The posters had long been taken down, the string lights unplugged for good. What was left were the remnants. A pair of worn pajama pants. A cracked photo frame. Perfume bottles with barely a drop left inside.

I knelt by the closet and started pulling out the last bits of what I could salvage. Pieces of clothing I didn't hate. Sweaters that still held some shape. A denim jacket that might still work in LA if the nights got cool enough. I folded each one with mechanical precision and stacked them neatly into a shipping box labeled *Keep*.

Everything else?

I tossed into a box for donation with the last pieces of my old life.

Leech jumped up on it and made a nest of the fabric inside. He flopped onto his side with a dramatic sigh like he'd claimed it all as his personal sacrifice.

I sat down at the edge of the bed, the mattress groaning beneath me. My whole body felt heavy. Soul-weary. The stress of everything was getting to me.

I rubbed my hands over my face and let them fall into my lap.

My eyes drifted toward the nightstand.

I opened the drawer.

BETWEEN FRIENDS

Right on top was a photograph...loose, a little curled, edges worn.

It was me and Andy. Nine years old, sitting on the lawn in our swimsuits, grinning like idiots with a sprinkler spraying behind us.

I stared at it for a long moment.

So much had changed.
And yet something in that smile still haunted me.
Like maybe some part of me still wanted that simple version of life. The kind with summer grass and popsicles and friendship that didn't end in tragedy.

I set the photo down and dug deeper into the drawer.

That's when I found it...the envelope from CVS with the word *Photos* splashed across it.

Only one picture was inside, and I slid it out.

Spring Fling. The three of us...Imogen, Olivia, and me...arms linked in front of the gym's silver tinsel backdrop, our arms linked, our smiles too big and too bright.

God, we looked *young*.

I studied it for a moment, letting the edges of memory settle around me.

Olivia was wearing that pale green Marchesa gown...the one she found at Goodwill and spent weeks altering. It looked like it had been made for her. Sweetheart neckline. Tulle that floated around her legs. Tiny, stitched pearls at the bodice that caught the light like stars. She looked luminous.

I remember her spinning in it, barefoot on the front lawn of my house, saying it made her feel like a 1940s movie star. I remember thinking it was unfair that someone who came from so little could look like *so much*.

But it wasn't the dress that caught my eye now.

It was the bracelet she was wearing. I hadn't noticed it that night.

Delicate silver. Thin chain. A single oval charm...glass, with what looked like a pressed baby's breath inside. Soft and feminine, almost too fragile to wear.

Something stirred in my chest.

It was eerily familiar.

I stared at it, something sharp stirring in the back of my mind.

And then it clicked.

Imogen.
Weeks before the dance.

We were sitting in her bedroom, cross-legged on her white duvet, both of us painting our nails with the same shade of Essie polish.

"My dad is having an affair," she'd said, so casually it didn't even register at first.

I looked up. "What?"

"I found a gift box in his briefcase," she said, like it was obvious. "At first, I thought it was for me or maybe my mom...this really pretty bracelet. Thin silver chain, little glass charm with a flower in it. You'd know it if you saw it."

I remembered blinking at her. "So? Maybe it *was* for you."

346

She shook her head. "He never gave it to me. I waited. Weeks passed. Nothing. Then one day I checked the briefcase again and it was gone."

She blew on her nails, smirking like the whole thing didn't even bother her.

But I remembered the look in her eyes.
It *did* bother her.
It burned.

My hands were trembling now.

I looked back down at the photo...at Olivia's soft smile, the way she tilted her wrist just enough to show off the charm.

And the question rose up inside me like a sickness.

Had Mr. Warner's affair been with Olivia?!

I didn't want to think it. Didn't want to say it. But the moment the thought formed, it dug in deep. Refused to leave.

Imogen said she found the bracelet in her father's briefcase. That it wasn't meant for her. Or her mom. That it disappeared.

And somehow...it ended up on Olivia's wrist.

I felt cold all over.

Suddenly, all the things she used to say...the stuff about finding *deals,* the constant *miracles* she found at Goodwill...none of it made sense.

The Michael Kors purse.
The designer heels she wore to Homecoming.

The perfume that smelled expensive.
The brand-name labels tucked into mix of her thrifted wardrobe.

She was being given those things.

And now, I couldn't help but wonder at what cost.

My chest felt tight. My mouth dry.

Every thought was a landmine now...every memory twisting into something darker, something sharp.

And just as I started to put the picture away, I heard it.

A knock. Hard. Sharp.
Authoritative.

My stomach dropped.

Andy wasn't supposed to be here yet.
He'd said he had paperwork and something about stopping by the station before dinner.
We weren't meeting for two more hours.

Another knock came. This time, wild and rapid.

I froze, the edges of panic already closing in.
Was this it?
Was someone here to arrest me?

Was this how it happened...your guilt finally caught up to you and knocked on the front door?

I slipped down the stairs and stopped outside of the door, my heart pounding in my chest.

Leech darted under the couch. I stood in the middle of the living room, breath caught in my throat.

When I opened the door, the wind hit first.
Hard and cold and *loud,* rushing inside of the house, curling around my body.

Rain whipped across the porch in sideways sheets, swirling around my ankles and driving straight into the doorway. My hair flew across my face. I had to squint against it just to see her.

Imogen was standing there, completely soaked. Mascara streaked down her cheeks in sharp black rivers. Her hair hung in wet ropes around her face, plastered to her forehead and neck. Her arms were shaking, either from the cold or fury or both. I had no idea.

She didn't say anything. Just stared at me like I was the thing she hated most.

She moved. Fast. No warning.

She shoved past me, shoulder knocking mine, shoes slipping slightly on the threshold.

Her perfume hit me a second later, sharp and cloying, mixed with rain and perspiration.

She dropped her purse onto the back of the recliner...it teetered there, crooked and off-balance, threatening to fall. She didn't care. She was already pacing, wet shoes clacking against the tile, arms flying as she started talking.

"He's so horrible, Maddie. So awful. All this time, I gave him the benefit of the doubt. I protected him, and for what? So, he could keep pretending like none of this was his fault? Because he wasn't the one who hid her body. He left us with the blood on our hands."

She spun on her heel, nearly slipping again.

"I'm done. You hear me? I'm *done* with all of it. The guilty will pay!"

She wasn't exactly talking to me. Not really. Just circling the room like her anger needed corners to bounce off.

I stayed near the door. My hand on the doorknob.
Held it like I might still turn it.
Like I could just slip out into the rain and disappear.
But I knew I wouldn't.

"Imogen...what are you talking about? What's going on?" I asked, afraid to know the answer.

She spun toward me like I'd asked something offensive. "Don't play dumb, Maddie. Not now."

The room felt colder suddenly. Or maybe it was just the storm outside pressing harder against the walls, seeping in through the cracks like it was listening. I could hear the tick of the old clock in the kitchen, slow and deliberate, out of place with the panic crawling up my spine.

Imogen's eyes darted around the room as she paced, her movements sharp and restless.

But everything stopped when she saw it. The whole world stopped spinning.

I saw it too, but much too late to do anything about it.

Andy's jacket.

His last name in white lettering stitched across the front.
Still sitting where I left it, draped over the arm of the chair last night.

She moved toward it, picking it up.

"What is this?"

I couldn't answer right away. My throat closed around the truth. She stood holding the jacket like it was the one that had betrayed her.

"We've been... seeing each other," I said finally. The words felt foreign in my mouth.

She didn't move. Didn't blink.

And for a breathless moment, I swore the room tilted.

"Maddie..." she said. My name came out like poison in her mouth.

My hand was still on the doorknob. Still an exit I wasn't brave enough to take.

"We've... been seeing each other," I stuttered, the words catching in my throat.

"Since I got back, I mean." I heard it in my own voice...the hesitation, the fear.
And worse, the shame.

She turned her head, slowly, like she couldn't believe what she'd just heard.

Her eyes narrowed as they landed on me.

"You've been *seeing* him."

It wasn't a question. It was an accusation. A blade.

Her lip curled. She let out a breath that sounded almost like a laugh...bitter, humorless.

"Of course you have."

She dropped the jacket and took a step closer. The rain still clung to her hair and her lashes. Her eyes were wild now...dark and glassy.

I swallowed hard.

"How perfect for you," she hissed. "You always did love the things I threw away."

I flinched, but she wasn't finished.

"You really think he wants *you?* The girl who left this town and came crawling back with nothing but guilt and a stray cat? What do you think you are to him, Maddie? Some tragic hometown redemption story?"

Her voice kept rising, words sharper, breath quicker.

"You're a warm body. A secondhand comfort. My leftovers."

She looked me up and down like she couldn't believe I was standing in front of her.

"You always were pathetic. But this? This is embarrassing."

I should've stayed quiet.
That's what the old me would've done.
Let her spit her venom and wilt under the weight of it.
But something inside me gave way.
Not loud. Not dramatic. Just final.

"I have always loved him, Imogen. And you know that. You've *known* that, actually."

Her mouth parted, just slightly. No apology. No denial. Just that practiced, unreadable stillness she always wore when cornered. But I didn't stop there. I couldn't. The seal had been broken.

"You took him back in high school because you could. Because you liked the way it felt to win. It was never about him. Not really. It was about me. About proving you could take something I loved and make it yours."

A pause stretched between us, heavy and electric.

"You didn't want Andy. You just didn't want me to have him."

She lurched forward.

"You are so *stupid,* Maddie. You always have been. Standing in the shadows, hoping someone would pick you. You're pathetic. You always were."

I shook my head, jaw tight.

"Then why did you date him? Twice?"

That froze her.
Just for a second.
A flicker in her eyes...something almost afraid.

"I know about the camping trip," I said.

She didn't move.
Didn't blink.

"How did you know that?" she asked, voice barely above a whisper.

"He told me."

That's when I saw it.
The shift.
The crack.
She wasn't in control anymore...and we both felt it.

She just stood there, breathing hard, still wet from the rain. Her mouth opened, like she was about to say something cruel again...but nothing came.

Instead, her face twisted. Her chin shook.
And she started crying.

Not delicate tears. Not the kind she could hide behind her hair or a clever line.
Real, heaving sobs.

She turned away from me, wiping her face with one trembling hand.

"You don't get it," she said. "I loved him."

Another sob escaped, hitching her words. "I did. I really did. But I couldn't be with a cop. Not someone like him. Not here. I had to get out...I had to *be* someone."

She shook her head, laughing bitterly through the tears.

"And after Olivia died everything changed. I had to protect Andy, but I can't any longer."

She looked back at me, eyes wide now, frantic. The tempo around her high again.

"Don't you see, Maddie? Andy's the reason this all happened. He's the one who did this."

The room tilted. I couldn't tell if she believed it or if she just needed me to.

"He would've done anything to protect that badge. You think he's innocent? You think he's *safe?* You have no idea who he is."

She stepped closer, her voice softer now. Less rage, more urgency.

"You don't see it, do you? God, Maddie...he's not with you because he cares. He's with you because he *needs* something."

I didn't answer. Just stood there, looking into her wild eyes, rimmed in red and determination.

"He's been using you. Ever since you got back. Every sweet little visit. Every question. He's trying to figure out what you remember."

She was shaking now, waving a finger at me.

"He thinks you know. That we both know. That one of us is going to slip and ruin everything."

My mouth felt dry.

"So, we... we hid the body to protect Andy?"

Her expression twitched. A flicker of hesitation...gone in a second.

"Yes. Of course we did. You remember that, don't you?"

I didn't.

But the way she looked at me...like she was handing me a lifeline, like we were still on the same side...it made me want to nod. To believe it. But Andy? It just didn't sit right.

"He's the one with everything to lose," she continued. "He's the one who left her there. We just... helped clean it up. Because we didn't have a choice."

Her voice dropped even lower, eyes locking onto mine.

"In the end, it's him who killed her, Maddie. And now he's with you, playing the good guy, just close enough to keep you quiet."

She started pacing again, shoes clacking hard against the floor, faster now. Her hands flew to her hair, pulling it back from her face, water flinging off in sharp little arcs.

"I told him I was coming here. I told him I was going to tell you everything. And the police."

She turned, eyes bulging, dark streaks underneath, lips trembling.

"He *freaked out,* Maddie. He lost it."

My heart pounded harder. My fingers flexed at my sides. I took a step back, toward the window, the storm still raging just beyond the glass.

"You confronted him?" I asked, barely recognizing my own voice.

"Yes! Of course. And I have evidence too. That's why he was so angry with me."

"No," I said, my breath catching.

The world suddenly suspended around me.
Heavy.
Awful.

Suddenly, my phone lit up and a long, hollow ring echoed through the room.

356

I glanced at the screen. Syndney Perry.
The new girl from work.
The one with the cop boyfriend.
The one who Adrienne said she could get the number traced, no problem.

My hand hovered for a second and I picked up the phone, cradling it in my hand like a lifeline.

Imogen was already mouthing, frantic...*What are you doing? Don't answer it. Hang up the phone.*

But something inside me...some flicker of instinct...moved my hand before I could stop it. I needed to know who had been calling my phone for weeks. Maybe make sense of some of this.

"Hello?"

The room was still except for the storm...rain tapping at the glass, wind beating against the house rushing against the siding.

"Hey, Madison," she said. "This is Sydney. Sorry to call so late. I'm with my boyfriend Todd right now and... well, he pulled up the number you wanted to know about."

I stepped away from Imogen, into the kitchen's dim light. My socks slipped slightly on the tile. The air smelled like coffee and metal.

"Okay," I said, my voice steadier than I felt.

"It's a burner phone, but the signal's still active," she continued. "And Todd just traced it to a location."

My fingers tightened around the phone.

"Where?"

A beat of silence passed, followed by whispers. And she spoke.

"It pinged in the vicinity of Magnolia Lane in Fairfield, North Carolina."

"That's where I live," I said.

"Well then, the phone is somewhere near your house. Right now. It is a live tracker he's using."

The floor felt cold beneath me, as lightning flashed right outside the window. My fingers tightened around the phone.

Somewhere near your house.

My heart stuttered.

There was no one else here but me.

And Imogen.

The realization hit hard, a dull thud in my chest. Imogen was the only other person in the house. The only other person who could've had the phone.

I looked straight at her and hung up.

The silence stretched, thick and humming.

But before I could think or speak, the doorbell rang.

Sharp. Sudden.
Echoing through the house like a gunshot.

Followed by a crash of thunder that shook the windowpanes.

The boom was so heavy it seemed to vibrate through the floorboards and into the soles of my feet. Rain lashed sideways against the house. Wind shrieked beneath the eaves. The porch light flickered once, then held steady. Shadows moved behind the curtain...tall, unmistakable.

Imogen's body went stiff, her gaze locked on the door.

Andy was out there.

My mouth had gone dry.

If Andy was here... Then, either of them could be the owner of the phone.

The house, the storm, the air between all of us...everything was charged. Wind howled against the windows, rattling them in their frames.

I could hear my own breath. Shallow. Uneven.

Imogen hadn't moved.

She stood completely still, but her eyes were watching me now.

Another bolt of lightning lit up the living room, casting long shadows across her face. For a split second, I saw it.

Something different. Something unrecognizable in her expression.

I took a single step back, toward the door. The old floorboard groaned beneath my heel.

She blinked. Tilted her head.

The doorbell rang again.

A long pause. And a single knock followed.

I swallowed hard and didn't look away from her.

From the other side of the door, Andy's voice came low and urgent:

"Maddie."
"It's me."
"Let me in."
"I need to talk to you."

Imogen eyes were wide, as she shook her head no.

And I moved without thinking...my feet carrying me toward the door like something inside me had already decided.

But before I could reach it, she jumped in front of me. Her shoes scraped across the tile, wet soles squeaking. Her arms flew out like a barricade.

"Don't let him in here. Are you nuts?"

Her voice was ragged, high-pitched...on the edge of something feral.

"You want to end up like Olivia?" she snapped. "We both know what he did, right? You understand what I'm saying?" Her breath came in fast bursts.

"We both know what he did. And he won't let us get away with telling on him."

Another knock...louder this time. The door shook in its frame.

Imogen whirled around, her back pressed flat against the door now, like she could hold it shut with her own body. Rain splattered against the windows. The thunder rumbled again, like a low growl.

His voice, muffled but clear, cut through the storm.

"Is Imogen in there with you? I saw her car out here."

"Maddie...don't listen to her. You can't trust her."

A pause.

"Just open the door. Let me explain."

My hand hovered in the air, suspended, undecided.

The wind howled harder now, screaming through the cracks around the doorframe. Rain pelted the glass like thrown pebbles. Imogen hadn't moved...still pressed against the door, shaking, her eyes locked on mine like I was the one holding a weapon.

"Maddie?" Andy's voice again, louder. Sharper.

The doorknob rattled. Once. Twice.

"Are you okay?"
"Just answer me, please!"

I said nothing.
Neither did she.

Only the storm answered.

Another rattle...harder this time. And a pause. I could almost feel him decide.

As if we knew what was coming, we both ran from the door.

And CRACK.

The door flew open with a splintered scream, slamming against the wall.

Wind came rushing in, wild and cold, carrying the rain with it. It drenched the floor, sprayed across the furniture. Curtains snapped. The house seemed to gasp.

Andy stood in the doorway, chest heaving, soaked to the bone. Water dripped from his hair, darkening the collar of his shirt.

His eyes found mine...wide, searching, wild.

And flicked to Imogen.
Back to me.

None of us moved.

The wind howled louder, rushing past him into the house, bringing sheets of rain and the sharp scent of pine and pavement and fear.

In a sudden burst, Imogen darted past him, shoulder clipping his as she shoved through the open doorway and disappeared into the storm.

And without thinking,
I followed her.

My bare feet slapped the wet steps, hair whipping across my face. The sky cracked open overhead...lightning streaked in jagged lines, lighting the trees in eerie flashes.

Imogen was a streak of black darting toward the driveway.
I chased after her, heart pounding in my chest.
She skidded to a stop near her car, panic flashing across her face.

"Shit...my keys," she muttered, voice sharp with frustration. "They're inside!"

Before I could catch my breath, she was already moving again.
Toward the woods, to that old, familiar path that twisted down the ridge.

She disappeared into the trees, and I was a few steps behind.

I was almost to the path when I heard him behind me...boots pounding against dirt and ground, his breath coming in fast succession.

He was chasing me!

Terror moved through me as I slipped into the forest.

"No! Maddie! Come back!" Andy's voice tore through the wind behind me.

I just kept running, lungs burning, heart threatening to break through my ribs. I didn't know what I thought he'd do. I just knew I couldn't let him catch me. Not now. Not after what I'd heard. Not after he kicked down the door in rage.

My lungs burned.
My breath came in broken gasps.
Branches slapped my arms, slicing cold lines across my skin.

Andy's footsteps pounded behind me, fast and closing in.

"Maddie!"
"Stop!"

But I didn't.
I couldn't.

The trees and darkness swallowed us whole. Pines clawed at the sky, swaying violently under the weight of the wind. Leaves spiraled down like falling daggers. The scent of wet bark and churned earth surrounded me. I ran without direction. Imogen was nowhere in sight.

My foot snagged something...root or rock, I didn't know...and I went down hard, hands scraping against leaves and twigs and cold wet earth. I gasped, turning over just as Andy lunged forward, reaching for me.

"No...get off me!" I screamed, heels digging into the ground, trying to scoot back.

"Maddie, stop...it's not what you think…"

Lightning flashed, lighting his face, just as he fell too, momentum carrying him down, his weight pressing into my chest as he landed. He looked at me and I saw the flash of fear in his eyes. Or was it guilt?

And then a sound...a sickening, heavy *crack.*
His body jerked.
And stilled.

I blinked, breath ragged. His eyes were open, mouth slightly parted. His weight slumped against me. Something wet soaked through the fabric at my shoulder.

I looked past him.

Imogen stood there, chest heaving, a rock slick with blood still in her hand.

She didn't drop it right away.

She just stared down at him...at us...like she couldn't quite believe what she'd done.

And she said, voice flat, breathless:
"Look what you made me do."

CHAPTER 35

Madison

"Imogen!" I screamed, my voice shredding through the trees. "You killed him!"

She didn't answer, her face, void of emotion.

"Oh my god…" I stumbled backward, breath catching in my throat. "Imogen...he's dead!"

Andy's body lay twisted in the mud, rain soaking his shirt, blood mixing with water and leaves. His eyes were open, unblinking.

My knees buckled.
I dropped to the ground, hands sinking into the wet earth as the sobs came.

"No...no...no…"
I couldn't breathe.
And I couldn't look away.

Andy. Not my Andy.

Imogen stood over me, hair plastered to her face.

"Get up!" she shrieked. "We don't have time for this. We aren't far from the well. You know the one. They're filling it in tomorrow."

"What?" My voice barely broke through the storm.

"I had no choice!" she screamed, turning to drag his body again. "He was trying to kill you, Maddie. Don't you get it?"

I froze, rain sliding down my cheeks, mixing with tears.

Was he?

Was Andy trying to hurt me?

I searched my memory...the look in his eyes, the twist of the doorknob, the way he yelled my name.
He was panicked.
Desperate.

Not violent.

But Imogen said he was, so he must've been. *Right?*

Imogen turned and started pulling at one of his arms. "Help me. We have to drag him. Come on."

The world blurred. Mud. Branches. The sharp sting of rain on my skin.

I found myself gripping his other arm, my fingers slipping against soaked skin. He was so heavy. My arms trembled. My body shook. The forest floor tore at him as we dragged him inch by inch through the darkness.

Imogen muttered as she moved, words low and fast and feral.

"He did this... he did this..."

I wanted to scream. To run. To disappear into the trees and pretend none of this was happening.

But instead, I kept dragging.

And the well waited.

Together, we shoved.
The weight of him slipped, heavy and limp, vanishing over the crumbling lip of the well.

A sickening thud echoed from below.

And the rain stopped.

Imogen stood still, breath ragged, arms streaked with mud and blood. She brushed her soaked hair from her face and wiped her hands down the front of her white slacks, now smudged dark at the knees.

Her voice came low, too calm.

"It's done."

But as she turned to look at me, something caught the dying light.

A glint.

There...on her wrist.
That same bracelet.

Beaded and delicate. With the flower inside of a delicate globe.
Olivia's bracelet.

The one Jason gave her.

I knew for certain she was still wearing it right before she died because she had it on in the Spring Fling photo.

So how did Imogen get it?

I didn't dare ask.

We didn't talk at all on the way back.

The silence stretched between us like a fault line about to break wide open.
The only sounds were the crunch of our footsteps on the wet leaves and the deafening chorus of frog songs, croaking loud and wild from somewhere deep in the woods. Crickets trilled in bursts, as if the forest itself were gasping for breath.

My clothes clung to me, soaked through and streaked with mud. My arms ached from dragging Andy, the strain still pulsing deep in my muscles. My hands wouldn't stop shaking, even as I tried to steady my breath. And my heart kept breaking, over and over again, remembering.

As we walked through the inky dark, with the sound the squelch of wet earth beneath our feet, something cracked open inside me.

A shard of memory pushed up inside of my grief.

Smoke. So much smoke.

The memory, so vivid, so clear...I thought the woods were on fire.

Thick, curling. Bonfire smoke.
It rushed back like a punch to the chest...the smell of cheap beer, the sound of laughter. It was all around me.

I could almost hear music in the distance, thudding, pulsing. Someone laughing. Someone yelling. A red Solo cup in my hand, tipped too far. The sharp tang of cheap liquor.

And bile in my throat. The heat of it rising.

The slap of a branch across my cheek.

BETWEEN FRIENDS

My stomach heaving. The world spinning.

Just as fast as it came, the vision faded, softening, as Imogen moved farther ahead.
I blinked hard, trying to clear the smoke that wasn't really there.

She was almost a shadow now, her figure barely visible through the blur of wind and branches.

I picked up my pace, feet slipping in the mud as I tried to catch up.

We came out of the woods behind my house, the windows glowing against the storm's dusk. I watched her climb the steps and go inside like nothing had happened.

My body kept moving, but my mind was unraveling.

The bonfire still crackled in my memory. Laughter, and yelling. Girls' voices rising in a fight. The scraping of branches. Cold air rushing past as I stumbled into the woods, heart pounding. Something heavy in my arms.

I leaned against the sink. Clumps of dirt and blood ran down the drain, spiraling and swirling like something alive. My hands were raw from scrubbing, the water scalding hot, but I couldn't seem to get clean.

Imogen ducked into the bathroom as soon as we got back. That was ten minutes ago.

Maybe more.

The faucet squeaked as I turned it off. The silence that followed felt louder than the frog song outside, pressing in on my ears, my ribs, my thoughts. I stood at the sink, long after I turned the water off, staring down into the empty basin like it might offer some kind of answer.

I stepped out of the kitchen, heart still hammering against my ribs, and moved through the living room. The floor was scattered with chaos. Muddy footprints, rain-soaked floormat, and puddles of water.

I didn't mean to touch it. Just meant to pass by. I was just going to get a towel to clean up the floor. But the edge of my arm caught her bag, still teetering on the arm of the recliner, and it crashed to the floor.

Lipsticks. Keys. Receipts. And a phone.

An older iPhone with a Wildflowers limited edition case. Circa 2013.

Olivia's.

I froze, my breath caught in my chest.

With shaking fingers, I picked it up and pressed the power button.

It lit up immediately. Fully charged.

Olivia's face flashed across the home screen. A selfie of her flipping off the camera.

I clicked the home button and then recent calls and there...at the top of the call log...was my name and number.

Over and over. My number and my name. Repeated calls. One after the other.

I didn't even feel the phone slip from my hands.

I just stood there, staring at it on the floor like it might explain itself.

But it didn't.
It didn't have to.

Because now I knew.

I picked it back up and was looking at the messages between Andy and Olivia when Imogen stepped out of the bathroom. She was barefoot and freshly scrubbed, my track suit on her body, mascara streaks faded now to soft smudges beneath her eyes. She froze mid-step, narrowing in on me. I fumbled, trying to shove the phone back into the open mouth of her purse.

"What are you doing?" she asked.

My voice came out thinner than I meant. "I knocked your purse over. I was just putting the phone back."

She watched me too long. That piercing kind of stillness, the kind that makes your skin crawl. But then she moved passed me, and crossed the room, as if nothing had happened.

I lifted my chin, "Imogen, we need to call the police."

The words hung there between us, raw and heavy.

Imogen blinked. Slowly. Like she was calculating her next move.

"We will do no such thing," she said, crossing her arms over her chest.

Her eyes narrowed. "We didn't *do* anything."

My throat closed, but I forced the words out. "We're not innocent. Not this time. Not with Andy."

Imogen's face twisted...not in rage, not in fear. Something stranger. Some mix of calculation and disbelief.

"We *are* innocent, Maddie. Do you understand me?" Her voice dropped to a whisper. "This isn't our fault. It never was."

I started to argue but stopped.

The sound of her voice, smooth, calculated, still carried that same undertone. The one she used to talk teachers out of detentions, to make boys lose their minds. The same voice that once convinced me to hand over my lunch money because she'd "forgotten hers," and then didn't offer me a single bite of the sandwich she bought.
She let me go hungry.
And smiled while doing it.

How had I not seen the truth of her before?

I stared at her. My brain not able to process the sudden realization of Imogen. The real Imogen.

The one that had just hit Andy over the head with a rock and killed him. The one who is calling herself innocent even though I saw what she did.

That Imogen.

And then it came, the tilt.
That slow, spiraling sensation like falling between floorboards in my own brain.
A dull throb bloomed at the base of my skull, spreading fast, heat behind my eyes.

The full memory hit.
Not gentle, not gradual.
It swallowed me whole.

372

BETWEEN FRIENDS

My breath stilled. My lips parted.
Smoke coiled through my head.
And beneath it, the sour taste of beer and bile, clawed its way up my throat.

I didn't want to see.
But I did.

Firelight blurred behind my eyes. Music thudded in the distance, too loud, too fast, too much. My stomach rolled again, sharp and relentless. I clutched my sides and darted away from the crowd, pushing through the trees. Nausea rose up and I knew I was going to throw up.

I couldn't let anyone see me like this. It was our last night of being high schoolers, I wasn't going to be remembered as the one that puked at our senior party. I ran toward the woods, so I could throw up out of sight.

Branches slapped at my arms as I stumbled deeper into the woods, heart hammering, breath catching. The smell of smoke clung to my clothes, thick and sweet and nauseating. I dropped to my knees beside a tree and threw up into the leaves, the sour taste rising up my throat, again and again.

I doubled over, clutching my stomach. The world around me spun like the tilt a whirl ride at the fair. I pressed my hand to the bark of a tree, the roughness biting into my palm, grounding me as my head tried to regain equilibrium. My breath came in shallow rasps, as I swallowed down the taste of something rotten clinging to my tongue.

Somewhere behind me, an owl screeched in the branches, and I shuddered.

And then I heard them.
Voices...two girls. Arguing.

"No! You don't get it. Do you?"
I recognized the voice. Olivia.

"You think you're special? You're not!"
And the second voice was Imogen.

My head jerked up. I wiped my mouth with the back of my hand, legs shaking as I took a step toward the noise. The trees were thick, shadows tangled around their trunks, but the moonlight pushed through just enough.

I heard a scuffle. A shriek. Leaves crackling.
And then I saw them.

Olivia was stumbling backwards, trying to get away, but Imogen was faster. She lunged, grabbed her by the hair, and yanked her so hard her body slammed to the ground. A sick thud.

"Stop!" I tried to say, but my voice caught. My throat was raw. My legs suddenly locked in place.

Imogen reached for something on the forest floor...a rock, heavy and jagged...and raised it above her head.

"No," I whispered. "Imogen, no…"

But it was already happening.

The rock came down. Once. A sharp, sickening crack that echoed through the trees.

And again. And one more time.

Olivia's body jerked. And then stilled.

And...Imogen looked up.

BETWEEN FRIENDS

Her eyes found mine in the dark.

Time splintered into fragments. And my body snapped into motion. I turned to run, but she was already after me, crashing through the underbrush like a wild animal.

"Maddie...wait...stop!"

I ran harder. Branches slashed my skin. My foot caught on something, and I went down hard, hitting the ground with a thud that knocked the air from my lungs.

And she was there.

"Maddie." Her voice cracked. "I need you. Please."

I stared at her, dirt in my mouth, vision swimming.

"This wasn't our fault. You know that, right?" Her voice dropped to a whisper. "We didn't cause this."

She reached out, and I was too shocked, too dazed to pull away.

She took my hand and led me back to the body.

I remember the way Olivia looked. One shoe off. Eyes wide. Hair tangled in the leaves. But still so beautiful. So unimaginably beautiful.

We dragged her under the rock overhang into our fairy cave. Our hands slipped, our shoes caked in mud. My arms burned from pulling her dead weight. I think I was crying, but it felt so far away. Like the tears belonged to someone else.

Imogen brushed the hair back from Olivia's face like she was tucking her in. Like this was some bedtime game.

And she looked at me. Her hands were shaking, but her voice was smooth.

"Remember," she said softly. "This is to protect us. To keep us safe."

She leaned close, her breath warm against my cheek.

"This is what we do to protect each other."

She smiled, her eyes wild.

"We keep it between friends, Maddie. Always." And she kissed my cheek.

When I snapped out of the memory, Imogen was staring at me. Eyes cold.

"What's wrong with you?' she asked, throwing herself down on the couch.

"My God, what did you do?"

She blinked. "What?"

"What did you *do,* Imogen?"

A pause. Just long enough for the air to go cold.

And she scoffed, a sharp, bitter sound. "What do you mean *what did I do?*"

My voice cracked. "You're the one who...who.... You're the reason we..."

"No," she snapped. "Don't you *dare* put this all on me. You should've never opened that door tonight."

"I don't mean Andy," I said, shaking now. "I mean Olivia."

Her name landed like a stone in the middle of the room.
Imogen's expression changed. Just slightly.

I felt myself pulling back, my voice barely above a whisper.
"Did you…kill her?"

Imogen's eyes flared, and for a moment, I thought she might cry. But her mouth twisted.

"Cut the crap, Maddie!"

"I need to hear you say it."

"You were *there*," she said, stepping toward me. "You saw. You *helped*. Don't act like you were some innocent bystander. You could've run. You could've screamed. But you didn't. You helped me knowing exactly what I did…and in a court of law that is the same thing as killing her yourself."

"I was in shock…"

"You helped. Period," she said, looking down at her nails.

I took a step back, heart pounding, ears ringing.
Because part of me knew she was right.
And the rest of me was screaming *no*.

Imogen got up and walked over to the fireplace, pacing in front of it.

My voice cracked as I whispered, standing on legs that barely held me,
"I don't understand… Why would you kill her? She was our friend."

I blinked hard, trying to steady the floor beneath me.
The air felt dense, heavy with the weight of the truth.

Imogen's hands flew to her head, fingers raking through her hair like she was trying to rip the thoughts out before they could speak.

"She was trying to become me," she hissed, eyes wild, voice shaking like a child mid-tantrum.

"She was trying to take everything away from me. First my father, then *Andy*. God, she was wearing *my* bracelet, Maddie. She acted like it was hers."

She let out a sharp laugh that fractured into something darker.

"She started *talking* like me. Did you hear her? She copied my voice. She was trying to replace me, and everyone was just letting her do it."

I stared at her, my limbs numb.

"You killed her… because you *thought* she was *copying* you?"

"She wasn't copying," Imogen spat. "She was *stealing*. And no one was stopping her."

She spun around. Her eyes glittered, unhinged and glassy. "She was after him," she said. "Can you imagine if word got out? That I lost my boyfriend to trailer trash?"

She tilted her head. "I was not going to let that little rat win."

The words hung in the air. Poisoned.

I backed up to the wall, arms wrapped around myself like instinct, as if I could somehow contain the wreckage. But the pieces didn't fit anymore. They hadn't for a long time. But now I understood why.

I swiped at my eyes, my vision blurred and stinging. I could barely see her face across the room. Just the outline. Just her shadow standing there. Imogen stood still, her back against the mantle, eyes tracking me like a cornered animal deciding what to do next.

Her hand clutched the edge of the fireplace as if she needed it to steady herself. As if the chaos finally looked unfamiliar even to her.
She didn't speak. Didn't come closer.
Just stood there. Watching me break.

I slid to the floor, my ribcage jerked tight. Breath caught halfway.
I tried to move...to sit up, to crawl away...but my legs wouldn't answer.
Everything inside me felt hollow, like something essential had drained out.

All I could think about was Andy. Out there, still. His blood darkening the leaves beneath him.
And now I *knew* he hadn't done anything wrong.

A low sound tore from my throat. A whimper, maybe. Or a prayer.

One thought clanged through my skull, over and over, louder than Imogen's panicked breathing, louder than the wind cutting through the trees.

What have I done?

Suddenly a force rose up inside me and I got up, stepping toward her.

"You told me it was Andy," I said. My voice shook, but I didn't stop. "You said he killed her. You said he was trying to kill *me*."

Her mouth parted, but nothing came out right away. Just a flicker in her face. Doubt. Maybe even regret. And it was gone, shuttered behind that cold steel of hers.

She squared her shoulders.

"I blamed him because I needed a fallback," she said, too fast. "In case it all came out someday. Someone to point to. Someone they'd believe could've done it and I had the messages. I had the evidence. And anyway, he was guilty either way."

"The evidence of what, Imogen?"

She crossed her arms, a bitter smile curling at her mouth.

"She was texting him. That little bitch thought she could take *my* boyfriend. And he was coming out there to meet her. I have the proof in the texts."

Her voice shook now, anger boiling over into something darker.

"She didn't belong here. Not with us. Not with him. Who the hell did she think she was? On top of that sneaking around with my father letting him buy things for her."

Her hands clenched into fists at her sides, and opened again, trembling. One lifted to her throat, like she could press the truth back down. Like she could force herself to stay in control. But her fingers twitched. Her jaw locked too tightly. The mask was slipping, just barely, but it was enough.

I crossed the room, heart pounding, and grabbed Olivia's phone from Imogen's purse, where I'd left it. My hands fumbled, slick with sweat, as I held it out to her. The screen glowed in the dim light.

"Here, look at what she said. She *threatened* him. She said she'd tell the academy that he did something to her unless he met her. You really think he wanted to go out there?"

Imogen didn't take the phone.
Her jaw tightened. Her eyes dropped to the floor like she already knew.

"This is his fault," she muttered. "His fault. He shouldn't have been texting her. Giving her rides. He was *my* boyfriend."

I blinked, shaking my head, trying to grasp her words...trying to find the version of reality where they made sense.

A bitter laugh broke in my throat.

"That's why you did all of this? Jealousy. Nothing but jealousy…"

I stared at her.
All the pieces were there now, just jagged and bloody.

She wasn't protecting Andy.
She was punishing him.

Her face twisted suddenly, lips curling, brows pulling in tight, eyes wild with something close to panic, or maybe fury. A sharp flush rose to her cheeks. The composed, untouchable Imogen cracked open for just a breath, revealing the desperate child beneath.

She held a shaky finger in the air and pointed at me.

"Anyway, don't start pretending you're innocent now, Maddie. You're not. You were right there with me. We're in this together whether you like it or not."

"I was drunk, Imogen," I said, my voice brittle. "Blackout drunk. I didn't remember anything from that night…except helping you. You and me, dragging her through the trees like garbage. That's all I had until tonight."

My throat burned. "And all these years, I thought maybe I did something. Maybe I hurt her. I had so much guilt."

Imogen spun around, eyes wild.

"You *should* feel guilty," she snapped. "Do you even understand what it means to be an accessory? It doesn't matter if you don't remember. You helped. You *hid* her."

She stepped closer, her voice dropping into a hiss.
"So don't start acting holier than thou."

Tears blurred my vision, spilling down faster than I could wipe them away.

"All the things I've done," I said, voice breaking. "All the years of pain.
The guilt. The silence. I've been carrying it like a curse...believing I was
the one who ruined everything. But it was you."

Imogen stiffened, but I didn't stop.

"You did this because you were jealous and why should it surprise me?
You were *always* jealous of Olivia. She was brighter than you. Softer.
Smarter. People saw her and *loved* her...and that killed you inside.
That's the truth, isn't it? But killing her because of it? That's just sick."

Her face changed...just slightly...but enough to know I'd hit it. The
nerve. The rot beneath.

Her voice came out low. "You better watch your mouth."
Something flickered behind her eyes, cold and sharp.
"Or you're going to end up like her. And Andy."

She stepped closer.
"You want to find yourself down a well too?"

My breath caught. I backed away slowly, every inch of me pulsed with
the instinct to run.
Because the look in her eyes…
She wasn't bluffing.

My hands came up, slow and easy. Not raised in surrender but angled
toward calm. Like I could smooth the air between us.

"Imogen," I said, voice low, careful. "I'm not calling anyone. I'm not leaving. I'm still here, aren't I?"

She didn't move. Just watched me.

I kept going, steady as I could. "You're right. About Andy. About everything. I just got scared. That's all."

Her jaw tensed. I searched her face for something, anything rational. There was nothing.

A beat of silence stretched between us.

"I'll follow your lead, okay?" I said, slipping back into the role she expected. The quiet one. The easy one. "Tell me what you want me to do."

Her eyes narrowed. Her lips pressed into a line.
But then...her phone buzzed.
She glanced down.
Chris.

Her shoulders loosened just slightly, and her expression shifted, just enough to let me breathe.

"He's on his way home, the game was rained out," she said, flipping her hair over one shoulder, already pulling her purse closed. "I told him I had a headache, so I have to be there when he gets home."

She turned to the door and paused.

"I'll call you in an hour," she said without turning around. "Answer. You hear me?"

I nodded.

Her shoes clicked across the wet flooring, fast, impatient.

The front door opened with a snap of damp air and a new burst of thunder boomed, rattling the house.

Suddenly, we were plunged into darkness. The lights cut out with a hiss. The quiet whir of the refrigerator silenced mid-breath. Even the ticking of the old kitchen clock hesitated, like time itself stopped. And when I looked toward the open doorway, lightning flashed bright enough to split the sky open, bright enough to catch every drop of rain mid-air, bright enough to show someone standing in the open doorway.

Olivia was there, standing on the stoop.
Soaked through.
And very much alive.

CHAPTER 36

Imogen

Lightning flashed white and sharp, nearly blinding me.
Followed by thunder, long and low, rattling the windows panes.

And suddenly there she was.

Olivia.
Alive and well.

My body went still, but my mind screamed.

Olivia was here. And very much *not* dead.

Olivia's eyes met mine and a small smile creeped across her face. My stomach turned, as the world titled underneath me. I wanted to run. Scream. But I didn't. I just stood there, cold creeping into my limbs. My mind grabbing for logic. For reason.

She stepped forward, slow and deliberate, like she had all the time in the world.
Like she was making a grand entrance.

My hands stayed at my sides, fingers twitching before curling tight into my palms. Sharp enough to hurt. Just to feel something real. To make sure I wasn't dreaming.

I blinked hard, trying to process what was happening.

That Olivia was actually standing in front of me.

And she looked exactly the same.
Not older. Not worn down.
Like time had skipped her altogether.
Skin clear, eyes bright. Like she hadn't spent a single second in haunted by the past.

And I hated that my first thought was how *young* she looked. Like the years had skipped her on purpose. Like she'd been preserved in glass while the rest of us faced the clock.
While *I* aged. Got lines. Shadows.

It wasn't fair.
She was supposed to be *gone.*
Not standing here, untouched, like a porcelain doll.

"I'm back," she said with a laugh.

Like it was some kind of announcement.
Like we should be *happy t*o see her.

Maddie made a sound behind me…part gasp, part sob.

I stood there, heart pounding, rage blooming beneath my ribs, like something I'd buried years ago was finally forcing its way up through the ground, wild and unstoppable.

"You were dead," I said.

The words came out low. Flat.
Not a question. Just fact. Like if I named it out loud, it might keep the ground from shifting beneath me. That somehow saying it would put me back in control.

"You *were dead*," I repeated, my voice rising. "We buried you in the cave. I saw your blood. I saw your body."

Olivia didn't flinch. She just stood there.

Composed and even more beautiful than I remembered.

And that burned me.
Every perfect inch of her felt like a slap.

"No," she said quietly. "You buried a version of me."

I felt the heat crawl up my neck.

Maybe I should've hit a little harder.

Maybe she wouldn't be standing here now.
Maybe I wouldn't be the one about to lose everything.

Because she was going to tell.

I could see it already, written across her face in quiet fury.
She was going to open her mouth and take everything down with her.

And for the first time in years…
I didn't know what to do.

Maddie turned on her phone flashlight, illuminating and morphing our faces into ghastly creatures. And maybe we all were.

Suddenly, memory rushed over me like a tidal wave.
The past creeped in through the cracks, wrapping around the moment, suffocating me.

Dragging me back to the woods.

I wasn't standing in the doorway anymore.

I was back there.

I could feel the humid air against my skin, heavy and close. The smoke from the bonfire clung to my hair, sharp and thick, curling into my nose. The party felt a million miles away, though I knew it was only a thicket of trees behind me.

It was too quiet. No crickets. No wind. Just the slow drip of wet branches and earth. And the sound of breath. Mine and someone else's.

I saw her before she saw me, Olivia, just a shadow near the tree line, pacing. Phone clutched in her hand, thumb dragging across the screen. Her hair was damp. Her jacket half-zipped.

I stepped forward, careful over the roots, my voice low but sharp.

"What are you doing here?"

She turned, fast. She looked up at me mouth parted, gaping. Eyes blinking too fast.

"Aren't you supposed to be on your way to New York?" I asked.

Olivia rolled her eyes. "That's tomorrow, you dumb twit."

My whole body went still.

Dumb twit?

She called *me* dumb?

The girl who barely passed algebra?
The girl who wore off-brand shoes and lived in a trailer with paper thin walls and broken porch steps?

388

BETWEEN FRIENDS

Who did she think she was?

My hands curled into fists at my sides, heat rising up my neck.

I moved toward her. My eyes caught on the glow of her screen. "Who are you texting?"

She pulled the phone back. "None of your business."

I reached for it without thinking, fingers curling around her wrist, trying to grab it, snatch it away. But she yanked it back hard.

And that's when I saw it.

The bracelet.

My father's bracelet. The bracelet he should've given me.

"What the hell is that?" I hissed.

She froze, just for a second. And looked down, slowly, like she'd forgotten it was there. "Oh. This?"

"Where did you get that?" My voice cracked. "My father…he had that bracelet."

She smiled. Cold. "I guess he wanted me to have something to remember him by."

"You're lying."

"He said I was special," she whispered, voice suddenly soft, like she wanted to hurt me with sweetness. "Said I was everything you weren't."

My breath caught.

My father would never say that.

But the way she said it. So calm, certain. It dug its way in.

Was she just trying to hurt me?

Probably.
I knew she'd always wanted to be me.
Imitated the way I spoke. Copied my handwriting.
Jealousy was practically her middle name.

So, it wasn't a surprise, really. That she'd stoop to this. Taking my father's money. Pretend like she mattered to him. I knew she would do anything if it meant winning.

And it was time to knock her off her high horse.

I stepped closer.

"Just so you know, stealing my dad's money doesn't make you rich, it just makes you a whore. And, Liv, news flash, you will never be me. So just stop trying. It's pathetic."

"You think I wanted to be *you?*" Olivia snapped, eyes blazing.

"I pitied you. All that perfection. Your hair, your body, your fake little smile. And still, you're not enough, are you? You've spent your whole life playing up to other people's admiration, but deep down, you know it's all a veil. Peel back the layers and there's nothing real underneath. Just a girl terrified no one will love her if she stops performing."

Olivia took a step forward, slow and deliberate, closing the space between us.

Her eyes locked on mine, "And for the record? I didn't steal anything. Your dad gave it all to me willingly. Said I made him happy."

"He was *using* you," I spat, my voice shaking. "He didn't care about you. You were just another mistake. Just another…"

"Oh?" she cut in with a laugh. "So, I guess Andy's using me too. He's who I'm waiting on, by the way. We're meeting here. So, I can say goodbye the right way."

I stared at her but all I could see was the white light of rage.

"You're lying," I said with a hiss.

"You're a washed up, has-been Imogen. Nobody cares about you anymore. Especially not Andy," she snapped.

And that's when I moved, blinded by crashing rage.

My hands were on her before I knew what I was doing, around her neck, shoving her back into the tree. She clawed at me, gasping, eyes wide.

We were both screaming.

She shoved me off, hard.
We both stumbled.

And then, there was a rock.

I don't remember picking it up.
I just remember the sound.
The sick thud.
The way her body collapsed, soft and heavy into the dirt.

And the silence that followed.

It was like the woods were holding their breath. Listening. Waiting. Every branch above me stretched long and still, shadows like fingers pressed to lips. Holding my secret.

But when I looked up, I saw Maddie standing at the edge of the clearing.

She didn't run. Not really. She turned, stumbled back a step or two, eyes wide and dazed. But I caught up to her easily. I always could. All it took was my voice, low and soothing, the way you'd talk to a scared animal.

I told her it was an accident. That we had to protect each other. That this was what real friends did. She didn't argue. She never did. Maddie had always been so easy to steer. A few careful words, a little pressure in the right place, and she folded. My favorite marionette. Loyal and willing.

She helped me pull the body deeper into the woods. Her hands shook so badly, but she still followed, still obeyed.

And right before we left Olivia hidden in the cave, among the trees, her hair tangled in dead leaves and her skin already paling beneath the canopy, I slipped the bracelet from her wrist. The one my father was supposed to give me. And I took the phone too. For insurance. Just in case someone decided to forget how this all went down.

Thunder cracked again, sharp and vicious, startling me from the memory. The boom rattled the windows of the house like a warning from the sky itself.

And Olivia took a step toward Maddie.

"Maddie," Olivia said, her voice teetering on the edge of sarcasm. "You going to say something or just stare at me like I am a ghost?"

Maddie stepped forward, her hands trembling. "I thought you were…"

"Dead?" she finished, arching a brow. "Yeah. I know. That seems to be the theme tonight."

She glanced between us, eyes trailing, like she was taking inventory of who we'd become.

"I've been in New York for the last twelve years," she said. "Working on Broadway. A backup dancer, mostly. But I have some turns at lead. Turns out I'm pretty good on my feet."

She smiled, a flicker of old charm crossing her face like a ripple.

"My sister Kristen called me a few days ago," she went on. "Said the police had found the clothes. The bloody ones. Said they were reopening my missing person's case."

She shrugged lightly. "So, I figured I better come clear this up before things got out of hand."

Before either of us could respond, a shadow stepped up behind her.

Logan.

Olivia looked over her shoulder, and back at us with a grin. "You guys remember Logan, right?"

She leaned her weight onto one foot, arms crossed casually. "He's the one who saved me that night. Even if he *was* a little stalker."

She laughed, an actual laugh, light and breathy like we were still eighteen.

"I was knocked out cold after Imogen hit me with that rock. When I came to, Logan was carrying me out of the woods. I asked him to take my bloody sweater back out there and leave it. You know... to punish you guys. So, you'd get in trouble."

Her eyes landed back on me.

"But I was just a kid back then. We all were. Right?"

I narrowed my eyes. That voice, that syrupy, self-satisfied tone. Like she was above it all. Like she was the one in control.

But that was me. It was always *me.*

I let my eyes slide over her. The wet hair. The thrifted coat trying to pass for vintage. I tilted my head, letting the venom curl behind my teeth. She needed to be cut back.

"Still dressing like you're seventeen, I see," I said. "That desperate backup dancer look must really look great from the cheap seats."

Olivia's smile widened, but her eyes sharpened.

"Are those wrinkles on your forehead, Imogen?" she said, soft and cruel. "God. I thought Botox was supposed to help with that."

I felt my breath catch.
Felt the flicker of heat rise under my skin like a lit match.

My fingers twitched toward the vase on the entry table.

For a split second, I imagined grabbing it and smashing it over her perfect little head.
Ending this.
Finishing what I should've finished that night in the woods.

But I didn't move.

394

"You don't belong here," I said, ice in every syllable.

Olivia shrugged. "Maybe not. But I'm here anyway."

And then she turned, walked out into the rain that was pouring again, with Logan trailing behind like a shadow.

They got in a car and left.

No words. No glance back.

Just gone.

As if she'd never been there at all.

Suddenly the power flickered back on. The lights too bright. I reached for my purse, fingers shaking just slightly.

I looked at Maddie, my voice came out calm. Too calm.

"This thing with Olivia will blow over. She's alive, so what are they going to do us?"

Maddie didn't speak. She just stood there like a lost animal.

So, I continued.

"And you better not say a word about Andy. No one knows but us. And we are going to keep it that way."

Her shoulders sagged, like she might collapse. And I didn't care.

"He's just going to be missing. That's it. No explanation. Got it?"

I turned to face her, eyes locking with hers. "I'll be back in a few hours. When I call you, be ready. We're going to drive his car back to his house. Leave it like he was never here. He parked out at the street. And since it was dark, no one probably noticed."

Maddie's lips parted like she might argue, but she didn't. She just stood there, small and useless in the middle of her dead mother's living room.

"No one will know," I said again, softer now. Almost a promise. Almost a threat.

Because I really didn't want to have to kill her too, but I would, if I had to.

And I walked out.
The door slammed shut behind me, and I was gone.

CHAPTER 37

Madison

I stood frozen in the silence they left behind, the echo of their voices still hanging heavy in the room. The air felt dense. Damp with rain. Close against my skin.
Everything around me held still.
Except my pulse.
That was already running.

Then I moved.

Not with thought, just instinct. Out the back door, into the night. I had to go there. Compulsively, I moved toward the well through the darkness. Not understanding why or how, just going.

Rain clung to the trees, falling in sheets so dense the world blurred. I pushed forward, half-blind, the wind tearing at my clothes, my skin, my soul. Branches slapped at my arms, as I ran. But I couldn't stop. I didn't know where the air in my lungs had gone.
Only that I had to keep moving.

If Olivia lived,
If she walked out of those woods, *bleeding but alive.*
Then maybe…

Maybe Andy was alive too.

My breath caught. My chest ached. I pushed harder.

We thought Olivia was dead.

We saw the blood, the way she fell, the way her body didn't move.
And she still survived.

So maybe, *maybe.*

But the thought cracked in my chest as fast as it had bloomed.

Because we didn't leave Andy in the woods…
We threw him into the well.

I winced, tripping over a root, catching myself against a tree.

The drop into the well was at least twenty feet. Maybe more.
A black hole carved into the earth.
No bottom in sight. Just stone and water and silence.

How could anyone survive *that?*

I clutched the side of my shirt, dragging in a breath.

But I had to know.

Even if it was too late.
Even if he was already past saving.

I had to try.

The woods swallowed me. Twigs cracked beneath my feet. Water
pooled in the hollows of the path. My breath came in ragged pulls, my
hands shaking as I stumbled past trees that had once been familiar, now
monstrous in the darkness.

Tears mixed with the rain. I didn't know which was which anymore.

BETWEEN FRIENDS

I just wanted it to stop. The lies. The fear.

I wanted to stop Imogen's control over my life.

"I've had enough," I whispered, voice shaking. "Enough."

Then... I heard something.

Faint at first. So soft I thought maybe I imagined it.
A sound rising through the stillness. Wet. Unsteady. Almost choking.

I froze, one foot still hovering just above the path, heart exploding in my chest.

There was another sound, not loud, but clearer this time.
A cough. Hollow and strangled.

I held my breath and turned slowly, my eyes locked on the well just ahead.
The dark mouth gaping open, black as the night sky, waiting.

There it was again, a stirring beneath the silence.
A whimper.
A groan.
Broken and shallow, but *there.*

The kind of sound a person makes when they're struggling to live.

I stumbled toward the edge, hand catching on a slick branch to keep from falling. My legs didn't feel like mine anymore. Neither did my voice.

But somehow, a word rose out of me.
It cracked from my throat, unsure and soft, but heavy with everything I'd been afraid to believe.

"Andy?"

Only silence returned.

My eyes searched the dark, straining.

"Andy!"
Louder now.
Shaking.

The rain poured down, as if the sky was crying out with me.

I moved closer to the edge of the well.

Please, I thought. Please let this be real. Let him be okay.

I scrambled forward, slipping in the mud, clawing my way, leaning against the edge, cold stone pressing against my ribs. I shined my phone light down into the abyss.

And there...through the shadows and the ruin...something moved.

Barely.

But he moved.

"Oh my God..." I dropped to my knees, hands gripping the edge of the stone. "You're alive. Oh my God, Andy, you're alive!"

I fumbled for my phone with trembling hands, fingers slick with rain and dirt.

The screen lit up, blinding in the dark.

911

I pressed the call with a shaking finger.

My voice cracked as I spoke to the dispatcher. "We need help. He's alive. He's alive. Please...please send someone...he's at the bottom of the well. He's...he's still breathing."

The forest spun around me. My knees sank into the wet earth. I couldn't tell if the roaring in my ears was thunder or my own pulse.

But Andy was alive.

They came fast...paramedics, officers, strangers with gloves and urgent steps. Just as they arrived the rain stopped again.

I backed away as they swarmed the well, still clutching the phone like a lifeline in my fist. My fingers were stiff, with dampness and fear. But my eyes never left the stone mouth of the well.

Ropes dropped. A harness. Shouting. Metal scraping. Bark snapping under the rush of boots.

They lifted him.

My Andy.

Crimson streaked his face. Blood caked into the curve of his jaw, the corner of his mouth, and his chest rose and fell in the shallowest rhythm I'd ever seen.

He looked dead.

But he wasn't. He was very much alive.

His head rolled weakly to the side, and his eyes...those soft, stubborn eyes fluttered open and found me.

A sound broke from my throat. Somewhere between a gasp and a sob, scraped raw from the inside.

"Andy," I whispered, but it came out choked.

His fingers twitched like they were remembering how to move. I fell to my knees beside the gurney as they lifted him, uncaring that my jeans soaked through with mud.

"Andy, I'm here," I said again, louder now, needing him to hear it. To know it.

His hand lifted, reaching out in the air like he was searching for something.

"Andy," I whispered, breath hitching, reaching my hand toward his.

His fingers wrapped around mine, clumsy but sure, blood-slick and trembling.

I squeezed back with everything I had.

Tears blurred my vision, spilling hot and helpless as the paramedics worked around us.
He was alive.
By some impossible grace, he was alive.

He tried to smile, that same crooked, boyish grin I remembered from years ago...but it faltered.

His lips parted.

"Maddie…"

And his eyes slipped closed.

"No...no, stay with me, Andy..."

"He's breathing! Let's get him out of here," one of the medics said. "We've got him. We've got him."

They wheeled him to the ambulance parked in the driveway. The lights flashed red and white, blinding me, as I watched them load him and close the doors.

From across the yard, I saw her. Colleen stood by watching, arms folded, phone limp in one hand. Her mouth was drawn, eyes sharp and glinting in the ambulance lights.

Our eyes met.

She didn't say a word. Just nodded...slow and deliberate, like she'd known the truth all along.

But it didn't really register.

All I could think about was Andy.

I felt his hand in mine long after they drove away, lights and sirens blaring, toward the waiting world, away from the darkness we'd just crawled out of.

Then the rain began to fall again, gentle and steady, washing away the trail of blood.

———————•❖•·———————

It happened fast after that.

The police swarmed the house. Questions poured in like floodwater...what happened, where was she, who knew what, when, how.

I told them everything. I held nothing back.

By morning, they had Imogen in custody.

They said she didn't put up a fight. Just sat there with her perfect posture and pale Dior trousers, pride on her face. As if she still believed none of it could hurt her.

And me? I made a deal with the police.

Full immunity in exchange for my testimony...every detail, every secret, every horror I'd carried inside me for twelve long years.

The story I'd never told. The memory I hadn't let myself remember.

It was the only way to make it right.

The only way to save myself.

This time, I wasn't going to hide.

Imogen would stand trial. I would take the stand.

It wasn't redemption. Not really.

But it was something.

A beginning of me choosing myself for the first time, maybe ever.

CHAPTER 38

Madison

A few final touches were left. A light wipe-down of the counters.

A last look through the cupboards.

And one glass of wine I'd poured without thinking. It sat on the counter like a dare. Red, rich, and taunting. A habit in a stemmed glass. I picked it up. Swirled it once. Watched the way it clung to the sides like it didn't want to let go.

Neither did I. But I had to.

I walked to the sink and turned on the faucet. Watched the water hiss as it hit the stainless-steel basin. I poured the wine out, slow and steady, watching the crimson spiral disappear down the drain. It looked darker than I remembered. Heavier.

Almost like blood.

The glass made a hollow clink as I set it down.

No dramatic declarations. No whispered promises. Just me and the hush of an empty kitchen.

But inside, I made the vow.

No more running. No more numbing.

No more alcohol.

I wanted to meet the next version of myself with clear eyes. With steady hands.

With nothing to blur the truth.

Just me.

The television flickered on with 6 a.m. news, casting shifting blue light across the living room walls. I hadn't meant to turn it on. I'd sat a box on the remote. Still, the screen lit up, full of color and sound. I stood there, frozen.

Imogen's face filled the screen.

Windblown mugshot. Mascara smeared beneath her eyes. Her mouth pressed into something that might've once been a smile. But there was no charm left in it now. Just shadow.

I clicked the volume button up with a shaky hand.
The anchor's voice broke through the silence, calm and crisp.

"...Imogen Warner-Smith is currently being held without bail on charges of the attempted murders of Deputy Sheriff Andy Marson and Olivia Mariner following a shocking series of revelations that have upended the quiet reputation of Fairfield."

They showed Olivia's school photo. That bright smile. The shine in her eyes.

And a picture of Andy in full uniform.

I had to sit down. I muted the TV and let the stillness sink in. My new reality pulsing.

An hour later, my bags were finally packed, zipped tight with everything I was carrying with me back to LA from my former life. My mother's ashes had already been shipped, along with a few boxes of clothing and trinkets.

I looked down at the photograph of my grandmother, peeking out from the side pocket on the side of my duffel, her wide, carefree smile frozen in time. My mother always said my grandmother was walking joy. That nothing could dim her spirit. So, I took the photo as a reminder, there was still hope for me too.

And if I kept trying, I could find my way to the light too.

I'd already survived the darkness.

And in that dark, I'd learned a few things.
How to sit with silence.
How to tell the difference between loneliness and peace.
How to listen when something in me whispered truth. And how to believe to believe in the sound of my voice. The one that had been calling to me this whole time.

———·◆◆·———

I sat on the porch, waiting for my ride, my hair blowing slightly in the wind. Morning mist curled low along the grass, lifting like slow drifts in the breeze. Somewhere deep in the woods, a bird called out once and went silent.

Leech sat beside me in a borrowed cat carrier, his green eyes blinking slowly in the soft light. I couldn't leave him behind. Not after everything. He'd picked me...showed up when I was most alone...and stayed. Over the last four weeks, he had become my family. A comfort I never knew I needed. And I knew he needed me too.

I reached through the grate and scratched behind his ears. "We're getting out of here, buddy," I whispered.

A hush fell across the yard, the kind that settles just before goodbye. My throat ached as I looked out at the yard one last time. It wasn't the town I hated, not truly. It was the version of myself I had been when I lived here. The girl who kept secrets just to feel safe. Who shrank herself down to fit someone else's idea of belonging. Who let fear wear her voice thin.

But I wasn't her anymore. She was the one that was dead and buried in the woods. And that's where she belonged. Because now it gave me the chance to be the me, I was always meant to be.

Behind me, the front door creaked open softly on its hinges, the sound low and familiar, as if the house was exhaling. Saying goodbye.

I turned back once more. "I know," I whispered. "You did the best you could."

And maybe it had. Maybe this house had held me, like a friend, all of these years. The only way it knew how, quietly, patiently, until I was ready to leave.

I heard the sound of his truck before I saw it. The low hum of the engine wound up the hill.

Andy pulled into the driveway, the tires spinning slowly as he eased to a stop. The truck door creaked open, and he stepped out into the morning light.

One arm was hanging in a sling. Thick bruises bloomed across his jaw and both eyes were blackened, the skin puffed and angry. A thin line of stitches ran along his hairline, pink and raw.

Still, he smiled.

BETWEEN FRIENDS

I groaned, as I lifted my bags and Leech off the porch.

"I got it," he said, rushing toward me.

"You really don't," I said, as he reached for the larger bag.

But he shook his head, shifting the weight of the duffel with one hand, wincing as he tossed it into the truck bed.

He turned back and crouched beside the carrier, tapping it lightly with two fingers.

"Hey, Leech. Ready for the next adventure?"

Leech blinked in reply.

I swallowed the lump in my throat, watching them.

He looked back at me as I eased open the passenger door.

"I wish you wouldn't go," he said quietly. Voice cracking at the edges.

My heart stopped for a second.

"I wish you'd go with me," I said.

His gaze went distant, thoughtful. "Elections are coming up, and the Sheriff says, I have a good chance at Chief Deputy if he's reelected."

The words hung between us like the echo of a promise neither of us could keep. I breathed deeply, letting the gravity of him tilt the world for a moment.

I leaned in, kissed his cheek, just beneath the bruising, and whispered, "Your dreams are coming true, Andy Marson. I am so proud of you."

His eyes closed for a beat. Maybe to hold it in. Maybe to let it go. I wasn't sure.

We pulled up to the departure terminal and he turned toward me, slowly, like the moment had knocked the breath from him.

"Maddie…"
He reached for my hand, careful not to wince.

"I'm going to miss you, Tiger."
His eyes shimmered with held back tears.

And without meaning to, I leaned and kissed him…long and deep.
Not the kind of kiss that asked for forever.
But the kind that said *please remember us.*

The kind that says thank you, and I'm sorry, and maybe, in another life.

When we finally pulled apart, his forehead rested against mine for a second.
A breath shared.
A goodbye unsaid.

I turned before I started to cry too.
Opened the truck door. Got out.
And didn't look back.

I was next in line for security when I heard them.
Footsteps. Fast. Echoing through the terminal.
I turned…and there he was.

Andy.
Running straight toward me.

People stepped out of his way as he weaved through the crowd, his arm still in a sling, face flushed with desperation.

I dropped my bags and ducked under the ropes, heart pounding as I met him halfway.

He didn't say anything at first. Just looked at me.

His eyes were glassy, wet with tears.

"I can't let you leave like this," he said, breathless.

I blinked, stunned, as people stopped to watch what was happening.

"My dreams might be coming true, Maddie... but what good are they if I don't have my best friend to share them with?"

"Wow," I said, a shaky laugh slipping out. "It only took you a decade to realize this?"

His lips parted like he might smile, but the emotion kept it from reaching his eyes

"I know," he said, voice thick. "I was young. Caught up in chasing dreams. Trying to be someone important. And somewhere in all that noise... I lost you."

He looked down, and back at me.
"But I always knew it was you. I just couldn't say the words. Not back then."

My breath caught.
"And now?"

He stepped closer. "Now I know I'd rather risk losing everything than live one more day without you knowing how I feel."

He took my hand.
"I love you, Maddie. I've *always* loved you."

And this time, when he kissed me...
It felt like coming home.

Standing there in the terminal, wrapped in his arms, I finally understood.
Home was never a place I was missing.
It was a person.
And my home was Andy.
It had always been and always would be.

No matter the miles that stretched between us or the obstacles we faced, I believed we'd find our way.

Our love was steady, tempered by time, and held fast through the fire.

What came before, would always be a part of us.

But this...
This was ours.

THE END

NATALIE BANKS

Other titles by Natalie Banks:

The Water is Wide

The Dark Room

The Canary's Song

The Moments Between

House of Lights

PS: COULD YOU DO ME A FAVOR?

If you enjoyed my book, could I ask you to take a minute and go leave me a review? I don't' have a huge publishing house behind me and reviews really help me to get the word out. It doesn't have to be anything fancy. Even just a few words, like I really enjoyed this book, go a long way.

Thank you so much for reading my stories!

I will see you again soon with my next book and in the meantime, I am sending you so many hugs!

Be sure to sign up for my newsletter at
WWW.NATALIEBANKSNOVELS.COM
to be the FIRST to know about upcoming titles!

Love,
Natalie Banks
xo

www.ingramcontent.com/pod-product-compliance
Lightning Source LLC
Chambersburg PA
CBHW070834260626
47170CB00007B/2365